THE YACHT PARTY

BENEDICT BROWN

Storm
PUBLISHING

This is a work of fiction. Names, characters, businesses, places, events and incidents are either the products of the author's imagination or used in a fictitious manner. Any resemblance to actual persons, living or dead, or actual events is purely coincidental.

Copyright © Benedict Brown, 2026

The moral right of the author has been asserted.

All rights reserved. No part of this book may be reproduced or used in any manner without the prior written permission of the copyright owner. This prohibition includes, but is not limited to, any reproduction or use for the purpose of training artificial intelligence technologies or systems.

To request permissions, contact the publisher at rights@stormpublishing.co

Ebook ISBN: 978-1-83700-263-4
Paperback ISBN: 978-1-83700-265-8

Cover design: Blacksheep
Cover images: Blacksheep, Shutterstock

Published by Storm Publishing.
For further information, visit:
www.stormpublishing.co

ALSO BY BENEDICT BROWN

The Marius Quin Mysteries

Murder at Everham Hall

The Hurtwood Village Murders

The Castleton Affair

A Body at the Grand Hotel

Arsenic and Old Lies

The Holly Village Murders

Lord Edgington Investigates…

Murder at the Spring Ball

A Body at a Boarding School

Death on a Summer's Day

The Mystery of Mistletoe Hall

The Tangled Treasure Trail

The Curious Case of the Templeton-Swifts

The Crimes of Clearwell Castle

The Snows of Weston Moor

What the Vicar Saw

Blood on the Banisters

A Killer in the Wings

The Christmas Bell Mystery

The Puzzle of Parham House

Death at Silent Pool

The Christmas Candle Murders

Murder in an Italian Castle

Death on the Night Train to Verona

The Alpine Christmas Mystery

The Izzy Palmer Mysteries

A Corpse Called Bob

A Corpse in the Country

A Corpse on the Beach

A Corpse in London

A Corpse for Christmas

A Corpse in a Locked Room

A Corpse in a Quaint English Village

A Corpse at a Wedding

A Corpse at A School Reunion

A Corpse from the Past

*For my brother, Daniel,
a true rock star whose resilience over the last few years
has inspired me every day.*

PROLOGUE

Now that everyone is dead, I pick my way through the bodies.

I can't say what woke me. To be honest, it's difficult to know anything with any certainty. The pain in my head is all-conquering. It feels as if I've spent the last day hooked up to a whisky drip and the hangover has just kicked in. I stumble from my room and along the corridor, clutching railing after railing to stop myself falling with the movement of the boat.

On the stairs above, I spot that unique shade of red in a great long splash up the wall. There's just enough blood to tell me everything I need to know; more people have died.

I remember now. Flashes of panic and anger come back to me and, a few moments later, I find the first body on the main deck. Following handprints and dirty red smudges, I make my way towards the back of the boat where a woman lies motionless. There are cuts all over her arms, but she's clearly fallen from one of the balconies above. Maybe the sound of her body smashing against the floor over my cabin is what brought me here.

A half-formed question of whether someone pushed her is quickly resolved as I look at the awkward position in which she landed. She's on her back, her legs twisted, and her arms stretched wide. Surely she'd be face down if she'd jumped. It could have been an accident but, given the circumstances, I truly doubt it.

Her face is pointed away from me, but I recognise who it is from her neat, unexciting clothes. I suddenly realise that I need a weapon, which isn't that easy to find on the deck of a fancy yacht. The décor is minimalist and, short of standing beside an immensely heavy chain and hoping the killer will submit to being knocked out with it, there isn't much at hand.

The fog in my head has, if not cleared, then at least parted for a moment. I remember that there are bedrooms along the walkway on this side of the ship, so I move to try the various doors.

The first I come to is a storage cupboard with nothing for me except an unwieldy mop. But I keep on. I persist. I won't give up. The wooden path curves around, and I find what I need. The door slides open a little too easily, and I stumble into a musty room and onto the bed. I push myself off the surprisingly hard lump under the covers, but I won't peek to see who's there. I really don't want to know.

The cabin is similar to my own, so I get to my feet to rifle through a chest of drawers on the off-chance one of my friends has brought a handy hunting knife or perhaps a small gun. Boxer shorts and T-shirts aren't going to help much, and I'm about to give up and try another room when I spot the bedside lamps. They're shaped like candlesticks, as they are in every bedroom. I grab the closest one and, with the shade removed and the cable detached, the metal body will just about do the job.

Back outside, I feel like every stupid hero in every stupid action movie I've ever mocked. I'm aware how ridiculous it is to even consider fighting a killer with half a lamp, but my friends are dead, and I have no desire to be next.

I hold the makeshift weapon in both hands and slowly mount the stairs to the bridge deck. My footsteps sound louder than at any moment in my life, and the wood beneath me creaks like it wants to let the killer know exactly where I am.

Just as I stop at the top to look around – just as I notice a knife on the floor and two definite pools of blood – a perfect shiver races through me.

I hear a sudden intake of breath, and a voice behind me says, "I didn't do it. I promise it wasn't me."

PART 1
BRIDGET

ONE

I am a drone. I am a worker bee. I am a cog in a machine.

This is what I chant to myself as I go about my work each day. As I sit in front of a computer screen in an office with as much charm as a motorway service station toilet, completing the tasks that the computer has assigned me.

At eleven o'clock, my deskmate Dan tells me, "I'm off to the loo, Bridget. Send out a search party if I'm not back in five."

I'm not sure whether he knows that he says the same thing every day, or he thinks the repetition makes it funnier. I never mention it. I just smile and pretend it's sweet. Dan and I have sat opposite one another at an S-shaped desk for two years now, and all I really know about him is that he does not have a particularly good sense of humour.

I am a drone. I am a worker bee. I am a cog in a machine.

That's not actually true. I'm more like the pin that holds a single cog in place, and even that suggests I'm in some way pivotal to the functioning of the machine. If anything, I'm one of those bits of transparent plastic that you get on the front of a router when the broadband company decides to send you a new one. If someone removed me, no one would notice the difference.

This is what occupies my mind as I try to make the day pass

quicker. And it works. It works oddly well. As boring as my job is, there's a sort of hypnotic beauty to it. I sit down in my chair at nine o'clock. At eleven, Dan goes to the toilet. At five past eleven, Dan comes back from the toilet, and at one fifteen I have my lunch.

In between all that excitement, I float through space. There will be a report open on my computer, and it will be more complete by the time I eat my ham and cress sandwiches than it was when I took my coat off that morning, but I would estimate that only 12 per cent of my brain is actively engaged with it. It's hard to say what the other 88 per cent is up to.

When I was a kid at home in Somerset, I had a tortoise called George. I liked to imagine what he was thinking as he sat chomping on lettuce leaves, saying nothing. Somewhere out in space, there are aliens watching me as I fill in box after box on my monitor, and I bet they're pondering the exact same question that I had about George. *Is there anything going on in that tiny head?*

My afternoons are pretty much carbon copies of my mornings, with the small exception that my best and only work friend, Tammy, comes by at three thirty and we go outside together so that she can smoke a cigarette and talk about how she should give up smoking. At five o'clock, I go home, and that's when things get truly bleak.

As I walk back to my one-bedroom flat – that had felt like such a milestone to buy and is now such a millstone to maintain – I think about my time at university when anything seemed possible. I think about the friends I had at Goldsmiths College and what they must be doing now. I think about Ade Okojie. Because really, that was the highlight of my otherwise pointless life: a drunken snog in a cupboard with a guy who went on to be a rock star.

And every night, when I close my front door behind me, I think, *Bridget, your time is your own. You have five hours before you need to go to sleep. Do something with it. Get your old notebooks out. Write something amazing, or draw a picture of somewhere beautiful that you dream of visiting.*

And then I make dinner and wash the dishes and realise that I don't have anything to write about and that drawing somewhere beautiful will only make me sad I'm not there. So I sit on the sofa to watch a film or read a book, but even that seems like too much effort, and in the end I stay right where I am, exercising my right thumb every ten to forty seconds as I scroll through videos made by people I would probably hate in real life, whose lives look so much more interesting than my own.

I am a drone. I am a worker bee. I am a cog in a machine. Not just in my job, but at home too. I am the eyeballs on the videos that make people rich. There are billions of others just like me, and it is our job to watch the occasional adverts that flash up on our six-inch screens so that more people make money in a manner I don't fully understand.

I am a cog in a machine in a room full of machines in a factory that makes machines.

Every day is the same... except today.

I get home at six twenty-five, as usual. I need eighty-five minutes, a bus and two trains to arrive because I can't afford to live anywhere near the place I work. This city, which once seemed so magical, but I have now come to despise, is approximately more expensive than anywhere else on earth.

I unlock my front door, pick up the assorted bills and ads from the carpet and walk into my apartment, with its stunning view of the car park where I could park a car if I could afford one. I can't afford one because I have a mortgage to pay. And I'm just about to tell myself that the next five hours belong to me when I realise that one of the bills in my hand isn't a bill.

I've never had a letter from abroad before. Actually, I don't think I've received a real letter here full stop. As much as I enjoy the missives from my bank telling me that I have just enough money to continue doing nothing with my life, and the kindly reminders from the electricity company of exactly where most of my pay cheque goes, this one surprises me.

There's Arabic writing on the postmark, and I can just make out that the stamp reads *Muscat*. I have no idea where that is, but my phone tells me it's in Oman, which a further search reveals is at the south-eastern tip of the Arab Peninsula. This is hardly the most revealing information, but then I remember I'm allowed to open the stiff, bulky letter and not just goggle at the envelope.

I was going to rip it open, but the paper is so thick and fancy that I change my mind. Whatever is inside deserves a touch of ceremony, so I go to the drawer in the kitchen and find my sharpest knife. As I insert it ever so carefully in the little gap at the side, I tell myself not to get too excited.

It's a scam. Bound to be a scam. It'll be from some Omani prince who needs to borrow my bank account to deposit ten million dollars. There is no chance I will come out of this well.

So you can imagine how I feel when I tip up the envelope and a plane ticket to Mauritius falls out.

TWO

I arrive at work at nine o'clock the next morning, as I always do. I hang up my coat, as I always do, and I'm about to sit down, as per usual, when I change my mind and knock on my manager's door.

Peter has bushy white hair that looks like it's been disturbed by a tornado. He is approximately seventy years old, and I can only think they built the office around him, as it's impossible to imagine him anywhere else.

"Morning, Peter."

"Ah... Bridget!" he says with a laugh. "And what can we do for you this fine day?"

The words are on the tip of my tongue. I know exactly what I want to say, but I've started to wonder whether I should lie. That would have been a great idea, but it's too late now. "The thing is, I need a week off."

He doesn't say anything. He just turns on his computer monitor, moves the mouse a bit, then *hmmms* a few times while I try to explain why I am worthy of an unscheduled holiday.

"The thing is," I say for the second time in the space of twenty seconds, "I've never been unreasonable with leave. I always work on bank holidays, and I try to be a real team player. But the thing is," three and counting, "the most brilliant opportunity has come up, and I don't think I can turn it down."

He finally glances at me.

"You've used all but two of your free days for the year. You went to see your mother in Shepton Mallet. You told me she was ill and needed a hand."

"I did, and she was. She's a bit better now, though she still has trouble with..." I stop talking because my mother's sciatica isn't what I've come to discuss.

"Then what's all this talk of a week's holiday?" His eyebrows rise above his glasses, and I feel as if I've committed some unforgivable crime. "You do know that it goes against company policy?"

"It's more like ten days than a week. But I totally understand if you have to take it out of my pay."

He folds his arms across his chest and rocks back and forth in his chair. I sit looking attentive, waiting for his next judgy comment.

"Tell me, Bridget, are you in some kind of trouble?"

I suddenly realise what he must be thinking, but before I can tell him that it isn't the Victorian era and the local landowner hasn't got me pregnant, he keeps talking.

"Or do you have a medical issue of your own? We here at Michaels and Mickelson are sympathetic to the needs of our employees, but you must tell me what's wrong if you expect me to help you out."

I'm still annoyed that the only thing he can imagine is that I'm ill or up the duff, but I maintain my saintly expression. "No, it's nothing like that. The truth is..." *Bad idea, start lying now!* "The truth is that an old friend of mine has invited me to Mauritius to travel on his yacht."

Peter is stupefied. "And are you a keen sailor? Is that the opportunity you simply can't pass up?"

Now I'm the one laughing. I'm trying to pretend that my request is no big deal. "Goodness me, no. The only boat I've ever been on is a pedalo when my family went on holiday to

Bournemouth." I laugh a little louder, aware that I'm starting to sound unhinged. Perhaps he'll let me go for the sake of my sanity. "No, the thing is..." I really have to stop saying that. "Well, the friend who has invited me is Adesina Okojie."

I wait for him to be amazed.

"I don't know who that is." Peter's eyebrows swoop back down. "Wait... is he the Ugandan fellow who works in the Swindon office?"

"No, he's a rock singer. Well, he's kind of poppy too. It's hard to describe." I sound like I'm fifteen again.

Peter shrugs. "I can't say the name rings a bell. But then I mainly listen to Classic FM."

"He's famous," I reply, a little shocked. "His band, Adesina, had a massive hit with 'Promises'. You must know that song."

I can see that he's already bored with the conversation. "As I said, I'm more a fan of Amadeus Mozart than Adesina..."

"Okojie," I reply, losing faith in my own argument.

Why didn't I lie? I could have said I was dying, or that my fictional grandmother in New Zealand was turning one hundred. I don't even mind pretending to be pregnant if it gets me off work. On the plus side, I came within seconds of belting out the chorus to Ade's best-known song. So at least I dodged that bullet.

I clear my throat and try to sound confident. "Anyway... never mind. The point is, he's invited a group of our friends from university to meet him on his yacht. It could even be a superyacht for all I know."

Peter isn't interested in superyachts or rock stars. He's got a caravan in Hastings and enjoys walking holidays. He's looking at his computer again. He's become distracted by an email or his to-do list for the day. I'm losing him. I'm losing my chance to escape.

"So is it possible?" My voice is full of casual cheer, and he just has to say yes, but I know he won't.

He sighs and leans closer over his sun-bleached keyboard. "When is it?"

That isn't an outright *no*. I can't believe it! I just need to get over one final hurdle, and it will quite literally be plain sailing.

"I leave on the fifteenth."

"That's next week!" The expression on his face matches the startled puppy's on the motivational poster on the wall just behind him. "Bridget, I really would love to say yes, but... no."

I immediately think of three possible arguments, but having worked approximately eight metres from Peter for the last... many years, I'm pretty sure none of them will work.

There's only one thing for it; I will beg. "I can't miss this, Peter. Please let me go."

That patronising smile is back on his face. He knows that he's in charge, and there's nothing I can do to change his mind.

"I really am sorry, Bridget, but the rules are the rules. It isn't my fault that you've already used all your holiday allowance." At least he didn't pat my hand. I might have had to punch him if he'd patted my hand. "Why don't you go back to your desk and forget all about it?"

What I want to do is grab his head and force it through the monitor. I want to pull the blinds down from his window and stamp on them. I want to do terrible things to his printer, but instead, I take a deep breath.

There's nothing you can do, I silently remind myself. *You are a cog in a machine.*

Except, there is one thing.

"Thank you for listening to my request, Peter. I do appreciate it, and with your response in mind, I'd like to tender my resignation. I will provide it in writing by the end of the day."

I push my chair back to leave as Peter flexes his eyebrow muscles.

"Bridget, are you saying what I think you're saying?"

"If you think that I'm quitting, then yes."

"But you've been working here for..." He looks back at the monitor to consult the relevant information. "... nine years."

"And I have no wish to make that ten." I consider keeping it professional, but this is my blaze of glory. It would be silly not to make the most of it. "For one thing, the cakes we have for anniversaries are disgusting."

"You're one of my most reliable workers." He stops short of calling me a good little drone, but I know that's what he means.

"Don't worry, Peter. The agency will find a replacement."

He is no longer bouncing in his chair so contentedly. "I don't think you would be best advised to—"

I interrupt him before he can say anything more. I'm scared that he might change my mind otherwise. "Don't worry, Peter. I'll see out my obligatory week's notice, and I promise to send a postcard."

I may sound like I know what I'm doing, but I'm already worried about my mortgage and the parking space that I'll never fill. There's a voice up here that keeps asking, *Do you really want to throw your life away for ten days in the sun?*

And though I'm terrified about what will happen when I get back, I find myself repeating a mantra as I leave poor, stunned Peter behind.

I am a drone, I am a worker bee, I am a cog in a machine no more.

THREE

Standing in Gatwick airport, about to get on the plane, there are approximately sixty things I could be worrying about. It's not just the thought of succumbing to Anne-Hathaway-in-*Les-Misérables*-level poverty when I return. As I wait to board, I realise that there may be a reason I haven't spoken to any of my university friends in a decade.

There were seven of us thrown together in our little apartment in the first year. It was me, Ade, Sasha, Tom, Jake, Clara and Dawn, and we went on to live together in a house after that. Of course, by the end of our second year, Dawn wouldn't speak to Ade, Jake and I had fallen in love and broken up, and Tom and Sasha spent their lives arguing. Am I a complete idiot to think it will be any different all this time later?

I wander down the gangway towards the plane, trying not to think about the last time that Ade and I spoke. I gleefully picture what it will be like to see my other friends again, forgetting that I have no wonderful stories that might amaze them or any interesting life achievements to share. I even consider the look of admiration on my ex-boyfriend's face as we reconnect for the first time since a long, messy break-up. I try really hard not to think of the arguments that tore our group apart, and I just know that everything will work out fine.

Even as I'm trying to convince myself that this is true, I catch sight of Sasha and Tom at the front of the plane. Trust those two to go first class. They are inevitably already tanned before the holiday has even begun. I stand watching them from that poky little spot where the cabin crew point the sheep left to green pastures and right to the butcher's shop.

"Welcome aboard," a slightly snooty voice declares before looking at me as though I'm the type to cause problems.

"Sorry," I mumble, then bustle towards economy as fast as I can without looking like a child running in the school corridor.

"Madam," the flight attendant complains, and I realise that I have no concept whatsoever of how to behave on a plane.

I slowly turn around, uncertain how I could have offended her so badly so quickly. Is there an etiquette guide you're supposed to study before flying these days?

Like she's channelling the Grim Reaper, she points a bony finger at me, and I instinctively look down, afraid that I've stained my clothes with the toasted cheese sandwich I had for breakfast.

"Madam, you have a first-class ticket. Your seat is this way."

Part of me assumes that she's made a mistake. A cleverer part of me remembers that the richest person I've ever met bought me my flight. Of course Ade paid for first-class tickets. He wouldn't know any other kind – just as I never questioned that I would be sitting between a twenty-stone rugby player and an old lady with a plentiful supply of fish-paste sandwiches.

There are tuts and eyerolls as I squeeze past my fellow passengers to get to the part of the plane where undeserving people take up all the space. I utter a few "Sorry... sorry! Sorrrreeee..."s but keep my eyes down.

The atmosphere here feels different. It's not just the pleasant music playing or the hushed way people talk. I swear the very oxygen around me is sweeter. The seats are in the form of white cocoons separated by retractable partitions, which admittedly do remind me of my office. I find my seat by the left-hand window, just behind my two former friends. I'm about to clear my throat and say hi to them when I realise that they're arguing, and I shouldn't interrupt.

"Do not start drinking immediately. It is so tacky." Sasha is beautiful in that far too toned and skinny way she always had about her.

"Ha! You're too late," her husband replies. "I had a cheeky G and T in the lounge when you went to the toilet. And let me tell you; it was delicious."

I watch his celebratory grin as I slide down into my seat. I can't see them anymore, but I can still hear them, and I can imagine the salty look that Sasha gives him.

I feel a bit sorry that she ended up with Tom, even though it was her choice. She set her sights on the poshest boy in our flat that first week we were living together. And besides, they didn't invite me to their wedding, so I won't feel too bad about it.

"This is a terrible idea," Sasha whispers to her husband. "We should never have agreed to come."

Tom is tall, and his head pokes above his seat as he gets comfortable. "Are you afraid I'll show you up? Afraid I'll make a fool of myself, and they'll all know what an idiot you were to marry me?"

"Yes." There is a pregnant pause. "That's exactly what frightens me."

"Poor, downtrodden little Sasha. Having to put up with such an obnoxious husband. You didn't seem to mind so much when my salary meant you could retire at twenty-eight."

It suddenly occurs to me that this argument is for the benefit of anyone within earshot rather than them. They know that they will be overheard and are trying to win over the silent jury. For the moment, I'm still with Sasha.

"You didn't seem to mind when I paid for you to—"

"That's enough, Tom."

She reaches forward to get something, and the argument is

over. She was never meek or contrite when I knew her, and I struggle to believe that she could have folded so easily.

"Hostess!" Tom clicks his fingers in the direction of the nearest crew member.

"You can't call her that." Sasha sighs, and I can tell this is one fight she has no hope of winning.

"At least I didn't say *trolly dolly*," he purrs in reply, just as a flight attendant arrives to see to his needs. "Hello, my darling, everything's included in the ticket, right?"

"Yes, sir," she replies most patiently, though I bet she's thinking, *Do I really have to put up with this goon for twelve hours?*

"Wonderful. Then I'd like two glasses of champagne." He turns to his wife to make the joke that everyone has already predicted. "Anything for you, Sash?" His laughter cuts through the quiet cabin, and the poor woman attending him has to pretend she hasn't heard this same line a thousand times before.

When she leaves, I catch a sliver of a glimpse of Sasha between the seats as she leans closer to him. "Listen to me, funny man. The first time you pass out drunk on that boat, if you've done the slightest thing to upset me, I will take your razor and do a very bad job of shaving your head." Her voice falls to a crisp whisper. If anything, this makes it easier for me to hear her. "If you do it a second time, that won't be the only thing I remove."

Tom is still gingerly touching his wavy hair when the young woman arrives with the two sparkling flutes. He clears his throat, hands one to his wife, and I feel the thrill of her victory.

Whatever else I might have thought about Sasha when we were at uni, she was always good at standing up for herself. In our first term at Goldsmiths, you could see that some girls weren't ready for the real world. At the freshers' fair in the first week, poor little creatures like our friend Clara were the field mice staring down a thresher. The hawks from sports societies and drinking groups circled in search of easy prey, and she would have been eaten whole if we hadn't been there.

Sasha was never a victim. She was bold and ballsy and always in control. I admired her, but she terrified me. When we met, I didn't ask what course she was studying because it was obvious she was an actress from the very first moment. She lived in the room opposite mine, and she walked straight over, her hand extended as though it were a business meeting.

"Sasha Bellwether," she said in a manner which suggested that this name should mean something to me.

I pulled her in for a hug for some reason. I'm not normally a hugger but must have felt somehow that she needed it – that her confidence was only skin deep – but I was wrong. Sasha was as strong as anyone back then, so it's good to see that being married to an odious bore like Thomas Ledger hasn't changed that.

The spiky back and forth between them has fizzled out, but Tom could never let things go and tries another avenue of attack.

"You can say what you like about my drinking, Sash. But I know that as soon as we get on board that boat, you'll have eyes for Ade alone. How do you think that will make me feel?"

I try to imagine the disdainful look she gives him in return. "It's not just a boat, it's a yacht, and I didn't hear you complaining when the tickets arrived. If anything, you were more excited to get the chance to see Ade than I was."

Tom shuffles again. "I have my reasons, and they don't concern you." His previous indignant tone has been replaced with a cagey murmur. "In fact, if you could stay out of my business altogether, that would be fantastic."

I settle into my reclining seat to continue eavesdropping, but then my neighbour arrives, and I find myself engaged in conversation with a gleeful divorcee from Milton Keynes.

I never imagined I'd get to fly in so much as economy plus, so lounging in this refined environment is fine by me – even if Mary alongside me has some lewd stories to tell about her ex-husband, Nigel.

Better still is the feeling as the plane accelerates off the tarmac, and the force pushes me back against my seat. We take to the air, and I watch Britain slowly shrinking in the evening light before it disappears altogether.

FOUR

Mary is a natterer, but I don't have the heart to press the button for the screen that closes the gap between us. Sasha doesn't have that problem. She immediately isolates herself, which might have something to do with the fact that Tom's snoring sounds like a chainsaw falling past a window every fifteen seconds.

I keep thinking that Sasha will hear me talking to my new friend and turn around, but it never happens. At some point between chats and meals, I take my nightly tablets to keep my world looking bright and soon fall asleep. When I wake up again, the colour of the sea beneath us is far more vibrant. Wherever we are, it feels like summer. It feels the way a holiday is supposed to feel. It's also a day later, and I realise that I'm looking out at a brand-new morning.

I try to adjust to the fact I'm half a world away from home. When I finally catch a glimpse of Mauritius rising up out of the Indian Ocean, it's almost too perfect. In the distance, it's easy to imagine that it is quite uninhabited – a perfect desert island with a turquoise ring around it and mountain peaks rising up here and there. It's tempting to believe that I've found paradise.

From the time that the captain switches on the seat belt sign until the moment it turns off again, Sasha and Tom revisit their earlier argument. I don't want them to know that I've heard everything they've said throughout the flight and so, as soon as it's allowed, I pop up from my seat, grab my bag and stand overeagerly by the door. I'm like a superfan camping outside a concert to run to the stage when the venue opens.

I am the very first off the plane – as the snarling hounds in economy are kept at bay by flight attendants with their arms outstretched to subdue them. I am also the first through passport control and the first to arrive at baggage reclaim.

I already know that this is where I will meet them again.

Oh, Sasha, Tom! Were you on the same flight as me? I will ask them. *I didn't spot you on board.*

I imagine the pretence that they will put on to suggest that they haven't been sniping at one another off and on for the last six thousand miles. I see their wide smiles as we reconnect.

That's not how it happens.

"The red case, Tom," Sasha is already screeching when she appears in the hall. "It's the Montblanc your mother gave me for Christmas. You know the one I mean."

She is wearing a black and white bodycon dress and stiletto heels which click percussively across the shiny floor. I can't imagine anything less comfortable to travel in, and I'm suddenly grateful for my baggy jumper and loose jeans. It is lucky that her husband sports more suitable footwear, as Tom must be plastered by now and keeps bumping into her as they walk.

They don't notice me watching them. I keep waiting for them to spot me, but it doesn't happen, and I just stand there with my mouth gaping open, feeling ignored. They come to stand right in front of me, even though there is plenty of room and it is obvious that I'm waiting for my case. They say nothing. They just stand watching the empty belt as if there are bags on it that only they can see.

"We should do something," Sasha declares when five minutes have passed and there is still no sign of our luggage.

"Like what, my dear?" he replies in that rather old-fashioned voice of his.

Tom comes from money, went to private school, and didn't fit in with our bohemian uni-mates one bit. I never found out why he went to such an artsy college when everyone knew that he was destined to work in the City like his father. Perhaps it was his form of rebellion against his parents.

Sasha doesn't answer his question, but six seconds later, the conveyor belt starts turning. Her red suitcase is the first one out, and Tom's is just behind. They load them onto a trolley, and I wait for the battered case that previously belonged to my cousin, who bought it years earlier from a supermarket. We're not big travellers in my family. Why would we need more than a few suitcases between us?

As my carefully planned reunion never materialises, I stroll out of the baggage reclaim on my own. All Ade's assistant told me in the confirmation email was that there will be someone waiting for me in the arrivals hall. I walk through a corridor of excited faces, and I suddenly dread the thought of my old friends being disappointed that I've come. Sasha could be painfully honest when I knew her.

Oh, you're here too, Bridget, I hear her mumbling in that deliberately nonchalant manner.

I find the driver who has been sent to collect us, but the others aren't there. He is holding a sign that reads *Mr Okojie's Party*.

"Excuse me, are you Bridget Hogg?" he asks in perfect English when our eyes meet. He is dark skinned and dark haired. He is neat and subtly handsome, as a chauffeur should be.

"That's right."

"I'm glad I found you." He bows just a little, and I want to tell him not to. "My name is Sendilen. I'll be your driver today."

"I'm sorry to interrupt," a teenage girl pushes between us to say. She points to the sign and blushes. "Are you Ade Okojie's driver?"

Still all charm, Sendilen remains professional. "I'm afraid I'm not allowed to give out that information, madam."

The British girl looks a little heartbroken, so I step closer to whisper to her. "But I am, and, yeah, he's Ade's driver."

She instantly starts bouncing about and her cheeks turn red. "Oh my goodness. Wait until I tell my sister. This will destroy her. Can I get a selfie with the sign?"

I feel like I've betrayed him just a little, but he looks at me for permission, and I smile before the girl explodes again.

"Thank you, thank you, thank you!" Cheesy grin, peace sign, click. "Is he here on the island?"

She looks back and forth between us and, as I haven't a clue where Ade is, Sendilen responds. "He's not far away."

The girl can't take it any longer and has to run off to see her friends.

"I'm sorry. Will you get in trouble for that?" I put my free hand out to touch his sleeve, but he doesn't seem too worried.

"Not I, madam. You're the one giving away Mr Okojie's secrets." I instantly like him, but then I always trust people too easily.

I'm about to ask him something about his life on this heavenly island when a deep voice sounds over my shoulder. "Mr Okojie's party? You better believe it, mate! I am here to *party*!"

I turn to see Tom dancing from the waist up. He's hardly changed since I first knew him. His face is a little fuller, but he has that same stupid goatee, the same aristocratic nose, and I bet his raisin-pip eyes are just as bloodshot as ever behind his shades. He's also still a terrible dancer.

"Take me to your leader," he yelps, and the trolley goes rolling away as he claps his hands.

"I'm sorry about my husband. He's an idiot," Sasha tells Sendilen before noticing me. "Oh, you're here too, Bridget." She holds me in her gaze for three long seconds and then opens her arms to pull me into her. "I am so happy to see you. I really am."

For a moment, I think she might cry. There was nothing in her tone to suggest it, and we were never so close that the emotion of this reunion deserves tears, but she holds me like she's been waiting for this moment since we parted.

"You too, Sash. It's so nice to see you again." My voice sounds bubblier than it has in years. I almost don't recognise it. "Bit out of the blue, all of us coming together like this, don't you think?"

Her eyebrows arch in concern. "It's not a coincidence, Bridge. Ade invited us too."

"I know that. I just meant—"

Tom speaks over me. "All right, Bridge? Been years." He leans in for a clumsy air kiss and almost topples over before righting himself and turning his attention to the man with the sign. "All right, mate. You the driver?" He sticks his arm out straight between Sasha and me.

"My name is Sendilen." My new friend shakes Tom's hand with that same in-built politeness that makes me feel guilty.

"Nice, nice. I'll call you Sendi." Tom is even less tolerable than I remembered. He is a walking red flag. "Sorry we're late. We had to stop because Sasha doesn't go to the toilet on planes."

Understandably, she punches him on the arm as hard as she can, and he finally shuts up.

Sendilen pretends he hasn't heard a word of it. He's good at pretending. "Shall we go?"

He graciously takes my case with the dodgy wheels and leads us off through the crowds. We are soon spat out of the glistening glass building into the heat of the Mauritian morning. A thermometer on an advertising hoarding tells me it's already twenty-five degrees at 10 a.m. I pull my coat off, already a little frightened of how red I will be when I return to Britain.

We reach the flash car that will take us to the yacht, and at least Sasha and I are impressed.

"It isn't a limo," Tom inevitably tuts. "I thought rock stars drove limos."

Sendilen is already tired of him. "It's a Bentley Flying Spur, Mr Ledger. I'm sure you'll have no complaints."

He goes to place our bags in the boot of that beast of a car, and Tom says no more. Personally, I associate limos with drunk teenagers on the way to an end-of-year dance and don't feel we're missing out.

Sendilen points me to the front passenger seat, and I clamber into the climate-controlled interior. There must be millions of people in the world who are so used to luxury travel that posh cars are no longer impressive, but I can only reiterate that I am not one of them.

Our driver pulls out of the parking space into a line of traffic to exit the airport as Tom bores him with boasts about his life as a day trader in the City of London.

"Are there more of our friends coming?" Sasha leans forward so that she's speaking straight into Sendilen's ear. "Or are they already on the boat?"

He hesitates this time. "I believe there are more people arriving on a later flight. I could not say exactly who they are." There's something a little mysterious about him, and it's hard to say if it's because of his professional discretion or there are secrets he's been instructed not to reveal.

To be honest, the whole thing is insane. Ade just expected us to travel halfway across the world with less than two weeks' notice. I might have been doing something important. I absolutely wasn't, and I'm so glad he invited us, but he couldn't have known that. I'd had to confirm my attendance by email to an unnamed assistant too. I couldn't even ring to talk it through with him.

We leave the city behind and are soon zipping down long, straight motorways between sugar fields. I only know that they're sugar fields because of a Wikipedia article I read. We don't get much of a sugarcane crop where I'm from. The English countryside isn't exactly known for its tropical climate.

"Dodos," I say aloud instead of just thinking it, as more of my reading comes back to me.

"I'm afraid you've arrived too late to see any." Sendilen sounds smoother by the minute, and Sasha finds this hilarious.

"I came here as a kid, and there weren't any around then either," she says, still smiling. "Maybe we bumped into one another."

Am I wrong in thinking that her voice has a hint of flirtatiousness in it? Either way, Tom doesn't care. His head turning back and forth, he looks out of the window, like a dog trying and failing to fix on one spot.

Sendilen, on the other hand, is good at everything. He knows just how to distract from whatever thought has entered Sasha's head by changing his voice to sound like a very dry tourist guide. "We're in the south of the island. Some of the wildest countryside on the island is down here. There's one walk in particular where you pass seven waterfalls. They're known as the Seven Falls."

He half turns to smile at me, and I feel that I've been let in on one of his secrets. His little speech has the desired effect: Tom and Sasha shut up, and the car falls quiet. Somehow, this is far worse than the chatter that preceded it. I keep having half-second flashbacks to the last time we were together – to when all the positivity of our first years at university was erased with shouts and arguments for reasons that I never fully understood.

The tone of Sasha's voice on the plane reminds me of her *I'm-so-over-this* posturing before we all found better people to live with for the final year. Tom's drunken slurring brings back the memory of when I found him in my room in the middle of the night, peeing in my rubber plant. And in and out of every other image, I see Ade.

We make it to the marina and pull up beside a sleek black boat that is bigger than my flat.

This still isn't enough to impress Tom. "I've seen swankier."

Our driver gets out of the car and shakes his head despairingly as soon as he's sure the idiot in the back can't see him. I leave the vehicle too, and I swear that it's five degrees hotter than when I got in. The air doesn't so much caress my body as give it a good slap.

"This is not your friend's yacht, Mr Ledger," Sendilen says as he opens the door for Sasha, and Tom climbs out on the other side. "This is the boat that will take us to him."

It's a fairly small marina with a few unglamorous fishing boats scattered around it, so perhaps a yacht like Ade's can't even dock in mere, everyday human facilities. The water is that exquisite blue I saw from the plane. The sun is shining and, now deprived of the car's air conditioning, I regret not taking the time to remove the heavy outer layers that I'd chosen for a chilly London spring.

I'm the last to clamber aboard and the boat zips away from the land. The wind rushes across my skin, and as soon as I have a steady place to sit, I yank off my jumper with a robin on it to avoid boiling like rice. I've already decided that I will never go home again. Why do so many people live in cold places when there are far nicer hot ones? With all the money that there is in London, couldn't we simply move the whole city to a desert somewhere, plant a load of trees to encourage rainfall, and be a lot happier?

A cheery captain waves from the controls as fine white spray splashes up in a regular rhythm. The only thing stopping me from pinching myself is the sound of Tom retching at the front of the boat. At least he had the decency to spare us that particular spectacle. Sasha looks out to sea, as if she's worried about what lies ahead, and I can't honestly blame her. Judging by the conversations I heard on the plane, and her reaction when she saw me, there are worse things in life than being single.

She and Ade were always very flirty too. That's something else that's come back to me. If she is anything like me, the thought of our imminent meeting is running on a loop through her head. And to make it worse, she has to insert the figure of her mess of a husband into any fantastical version she can concoct.

Sasha was always a bit of a mystery to me. Her thoughts were rarely imaginable behind her dark eyes. Perhaps it was the confidence that comes with being so beautiful, but I remember finding her strangely distant, even as she left her mark on every party and night out we ever had. I want to ask if she's okay, but something stops me. I feel as if whatever small connection we once shared has been severed by time, and anything I say now will be intrusive.

"Was it easy for Tom to get time off work?" I ask this perfectly banal question, if only to cover his moaning.

Her head whips in my direction so fast that I'm sure she must have hurt her neck. She examines me for a few seconds, just as she did when we met at the airport.

"Off work?" she answers, and then the world comes rushing back to her. "Oh, yes... I mean, no, it wasn't difficult." She adjusts her tone. Her demeanour changes with it, and she suddenly plays the proud wife. "He's hugely respected at his company. When he says he needs a holiday, the bosses accept it."

Perhaps it's his drunkenness that makes her show off Tom's credentials. I can see how badly she needs to prove that, despite appearances to the contrary, the dear fellow is a terribly big cheese.

"And you don't act anymore?" I hope that my voice is light and only mildly interested, but as I say the words, I realise that I shouldn't know this about her. I only found out because of the conversation I overheard on the plane.

She tilts her pretty head and glances at me across the bench in the middle of the boat. "That's right. I gave it all up to focus on..." She hesitates then changes what she was going to say. "I needed some *me* time, so Tom goes to work for the both of us."

I want to ask how far she got in her acting career, but as I know the end of that particular story, there's no way of phrasing it without sounding unkind.

"What about you?" she asks when I don't say anything for a few seconds. "Are you still writing?"

It's hard to know whether she really cares about the answer, or she is playing the part of someone who cares, but I tell the truth.

"No, I..." Well, I hesitate for about five seconds and then tell the truth. "I've been doing the same job for nine years, and I hated it more than I can say. So when Ade sent me the invitation, I quit."

"Wow." This apparently wasn't what she was expecting. Her

truly green eyes widen and her lips part. "That's just so you, Bridge. You're amazing."

That certainly wasn't what *I* was expecting, and I fail to produce a response.

"You were always more liberated than me," she hurries to explain. "I'm not the kind of person who could give up a job on the spur of the moment. I would need to sit down and write out a list of pros and cons. And even then, I would agonise over the decision for months."

"There's nothing special about me." I don't mind compliments if I'm worthy of them, but I feel the need to correct her. "I haven't written so much as a limerick since we left uni. I took a mindless office job to forget the fact I have no talent."

Her eyes glisten, and I'm afraid she really will cry this time. I suddenly feel as if it's her I was insulting but, before I can apologise, there's a shout from the front of the boat.

"For goodness' sake," Tom complains, and Sasha instinctively shoots to her feet. "I can't actually believe it."

"What's the matter?" Sendilen pokes his head over the windshield (or whatever sailors call that part of the boat).

Tom staggers back to us, looking as white as a sail. It's hard to say whether it's his drinking, the recent sickness or what he has now glimpsed that has brought about the transformation. He slowly raises his arm and extends one finger to reply. "That."

I see what's caused his outburst a moment before he explains, and I'm a little light-headed myself. Ade's yacht is titanic.

"That's not a boat," Tom says in a voice distorted with envy. "It's the lost city of Atlantis."

I wander closer to the prow to make sense of the colossal vessel that, in two minutes' time, will block out the sun as we pull up to it. It has at least six storeys, all glossy, shining white, and I think I might know why the top decks are cut off at such a dramatic angle. Now that I think about it, it was kind of cheap of Ade not to fly us here by helicopter if there's a helipad on board.

The whole thing looks like the image of a space yacht that a child might draw. There are spinning things and antennas on the roof of the bridge deck. And each level has long rows of windows that I bravely predict will give the most beautiful views of the Indian Ocean. I'm already picturing the swimming pools, bowling alleys and champagne bar that we are about to discover.

I've never been a materialistic person, but that's probably because I've never seen a ship like this before.

FIVE

"I'm sure that you'll enjoy your time on board the *Tanis*," Sendilen tells Sasha as he helps her from a very expensive boat onto an impossibly expensive one.

"You mean you're not staying?" There's a hint of alarm in her voice, and I wonder what she was hoping would happen. Had she set her heart on leaving her husband and enjoying island life with the handsome Mauritian driver?

"I have to meet more of your friends at the airport, but I'll see you again."

There are two staircases that sweep down from the deck above and a low platform at the level of the water for people to board. Sendilen offers me his hand next, and I lunge across the gap.

The yacht's name is printed in large black letters on the hull. '*Tanis*' means nothing to me, but then I haven't seen Ade for a decade, so that's hardly surprising. It could be the name of his girlfriend or his niece, and I'd be none the wiser. The papers – and yes, I have read practically every article ever written about him – always describe Ade as a perpetual bachelor. Rumours of links to a tennis player and a couple of famous actresses came to nothing, but it wouldn't be a total shock if he'd called us here to meet his smoking-hot fiancée.

I don't know why I'm crossing my fingers that this isn't the case. I swear I've never dreamt of becoming Ade Okojie's wife. If anything, I think it's the potential awkwardness of having to watch my friends' reaction to such a scenario that makes me cringe.

Either way, there is no terrifyingly lithe Swedish supermodel here to welcome us as we look up those shiny black stairs. Instead, an approximately teenage waitress in an anonymous white blouse and black skirt stands at the top with a tray of drinks.

Tom sees his prize and pushes us out of the way to thunder towards her. It's almost comical, but for the fact the man is clearly a mess. I don't think I've ever wanted something so much in my life as he wants a helping of wine just a few hours after his last glass.

"Tom, would you give it a break?" Sasha begs.

"We're on holiday," he shouts back over his shoulder without looking.

"Yeah. Holiday..." His wife shakes her head, and this time I can't help it. I put my arm around her and guide her up the opposite staircase to the one Tom just mounted.

"Don't worry, Sash," I tell her with a smile. "It's a big ship. If he keeps getting under your skin, we'll divide it in two. You can have the top decks, and we'll lock him downstairs."

Like the sun coming out from behind the non-existent clouds, Sasha's face brightens. She doesn't say anything but squeezes my hand as we walk up the stairs.

"Sparkling wine, ladies?" the girl asks in a South London accent. I'm still not used to being waited on like this.

"It's not even champagne?" Tom complains because, apparently, that is what he does these days. It doesn't stop him pouring the drink down his neck. "Where's Ade?"

The poor girl – I now feel sorry for anyone who interacts with Tom – doesn't look like she knows what to say, and so I step in to make it better.

"Thank you so much for the wine. I'm Bridget."

"Phoebe," she hesitantly replies, but I have a feeling this will be the extent of our interaction.

Tom huffs and puffs his way up another flight of stairs. I hadn't noticed it before, but his whole frame is bulkier than when we were younger. He was always a big guy, but there's an extra broadness to him now. I guess traders sit at a desk all day, and he's clearly not the type to spend his free time sweating in a gym.

There's a flat section on the main deck where the helipad is located. Towering over it are the four raised levels of the ship with the control tower at the top. At the front, each deck is a little longer than the one above, but at the rear of the boat, they end quite suddenly to give the currently absent helicopter room to land.

"Welcome aboard," a man whose manner is uncannily similar to Sendilen's says in a soft voice. He stands in the middle of the large white H on the deck and holds his hands out as if to say, *This is your home for the week*. "My name is Shabeer. I am the chief steward, and anything I can do for you while you are here, I will."

His sentence is a little wonky, as though he wasn't certain what he wished to say when he started speaking. I know from Wikipedia that, if he comes from Mauritius, he's likely to speak multiple languages, so who am I to complain? I got a B in my school French exams, and the only thing I remember how to say is "What a beautiful bookshelf, madam. Where did you get it?"

"Hey, Shabeer? Get us a—" Tom begins, but Sasha elbows him in the guts before he can make a very obvious pun on the man's name.

"Is Ade on board?" she asks. "We're all eager to see him."

Shabeer's smile tells us that everything is fine and there's no need to worry. "Mr Okojie is being a little busy at the moment, but he will come to find you forthwith. Perhaps if you'd like to see your cabins, you can follow me."

Before I can ask whether anyone brought our possessions on board, a figure wanders over from the side of the yacht. There's a half-second's excitement before I realise that it isn't our host.

"I'll look after our guests, Shabeer," the shabby character exclaims before turning to us. "I'm Mick."

The newcomer definitely thinks we should know who he is,

but Sasha and Tom don't have a clue. He does the same arms-apart welcoming gesture as Shabeer did, but his eyes never quite settle on us. He's wearing a yellow sleeveless vest and brightly patterned shorts. His beard is unkempt, his arms covered in tattoos, and he isn't the kind of person I expected to meet on a luxury yacht.

"Mick!" he says again and then he pretends to play the drums for us. To be fair, he does a pretty good job of it.

"Mick." It finally clicks, for me at least. "We met once. It was backstage at the Astoria."

"The Astoria! That takes me back." Mick claps his hands, and I notice that there's something not quite right about them. They're darker than the skin on his face and legs, as though they've been trapped in a door. He's about ten years older than the rest of us, but I doubt that's the reason.

He stands there, frozen for a few beats longer than normal. I guess we're both thinking back a decade. Ade put me on the guest list to meet him after the show, at which point he ignored me entirely and made a big deal of hanging out with his far cooler friends. He looked at me like a stalker when I told him that I had to go home. For a long time after that, I just about hated him, and I wasn't the first to feel that way.

"Mick is the drummer in Ade's band," I explain to the others in case they've failed to work this out. "You've been with him since he got big, right?"

Mick's jaw juts out proudly and he nods. His wild, curly hair bobs as he does so, and we wait for him to say something more. There's clearly a delay somewhere. Everything with Mick takes that little bit longer than you would expect.

"Yeah. It was me, Ade, and Jake when we signed with the label. We've got a whole different crew now. You wouldn't believe it." I think he must realise that he's kept us waiting long enough, as he points to go. "Shall we...?"

Sasha looks relieved that this conversation has concluded. She was never one of Ade's groupies – never a rock chick. They used to hang out despite his music, not because of it. She walks alongside

Mick as he crosses the helipad and starts to describe the features of the yacht.

"I've only been on board for a few days, but I love it here. There are three different jacuzzis that I know about, so I've spent most of my time in there." He holds his discoloured hands up to show that his skin is still wrinkled from his last dip. "Then downstairs there's a gym and library. The bar is amazing. Wait until you see that. And there's all sorts of fun and games hidden about the place."

He stops as the walkway we've navigated ends, and we come out on the sun deck. The jacuzzi is surrounded by a white padded bench for lounging on, and the floor is made of glossy wood.

"All the wood here is the finest teak," Mick announces, as if this is just as impressive as the fact our friend owns a ship with its own gym and library on board. "And up there is Captain Andy. Give him a wave."

Dutifully, if hesitantly, Sasha and I wave up to the bank of windows on the second staggered deck above us. We see a shadow move on the ceiling, but little else.

"Where is—" The question we all want to ask forms on Tom's lips, but Mick cuts him off.

"I'll show you to your cabins. Prepare to have your minds blown."

We turn back on ourselves to reach the main salon, which I would tell you was bigger than my flat at home, but I'm growing tired of that comparison. Mick chatters as we go, talking of the main deck, bridge deck and upper deck as if they were terms he'd always used.

I feel like we're walking through a show home. As I peek into a huge lounge, with its TV wall and bar, I have that same feeling of mild disgust that I'd had when I boarded the plane. I can't help wondering whether, if I had fifty million pounds, or however much this stupid, beautiful ship cost, I would blow it on a floating hotel. I like to think I'd buy a huge swathe of the rainforest to protect it for future generations, but I'm probably more selfish than I know.

"There are three suites on this floor and four smaller ones on the deck below." Perhaps Mick is no longer a drummer and now works as a yacht salesman. He points to the next windowless door we come to. "This one is mine, and the one we just passed is the master suite where our mutual friend is having a lie-down."

This news sets my teeth on edge. We've come all this way to see Ade, and he hasn't bothered greeting us because he needs a nap. Is that the behaviour of a normal person? And for that matter, does a normal person send his friends plane tickets rather than just picking up the phone? I know rich people have a special licence for being eccentric, but the same question keeps throbbing in my head: why did I ever think this would be a good idea?

"This one's for you two," Mick tells my companions with a smile as he bangs on the next door.

Tom puts his arm around Sasha, who is so excited that she doesn't even mind. She darts forward to push the sliding door aside and practically falls into the room. Unsurprisingly, it's a big space with lots of expensive stuff in it. The bedside lamps look like antique silver candlesticks. There are two crossed oars above the bed, and I'm pretty sure that a concealed television will rise up from the floor if you know which button to press. None of this changes the fact that much of the decoration is decidedly tasteless.

There are three prints in Day-Glo colours with ridiculous slogans on them. One says "21st Century Chastity Belt" on a plain blue background. Another has a picture of Salvador Dali grinning with the words "All men are legends, but not all legends are men" painted over him, and the third is just the word "Art" with an upside-down question mark on either side of it.

All in all, they make me feel empty and a little bit sad. Is this soulless hotchpotch of styles really the best that money can buy? I'm tempted to rip the prints off the wall and throw them out to sea, but I'm not that bad a guest, and Tom stands nodding as if he finds them thought-provoking.

"Come on, kid." Mick pokes me in the shoulder for some

reason as Sasha copies the expression of the grinning artist on the wall. "I'll take you down to your cabin."

He walks off before I can say anything, so I leave my friends in their room and scamper after him.

"I've spent most of the last decade touring. I'm glad of the break." He sighs the sigh of a truck driver who has just completed a round trip to Mongolia. "You know how it is."

His beard obscures half his face, but I try to work out how much older he is than me. I remember that Ade met him gigging in London rather than through the university, and he'd already been in a load of bands that never made it big. As he rattles on about his time as a famous drummer that no one has heard of, he gives off those *old-man-who's-seen-it-all* vibes. I get the feeling that, if he hadn't fallen in with Ade, he'd be propping up a bar somewhere, thinking back on the glory days that never were.

"This is yours," he says as we reach the deck below and he opens the first door on the right. "Not too bad, is it?" Before I answer, he hits his forehead with the ball of his hand and begins to walk away. "Sorry, I've forgotten something I have to do... Shabeer? Shabeer?"

He goes off, shouting the name over and over, though the chance of the steward hearing him on such a big ship is surely very small.

Once I'm alone, I look around the room, which is a slightly smaller version of the one I've just seen. It's all black and white and ever so plush, but I'm tired of artificial neatness, and wish it was more lived-in. The only real thing in here is my tatty suitcase, which has already been delivered by some unseen minion. The whole room is unbalanced; the bed is too close to the door, and there's a wall giving onto the side of the boat that is strangely free of decoration.

For some reason, I have a burning desire to know where the TV is hidden. If there's one thing I know about rich people it's that they love hiding their TVs, so I grab the two remotes from the nightstand and click the buttons like crazy.

Just before another ugly painting retracts to expose the telly, the big blank wall slides away and there's the ocean, right in my bedroom. Well, there's a swish balcony with seating for six, but the water is just beyond it. There's even an extendable diving board you can jump off, which reminds me of a pirate story that used to scare me when I was a kid.

My nerves haven't exactly settled when the whole ship shudders. The sound of a lifting chain clanks across the bow, and we start to move.

I'd say there was something magical about this, but that would be inaccurate. There's something mechanical about this. The change from stillness to motion without a single person appearing before me is proof of just how much is going on out of sight. I suppose I'll have to get used to the fact that I am no longer a cog in a machine. I'm a passenger on one.

SIX

I keep my eye on the land in the hope that I'll catch sight of Sendilen bringing the others to the yacht, but we're already moving away from the shore. Does this mean that they're not coming? Will it just be me, a warring couple, a reclusive rock star and his seen-it-all drummer?

I wonder whether I'm being kidnapped without even realising it.

This seems like a good moment to tell myself not to get worked up unnecessarily. And for once, I listen. I spend five minutes wondering whether I will look an idiot if I put on a bikini and sarong, before spending a few more worrying that I will look a total idiot if I don't. I plump for the former and head off to explore.

It turns out that the ship was fairly busy when we arrived, but it's truly dead now. I feel like I've been called here to haunt it. I keep hoping that I'll bump into Shabeer, or Sasha will emerge from her suite, but I don't even see the girl with the wine again. I sit beside the jacuzzi and wave up at the captain to remind myself that I'm not totally alone in the world.

The quiet of this immense vessel, as we glide across the Indian Ocean, is oddly unnerving. Even the warm breeze sends a chill through me, and I may be the first person in history to have goosebumps in twenty-eight-degree heat.

After a while, I go back to the main lounge and try to work out how to turn on the TV wall. I've honestly seen smaller screens in sports stadiums. It kind of surprises me that the channel that comes on is for kids. Fred Flintstone's head is the size of a fridge, but I don't care. I just can't stand the silence anymore.

The sound of canned laughter and things breaking provides exactly what I need. Perhaps if people did this to calm themselves down in horror films and indie dramas filled with existential dread, those stories would turn out a lot better for everyone involved.

The Flintstones' pet dinosaur bites his master's hand, which makes Fred jump into the air and sort of hang there for a few seconds as his toes wiggle in pain. I know how he feels, suspended like that, but then I click the button about fifty times until I find a music channel, and Ade is there with me at last. His face fills the screen, and he looks me dead in the eyes with all the soulful understanding he ever had when we were friends.

It's only when I hear the repeated thwack of a helicopter blade growing slowly louder that I pull away from the comforting glow of the billion-pixel screen. Tom and Sasha hear it too and get there before me, but I reach the back of the ship just in time to see the small black aircraft coming in to land. Just like Fred in the cartoon, it hovers in the air over its landing point for a few seconds and then drops straight down.

I can see Sendilen sitting beside the pilot in the cockpit, so I guess his duties extend to more than just driving, but I won't be able to ask him because he stays on board. The rotors keep spinning, and the doors at the side of the helicopter open. A bag flies out before I see anyone, then Jake jumps down, making sure to protect his head as he does so.

I've been trying not to think too much about my ex-boyfriend, but there's no longer any way to avoid it. He hasn't changed. He still wears a black leather jacket, just like when we dated. Still has that shifting glance, as though he wants to check that no one's watching him, and he's still kind of adorable. I feel a sting inside me as he looks back at the helicopter and helps the other guests down. I try to ignore what might have caused it.

I know who I'm expecting next, but she's not there. Of the seven of us who used to live together, only six of us are here, and Dawn isn't one of them. She was our unifying force – the popular, positive heart of the group – and it feels instantly wrong to be here without her.

In her place are our ex-flatmate Clara (who I've felt guilty about not getting in touch with for approximately the last eleven years) and a shy, chubby-cheeked guy I barely remember. I think he was a drama student with Sasha, and his name was... Adam, maybe? I have no idea why he's here instead of Dawn.

"Jake, you old tosser!" Tom says, because this is the kind of thing that Tom says. He rushes past me, shoulder-barging his wife out of the way as he goes.

"All right, Tom." Jake is understated and in control even as the man-child darts towards him.

Tom is not. He picks up his old flatmate and spins him around like they're lovers reunited after a war. Even this doesn't faze Jake. He looks askance as he waits to be put back down. His failure to enjoy this spectacle does not sit well with Tom, who immediately moves off to the next newcomer.

"Clara, it's great to see you." Something about the way he talks is off. I don't know if it's the drink that is coursing through him or something more, but he's enthusiastic to an artificial degree. He rushes off to the final member of the group, who looks serious as he untangles the strap on his bag.

"And Alan!"

"It's Ryan," he corrects him. "My name's Ryan."

"That's right, Ryan." Tom acts as if the guy had misheard and then stands there looking uncertain as to what more he can possibly say. "You're here too."

This uncomfortable scene is interrupted by the sound of the helicopter taking off again. Sendilen offers a wave through the window. I bet he's glad to get away from us. He must be used to spoilt individuals in his line of work, but Tom is something else.

When the noise dies down, there's a sense of uncertainty in the group. There are pieces missing, and we don't know how to act without them. Ade and Dawn would have made this feel okay, but there's no one here to tell us what comes next.

To break the stalemate, I run over to Clara and smother her in a hug.

"It's nice to be here." She's so shy that she blushes, but I think she's pleased to see me.

"All right, Bridge?" Jake has waited his turn, and we stand in front of one another, unsure whether to hug or shake hands or kiss each other's cheeks.

"Hello, old friend." There are more awkward responses I could have fashioned, but not many.

He grins back at me all the same. His brown eyes are lighter than I remember, with flecks of orange and hazel. Up close with him for the first time in forever, I'm surprised by just how much the reunion affects me. My body's become stiff, and I instantly regret being so standoffish.

After waiting so long, it's a relief when I hear a noise on the deck above us, and there's the man we've come to see.

"Look at you all," Ade shouts down, and his frighteningly handsome face is only enhanced by his whitened smile.

Just as suddenly as he popped up there, he points over his shoulder and disappears from view. It occurs to me that this scene has been stage-managed. Ade was only standing on that balcony for effect – the helicopter was only deployed for effect. His cabin is on this level, and I doubt he had any reason to go upstairs except for the impression it would make. He was saying, *Now that everyone's here, I will honour you with my presence.*

Sasha is chatting to Ryan. She's the only one of us who knew him particularly well, though now that I think about it, I can remember him leading a pack of unshakable groupies that Ade's band picked up before they were famous.

"Of course, I was always very lucky when I was acting because of my unplaceable ethnic identity," Sasha explains, pointing to her naturally tanned colouring on the off-chance we hadn't noticed it. "I could play everything from Arabic to Italian, and I was told that casting directors adored such flexibility."

"Good for you," Ryan mumbles, and it's clear that he feels even more out of place here than the rest of us.

"I'd forgotten that." Tom wears a pensive look, and I can tell from his tone that he's about to say something irritating. "You were the token non-white person in a bunch of things, even though you're actually white."

Sasha has no time for a withering look or even a tut, as our host now appears. Ade glides around the corner, and I imagine that, in his head, he's walking out to a crowd of thousands. He somehow looks cooler than I've ever seen him. His dreadlocks are short and dyed in a scale from blonde to bronze. They're swept forward on top and shaved close at the sides. The artificially light colour makes his blemishless skin all the blacker.

"Look at you all," he says again, and I get the feeling he took a long time planning his opening line and wants to make the most of it. "You're beautiful."

It would be easy to roll my eyes and call him a flatterer, but he speaks with such sincerity that a wave of gratitude sweeps over us, and we all smile back because the man who was once voted *GQ* magazine's man of the year just said that we are beautiful.

Tom is suddenly on his best behaviour. "Mate, it is so kind of you to invite us here." He extends his hand formally before Ade takes it in both of his.

"This is amazing." Sasha looks around the ship as she awaits his attention.

The rest of us are more restrained, but I can see that even cool-as-Pepsi Jake is anticipating his moment. This is our reunion. It's all we've been thinking about for the ten days since the letters arrived. It's all we've been thinking about for the last ten years.

"It is my pleasure." Ade is grinning so much that his sparkling teeth are still on display. Has he had work done on them? I'm pretty sure they were never that white or straight before. "It's just so incredible to see you all. I can't believe you came."

"Get over here, you." Sounding like a grandma, I pull him in for a hug.

The last time I saw Ade, he was an about-to-be. Now he's a genuine rock star. I don't know if it's a filter that I apply when looking at famous people, but there's a magic about him that you don't often encounter. His eyes are brighter than anyone else's. His skin is smoother. He's almost unbearably perfect.

It's not just the way he looks. His cologne is as fresh as the ocean, and his muscles feel impossibly firm as he hugs me back. It reminds me that there was always something just a little bit dangerous about him. It wasn't as if he was cruel, but it was impossible to say what he was thinking. I never quite knew what was going on behind the mask.

"Thank you, Bridget," he whispers in my ear. "Thank you for coming."

For years after our last meeting, I felt nothing but anger towards the great Adesina Okojie, but seeing him now makes me feel like I'm home again after a lifetime spent away. We pull apart and, even though he's standing right in front of me, I miss him more than I ever have before. I can already tell that, when this trip is over, his absence will be intolerable.

Jake's still cagey. He's barely said anything since he arrived, and when his turn comes to shower our guru with attention, he doesn't quite deliver.

"It's good to be here," he says in his typically rough, ironic tone, as though he's embarrassed to express even this limited emotion.

I notice that he doesn't say, *It's great to see you.* In fact, he can't bring himself to look at the man who has paid for all this, and Ade might have seen it too if it weren't for the fact that he keeps looking over at Ryan, who stands back from the action, out of the circle a step or two.

"Hi Ade," the outsider says, and the two exchange a nod and a brief handshake.

I have no idea why this is happening. Ade knows the guy well enough to invite him to sail off into the sunset with us but is acting like they've never met before.

"Are you going to tell us what we're doing here now?" Tom's directness almost makes me like him. I'm sure it won't last.

Ade is holding Clara by the shoulder and looking at her like she's the prize at the end of a quiz show. When he comes back to us, he tries to distract Tom by pointing to Phoebe, who has returned with a bottle and a tray of wine glasses. His knowing gesture makes me wonder whether Ade's done his research on what each of us is up to these days:

Tom is a drunk.

Jake has been frozen in time since the last day of our final term.

I have no life...

You get the idea.

"We're going to get reacquainted," he announces, still grinning, still apparently overwhelmed at seeing everyone again, "and it's going to be incredible."

SEVEN

The sound of Ade playing an acoustic guitar is picked up by the breeze as we laze around the oversized jacuzzi. For the moment, we're all still faking it. Everyone's so amazed by the man and his world that we're pretending that we're the best of friends and there is nothing strange about us hanging out together. There's a sort of forced positivity to everything we say that helps us gloss over any drama that occurred back when we were still in one another's lives. No one mentions the end of our time together. No mentions anything of any real importance.

"Have you got a boyfriend now, Bridget?" Sasha asks ever so innocently.

She is kneeling in front of me with her chest beneath the water so that she looks even more toned and fit than before. Her electric blue bikini is like a flashing sign directing all eyes straight at her.

"I actually just broke up with someone." This seems like an honest answer, but then I realise that a whole year has passed since Paul moved out. "I'm enjoying being single for a while." I fail to not look at Jake as I say this.

"It's kind of weird that none of us have children," Ryan puts in from across the pool. "I mean, we're old enough, but here we are. Free to jet off at a moment's notice."

In response, Tom looks at his wife with a wounded grimace. Clara looks away altogether, and Jake tips his head back to challenge him.

"How do you know I haven't got kids?" There's an edge to his voice, and it's clear he's taken it personally for some reason. It makes me wonder once more why Dawn isn't here to stop this kind of thing.

"Sorry, I just assumed—"

Jake bursts out laughing, which somehow makes the atmosphere worse. "I'm only joking, Ryan. I mean, you shouldn't make assumptions, and I do have a kid, but I'm messing with you."

Tom turns to look at him. "*You* have a kid?" He does nothing to hide his surprise. "How old is he?"

"It's a girl, not a boy," Jake answers with a smile. He has made an attempt to look summery, in that he's wearing shorts and a T-shirt, but the fact that they're both black and the T-shirt has a picture of a snake escaping from a skull limits his laid-back vibe. "Heather's thirteen."

"Thirteen!?" we all want to say, but only Sasha does. "You had her when we were in our first year at uni?"

Jake wears the same reluctant smile he had when meeting Ade. "In a way. Though, in a far truer way, I got a girl pregnant, denied that the baby was mine and had nothing to do with my daughter until I got my head together a few years back."

The hush that now falls is so loud that it drowns out the sound of the wind and the waves as the boat pushes on. Even Ade's tuneful strumming does nothing to make it better.

Jake always liked awkward moments and waits a few seconds before continuing. "The mum was a girl on my music course. She dropped out after the first semester and raised the kid without my help. I was a pretty terrible person, to be honest, but I'm trying to make amends. I spent most of my twenties a total mess, but drugs and drink and feeling sorry for yourself will do that to you. It's a good thing you got rid of me from the band when you did, eh, Ade?"

His stare is so intense that I half expect him to lunge forward and smash the guitar over Ade's head. For his part, our host shows no sign of having heard. He just keeps sliding his fingers up and down the strings with that metallic scrape you hear on intimate acoustic recordings.

When Jake laughs next, he wants us to think that it's not a big deal, but I can tell it is. He looks over at Mick, who is lying on the white sunbed in nothing but a pair of tiny red Speedos. I finally think of an explanation for the weirdly purplish colour of the drummer's hands. I look at his body for track marks, but the light's too strong, and I can only see the black hair that covers him like a suit.

Sasha changes the topic to avoid any further confrontation. "You always were a wind-up merchant, Jake." She shakes her head encouragingly. "I reckon you're a big kid at heart."

He leans back and takes the half-compliment, half-insult with a smile.

"Dawn has kids," Ade says, and his contribution makes everyone turn to look. "I invited her this week, but she couldn't come. I called her to catch up instead."

This almost makes me laugh. A phone call? Why didn't the rest of us get one of those?

"She sounded good, you know?" Ade flashes his pearly whites. His voice is thick with nostalgia. "The same old busy little bee, organising her family now instead of us."

Perhaps that's why he brought us here: for old times' sake. This doubt hangs over us, and when no one knows how to continue the conversation, it fragments. Sasha paddles over to stare adoringly at Ade, who guffaws at whatever she says as her husband glares. Tom distracts himself by talking about football or rugby or something that makes Ryan look intolerably bored, and I turn to Clara, who's hiding under a parasol beside me. Near-transparent people like us know not to mess with ultraviolet rays.

"I'm really glad you're here," I say, having decided that there's no need to apologise for losing contact because friendship goes both ways. "And I'm sorry for not getting in touch." Fine, I instantly abandoned this resolution. "I don't know where the time's gone. It's been years."

Her golden-brown eyebrows curve, and her shyness rises to the surface – much like Sasha's possibly enhanced cleavage. "I'm sorry too. I moved home after leaving London, and I felt so stupid for not doing more with my life that I stopped talking to anyone from back then."

"It was a bubble." I suppose I identify a little too closely with what she's said as, instead of immediately explaining what I mean, I stare up at the sky. "We were surrounded by all those talented people, and we convinced ourselves that creativity was all that mattered."

"I know exactly what you mean." She smiles, and it makes me happier. "When we were at uni, it felt as if only the artists with their own gallery shows and the writers who already had short stories published would go on to change the world. I always saw myself as so inferior, but when it comes down to it, everything is just as messed up now as it was before. We may be sitting on Ade's billion-dollar yacht, but he's just another pop star, like all the others. There are still wars and hatred. At least my work at the old people's home helps in some small way."

"So you stopped painting?" I ask a little too keenly. I hate that I want her to say yes so that I don't feel bad about my own creative inertia.

"No, I still paint." She looks at the horizon as if searching for a colour to daub over a canvas. "I just don't show anyone anymore."

My throat is dry, and I wish I could continue our friendly conversation in the same tone as before, but the only comments that come to mind sound trivial or mean, so I hold my tongue.

"I still see Dawn sometimes," she explains in a more serious voice. "She was always so good at looking out for us, wasn't she? She even brings her kids to story time in the home on Saturday mornings. We're quite good friends these days."

I forgot that she and Dawn came from the same place. Chester or Chelmsford or Chichester or somewhere. I suddenly feel left out of their cute little meetups, and before I can reply, Tom's loud voice interrupts us.

"No, just a normal beer."

"I'm afraid we only have alcohol-free, sir." Phoebe the waitress is holding a tray with a can and a glass on it, and her eyes stray over to her boss, who just keeps strumming.

"What do you mean?" Tom's little mind is working away. I bet he's thinking back to the wine we had and wondering what was in it. He's about to open his mouth to complain when Ade starts singing.

"Yeah, I broke all my promises."

If he'd chosen any other song, it wouldn't have worked. Tom would have thrown a tantrum like a two-year-old, and there would have been nothing we could do to repair the mood.

"I did it all for me."

But like the star that he is, he knew exactly when to play us his biggest song. He knows the power it has. Because even though he's had three massive albums since then, and each has had its own stratospheric singles, he'll always be associated with the enormous hit that made his name.

"I left you crying, left you alone."

If you go onto setlist.fm, you'll see that he's finished every single concert he's ever played with that song. It would be insane not to, and that's why he brought it out right now.

"I chose to set myself free."

Ade has a voice that's part Tracy Chapman, part Jagger. It's coarse and tortured and, even though "Promises" is all about betrayal, it's somehow the singer you end up feeling for. It's so potent that Mick wakes up from his doze and starts drumming on the bench just at the moment that the digital beat comes in on the record.

That was what helped Ade break through. He was the indie darling who embraced the club scene. The remix of his biggest single helped him sell ten times as many copies as the original version. And after a few bars of that breakbeat, a bass line starts pounding, his voice gets all distorted, and it sounds as if he's singing through tears. When you're jumping about to it with your mates, you forget all that, but the emotion is still there.

Sasha isn't worried what the lyrics mean as she grins up at our hero, and she certainly isn't thinking about her husband's desperate need to continue his bender. I doubt she's even questioned what the possible absence of alcohol on the boat might mean. She is in love with Ade and with this moment. She is happy.

I feel as if I'm watching this whole thing on television, and, in keeping with the high production values, a desert island comes into view. I stand up next to the jacuzzi to make sure it's real. Long-tailed white birds swoop along the coast like arrows shot from the heavens. There's a perfect beach that a child might have drawn, studded with large rocks and a neat treeline with swaying branches. At the far end, an immense cliff face rears up, seemingly out of nothing, and I want to jump from the yacht to swim out and claim the place as my own. I want to live there for ever.

Just as I'm thinking that this really is paradise, there's a thud on the parasol above me, and I jump out of my skin as an immense black bird slides grimly off it to land on the deck in front of me.

EIGHT

We all stare at the unearthly, bat-like creature with its dirty red breast and huge curved wings. It's intimidatingly large and must be a metre from the tip of its tail feathers to its beak.

"Is it dead?" Sasha asks, pulling herself up and out of the water to inspect the intruder.

"Its eyes are moving." Tom is clearly freaked out and carefully moves behind the girl with the tray when he thinks no one is looking.

"I'm pretty sure that's an albatross," Clara whispers, and the literary significance is lost on no one.

The bird slowly turns its head in our direction, and I remember how scared I was watching the first vampire film I ever saw when I was a kid.

"Looks more like a pterodactyl." Jake laughs the laugh of someone pretending he isn't scared.

Ryan is braver than the rest of us. He walks a little closer and tries to put our minds at ease. "It's a male frigatebird. Albatrosses are plumper and don't have red plumage. Pterodactyls have been extinct for millions of years."

I expect someone to challenge him on this. I was sure that Tom would say, *Who are you to say what it is?* But as we know so little about Ryan, it's perfectly plausible that he's an ornithologist.

Ade puts down the guitar and approaches the creature from the other side of the pool. "Hello, buddy. There's nothing to—"

Before he can finish the sentence, the animal launches itself at him, and my screams follow Tom's. The frigatebird shows its talons and flaps its wings, but Ade ducks just in time to avoid it. The bird rises through the air unsteadily before finding its rhythm and circling the boat with a judgemental call.

When it disappears behind the upper levels, the silence breaks and Ade's full, tuneful laugh fires up.

"That was ridiculous," Tom says, trying to be cool.

"You're ridiculous," his wife tells him and, though this could make everything awkward again, we're all relieved that the bird didn't scratch anyone's eyes out, and our laughter travels around the group.

"It was an added bit of excitement." Ade goes to give Tom a reassuring pat on the back, and the drunk pushes his hand away. "But I think I have something more entertaining for us this afternoon."

When we follow him to the back of the yacht, it is not to jump into a speedboat that will take us to the island I'd spotted. It turns out that rich people use such idyllic places as mere backdrops.

"You can head over there if you really want to," he tells us as we descend to the lower level. "But there's not much to see, and we can have a lot more fun right here."

He presses a hidden button, and the seemingly unspectacular area where we boarded is transformed. An electric door opens up between the two curving staircases, and we are introduced to the beach club of the good ship *Tanis*.

"Marco is ready to take your requests." Ade points to a DJ who's stationed at a bar at the end of the long room. "Phoebe will ply us with cocktails." He hurries on to his next point before Tom can ask any questions. "There's a barbecue almost ready, and games to enjoy. Oh, and you can swim right off the boat, of course."

With this, he throws off his cotton robe, sprints along the platform and somersaults through the air to splash into the water.

"You're still a show-off," I shout at him when he comes up for air. My sarong is soaked, but he grins up at me, and I fall under his spell.

Jake lingers on the staircase, watching the two of us, but that awkward smile is still plastered to his face. I get the feeling he'd like to talk to me, but he keeps his distance.

"I know you must be wondering what the plan for the week is." Ade shows no remorse for keeping this from us. "We're going to cross the ocean to get to the Maldives by Friday. There'll be all the island-hopping you want over there, but this is just a quick break before we start the journey in earnest."

We chatter between ourselves like schoolkids who've just been told about the end-of-term trip. We are so easily pleased.

As Ade's speaking, a young, athletic guy in a smart blue polo shirt manoeuvres a floating disc on a chain into the water. It has a target standing on it and, with Ade's help, he pushes it further away from the ship. Tom's competitive instincts kick in, and he rushes to the edge of the platform as Jake comes to see what's happening.

"I thought you might fancy a spot of archery." With beads of water dripping from his expertly chiselled chest, Ade pulls himself up a short ladder and back on board. "The only rule is that, if you miss the target, you have to swim out and get everyone's arrows."

The deck hand or cabin boy or whatever he's called goes into a concealed cupboard and returns with several bows.

Tom eagerly follows him and reappears with a bloodthirsty smile on his face. "What?" he says when we all stop to gawp.

"You look like a psychopath," Ryan tells him, and Tom's wife shrugs but doesn't disagree.

Tom has a loaded crossbow in either hand and is pointing them up at the sky like he thinks he's Rambo.

"I'm not going to shoot anyone, you muppets." He glances down at the primed weapons. "But they are pretty cool."

Sitting on the stairs, Jake and Clara shake their heads in perfect synchronisation. It was always like this. Tom always said the wrong thing and upset people. The only reason we hung out with him was to see Sasha, but now even she doesn't seem to like him.

"Put them down, idiot." Ade doesn't mince his words. "They're easier to use than normal bows, but more likely to go off by accident."

I almost feel sorry for Tom. I considered myself an outsider at university because I wasn't as cool or capable as the others, but he couldn't have been further from his natural environment. The fact he proceeds to shoot a bolt up into the air so that we all have to duck for cover promptly banishes this sympathy. It lands in the water without causing any damage, and Tom smirks like we're the stupid ones.

Shabeer organises a table for lunch as a chef sees to the barbecue on the deck above. Even this is for show. It has clearly been cooking elsewhere for some time, as we're told that the meat is almost ready, and the barbecue wasn't there when we arrived.

In the meantime, Ryan opts out of the game by going for a swim some distance from the target, and the rest of us wait our turn to shoot. Sasha is already making a big fuss about how poor she will be – before no doubt amazing us all with her natural talent – whereas Clara is the first to have a go with one of the crossbows and just about catches the edge of the target.

"It's actually easier than I thought," she says as the unnamed worker reloads the weapon without making eye contact with any of us.

It makes me want to grab him by both cheeks, look at him dead on and tell him he isn't invisible. It makes me wonder what kind of training these people go through to prepare for a job in which they're treated like extras in a movie.

Clara's second shot hits one of the inner rings of the target, and then Jake steps forward with an actual bow. He needs no advice as he raises it to his eye, holds his breath and releases without flinching. The string twangs, the arrow shoots forth (as straight as an arrow), and he is just centimetres away from the yellow bullseye.

"Beginner's luck," Tom is legally obliged to comment.

"There wasn't much else to do in prison." Jake is the master of the deadpan comeback. "I got pretty good."

His bow hangs from his finger, and he holds it out to Tom before winking to muddy the line between reality and invention.

"At least half of what you just said was the truth," I whisper when he comes to stand next to me.

"Oh yeah? Which half?"

Jake lived in the room next to mine in halls. We dated for eighteen months, and I still feel like I know him better than anyone else here, even if we haven't exchanged so much as a Christmas card in years.

"Well, they're not going to give prisoners a bow and arrow," I conclude like the master detective I am not. "So that's a lie. But I reckon you genuinely were in prison."

He rolls his shoulders back as though trying to adjust the leather jacket he's no longer wearing. It's not often that he shows his true smile, but it happens now. It carves up his whole face, and the chipped tooth at the front of his mouth is briefly visible.

"You've always been a clever one, haven't you, Bridge?" I'm not sure whether this is a good or a bad thing.

"What were you in for?"

He doesn't look away, and for a moment, I think he will confide in me. "I'm a world-famous arms dealer." His cheery expression remains as he pulls off his T-shirt to dive into the ocean. I try not to look at his chest and fail.

Tom is still preparing to take the shot. He keeps getting distracted by Jake's strong arms as they arc out of the water, and I worry for a second that he's going to turn the bow and shoot the only guy I've ever loved. That's the problem with Tom. It isn't the money he comes from, or the trouble he always got into when he was drunk; he has a thin skin and can't stand the idea that someone might be laughing at him.

When he finally lets the arrow fly, it hits the second to worst circle. He has achieved mediocrity, just as we knew he would. Ade has apparently lost interest and is chatting to the DJ in the bar, so Sasha asks the instructor to help her with the bow. He whispers in a way which might sound seductive if what he was saying wasn't so entirely free of innuendo, but he manages to coach a better result out of her than her husband achieved.

When it comes to Mick's turn, his hands shake as he holds the bow, and he has to re-nock the arrow a couple of times before finally unleashing his first shot. It limply pings off the string and falls into the water a few metres from the boat. His second isn't much better, but at least he reaches the target before meekly swimming out to retrieve everyone's arrows.

It's my go next, and after poor Mick's embarrassing display, I opt for the crossbow. Ade said it was easy to use, and after some helpful mumbling from John Doe, I get two bullseyes in a row. It's definitely a fluke.

"William Tell couldn't have done any better." Sasha stares at me like I've cheated, and I remember the other side of her character – the catty, judgemental part of her that she used to hide until she couldn't any longer.

I've even caught Ade's attention, and he strolls over to us. "Good going, Bridge." The muscles on his arms and chest are still glistening in the sunlight as he stands next to me. "I suppose that means I should have a turn."

He comes pretty close to equalling my score, even with the more difficult apparatus. But this is hardly a shock, as Ade is good at everything. He always was. It surprised a grand total of no people whatsoever when he signed a record deal while still in full-time education. I doubt that even his grandmother would have flinched when the news of his first number one came on the radio. *Yep, that sounds about right for our Adesina*, I can imagine her saying, if she exists.

"Not bad." His laughter fills the air once again. "Who's next?"

We eat in little groups about the place. Clara seems to have taken pity on poor Mick. They chomp away at their steaks with their feet dangling off the platform into the just warm enough water. I catch snatches of their conversation. Mick tries to show off about the endless list of places he's visited on tour, and Clara says all sorts of sympathetic things that make it sound as if she is the one with the satisfying life and he deserves our pity.

Sasha and Tom have barely spoken to each other since we arrived here, but he watches her interactions as he stuffs his face. I can't quite picture what's going on between them. Did Tom have an affair and mess everything up? Is Sasha addicted to diet pills? Or is it just your common-or-garden seven-year itch?

Sasha wants us all to know how much she's enjoying herself and pulls Ade up to dance with her. If Dawn were here, it would be all right. She would clap along, and the scene would feel natural. Within a minute or two, we'd all be joining in. But she isn't around to act as our entertainments manager, and Sasha's grinding just looks seedy.

I try to imagine why Dawn didn't come. Was it really just her kids that kept her away? Or did she simply not want to see us? I know that she and Ade fell out in our second year living together, but that was a long time ago. Whatever the reason, she's not here, and Jake and I sit cringing as beautiful, capable Sasha walks her fingers up the rock star's muscly chest.

I'd like to think that, deep down, Ade's sorry that she feels the need to act like this, but celebrities must love being the centre of attention more than anyone, and he smiles throughout. Tom picks up the bow again and pretends not to notice.

I don't eat much but go into the sea instead. As the water warms my body, and I think how lucky I am to be here, the others make their excuses and disappear back to their cabins. Mick is the first to go. He walks off muttering about catching forty winks, and Ade watches him curiously without responding. I wonder if there's a hint of disdain in his gaze – if he's tired of supporting his junkie friend – but it soon passes, and he turns back to us.

"We leave here in half an hour and dinner's at eight," he says, as if to cover whatever he was thinking. "In the meantime, the boat is yours. You can do whatever you like."

He claps his hands together in anticipation and hurries up the stairs. Presumably desperate to forget his continuing inferiority with a crossbow, Tom picks up his shirt and chases after the star.

"There's actually something I wanted to talk to you about, mate." He puts his arm around Ade at the top of the stairs, and the two walk off together out of sight.

Ten minutes later, Ryan, me and a couple of sea turtles are the only ones left. We swim around in silence for a while, but that feels rude, so I paddle over to talk to him while the turtles ignore us entirely.

"It's nice to see you again," I tell him, and it's not quite a lie. I just wouldn't have expected it to happen. "I didn't realise you knew Ade that well."

He turns onto his back and flaps his arms and legs to be able to stay afloat while looking at me.

"Neither did I." He has podgy cheeks that puff up in surprise. "To be honest, I can't believe I'm here. I honestly didn't think he liked me. When I got the plane ticket, it blew my mind."

This makes me laugh a bit more than is polite. "Don't worry, I thought pretty much the same thing."

"Yeah, but I'm basically just a fanboy. I used to run a website dedicated to him. I got in trouble once for selling bootleg recordings of his gigs. Ade and I never hung out together, but you two were besties, weren't you?" He has a soft, slightly camp voice that I remember people teasing him for behind his back and occasionally to his face.

I flap my arms to keep me in the same spot and consider the question. "We were once. I was dating Jake when they formed the band. Ade and I were like brother and sister, and I really thought I loved Jake, but—" I realise that I am going off topic and switch back. "The last time I saw Ade, his first single had just come out. I went to one of his gigs, and he pretty much blanked me backstage."

"At least he put you on the list, eh?" When he smiles this time,

I remember that he's a nice guy. "I went to see him every chance I could and, except for one experience I'd rather forget, I paid for every ticket."

This information floats between us for a moment.

"I suppose you're right," I concede. "It's not as if we ever argued or anything. He was with all his swanky friends, and I turned up wanting to talk about the time Tom vomited in our professor's office. Maybe I made a big deal out of nothing."

"Maybe." Ryan turns to stare up at the sun as though he's decided to blind himself. "In my experience, famous people are some of the biggest nutjobs in the world. All that attention drives them insane, and yet we keep praising them like they're better than us." The belligerent edge to his voice forces me to question my previous good impression. "Imagine not being able to go outside your own house without someone begging you for a favour. *Ade, can I have a selfie? Ade, can I have an autograph? Ade, can I have your baby?* It's enough to make anyone lose it."

It's a bubble, I almost say, but I remember the conversation I had with Clara and change my mind. "What do you do?" I ask instead.

"I work in artist development for a record label, but it's not as interesting as it—"

There's a scream followed by a loud splash from around the side of the yacht, and whatever he was about to say is cut short. Our necks whip in the same direction, and when we don't hear anyone coming to help, we burst into life. We swim towards the ship as fast as we can, but it's clear that Ryan doesn't have the lungs to keep up with me. I'm surprised at my own strength, as he tails off to climb onto the platform, and I keep going in search of whatever or whoever fell into the water.

Ninety minutes a week at my local council-subsidised swimming pool has apparently paid off, and when I get closer to the point where I think the noise came from, it's hard to know where to look. I can't see anyone on the yacht, but there's a red stain on the shiny white paint a metre or so down from the main deck, and so I swim to the point underneath it.

"Hey!" I shout when I'm near enough to see the mark more clearly. This is a perfectly stupid thing to say. It would have been all right if someone had stolen my purse or pushed in front of me getting on a bus, but it's all wrong on my way to save a life.

It gives me impetus all the same. My arms cut more easily through the waves, and I get to the exact spot and put my head under to see if there's anything there. The water is perfectly transparent, and I can see someone deep down beneath me, but she's not moving.

My heart is beating too fast, and there's acid in my veins. For a moment, uncertainty paralyses me. The panic that I've successfully suppressed until now starts to overwhelm me, and all I can think is that I'm too slow, too weak, and Clara is dead.

NINE

As I hear calls from up on the boat, I take a deep breath and plunge beneath the water. The hush down here is soothing. For all his talent, Adesina Okojie will never write anything quite so beautiful.

It doesn't last long. As soon as I get hold of Clara's arm, it jolts her into life, and she starts thrashing and fighting against me. I can see traces of blood in the water, and I know that, if I don't calm her down, she'll keep falling deeper.

I let go just long enough for her to look at me. It works. To my genuine surprise, it works, and she sees that I've come to help. Before she freaks out again, I put her arm over my shoulder to pull her up towards the surface.

When the silence breaks and the noise comes rushing back into my ears, it feels impossibly loud. Clara is still panicking between coughs, and I do my best to support her. There are voices from on high, but I can't make sense of them. After a few moments of disorientation, there's a splash just behind me in the water, and I know what to do.

"Are you all right?" Ryan shouts down, but I'm still catching my breath and can't respond. "Is Clara okay?"

I grab her by the collar of her T-shirt and manoeuvre the life ring over her head so that she can do the rest. She pushes her arms through the hole, and she is safe now. We both are. I hang on to one side of the ring, and we fall silent to find the calm that we both need.

I hear someone splashing towards us through the water, and Jake works his way over to us from the dive platform. As soon as I see him, I feel better, and I'm so glad that he's the one to come out to us.

"What happened? Are you hurt?" he calls from ten metres away, and I turn to Clara because I really don't know what to tell him.

There's blood running down her face. She must be aware of the pain too, as she clutches the top of her head to stem the flow. Despite the warmth of the air and the sun beating down on us, she's shaking. So instead of answering Jake's questions, I pull her back to the ship directly.

Ade is standing with Ryan, and I assume that he was one of the people I heard calling down. They've stopped now, but the way they watch as we drift back to the platform sends a chill through me. They look like pedestrians gawping at a ten-car pile-up, and I can't help but wonder whether they're a little disappointed that everyone is okay.

When we're sitting in the beach club – now without the unnecessary DJ – Ade rushes down to us with an ice pack.

He wraps a towel around Clara's shoulders and kneels in front of her before asking the inevitable question. "What were you doing in the water?"

"I..." She looks at me for support, but I can't answer for her. The blood that is already staining the fluffy white towel makes the question mark on the end of his sentence all the heavier. "I was just standing at the side of the boat, looking down into the water. I felt myself keel forward. I don't... I really..."

I hadn't noticed him until now, but Ryan is standing on the staircase peering into the room. "Was anyone up there with you?"

In a frightened, birdlike movement, Clara turns her head to look at him. She is more agitated now than when she was underwater, and I'm surprised she doesn't take the towel and hide beneath it.

"I can't remember. I think I hit my head as I fell." She glances back at me as her ally – she doesn't know that Ryan did his best to help her too. "I remember being on the deck below the helipad, and then I was in the water. All I know is that my body tumbled forward, as if I was..."

She doesn't finish her thought. Perhaps it's the way that Ade is looking at her or something in Ryan's question, but she suddenly becomes defensive. "I didn't jump, if that's what you're thinking. You've probably always seen me as a neurotic little weirdo, but no one is—"

"So you fainted?" Ade suggests, and every word he says seems to push her away from us.

I decide to stop the questions before they make her more anxious. "It doesn't matter now, does it? The important thing is that Clara is okay."

I rise to look at the top of her head, and even through her long, mousy brown hair I can see the cut.

"It doesn't look too deep," I say, based on my complete lack of medical knowledge, before Ade finally leaves to get help.

"I'll fetch the first-aider. Do you think you can walk to your cabin?"

Clara doesn't answer, but he heads back to the staircase and disappears regardless. She waits for Ryan to do the same before saying anything more, and I feel I have to reassure her.

"I was talking to Ryan when we heard you fall. He got back on the ship and threw down the life ring."

Clara pulls her hair together at the back of her head to tie it in a loose knot before taking the towel and pressing it against the wound. The trickle that had previously promised to become a stream seems to have dried up, but I can only imagine how frightened she still is.

"You must have fallen about ten metres before hitting the water."

"I didn't fall." Her tone is curt, her expression fierce, and I don't know how to respond. "I mean... Oh, Bridget. I don't know what I mean." Her breathing becomes louder, and I move to put my arm around her.

"I don't blame you, sweetie. No one does."

There are tears in her eyes, but she doesn't sob or cry out. What I haven't said is that she came seconds away from dying, but I don't want her thinking about that. She was the innocent, slightly vulnerable one in our group of friends, and all that matters right now is that I get her checked out. The thought that she could survive nearly drowning but end up with a dangerous concussion enters my mind, and I push it back down.

"Come on. You'll be more comfortable upstairs." I realise for the first time that the boat has started moving again, but not before I mistime my step and have to grab hold of the wall to get my balance. "I'll stay with you for as long as you need."

It's wrong to say that she starts smiling, but the fear on her face diminishes somewhat, and I help her to her feet while she has the courage.

Ryan is standing at the top of the stairs. I can tell there's something he wants to say, but, just like me, he puts on a brave face for Clara as he accompanies us through one of the yacht's countless lounges towards the central corridor where our cabins are located.

When we get to Clara's room, Ryan makes the universally recognised flicking-eyes gesture to show that he wants to talk to me alone, but I can't just leave her. I wave him away and help Clara through the door as he looks on, bemused.

When the man who'd taught us to shoot the crossbows comes to the room a few minutes later, he has a small red bag with bandages in it and a skinny torch for shining in Clara's eyes. His name is Steve, and he certainly acts like he knows what he's doing.

"I know what I'm doing," he says to confirm it. "I'm a formally qualified medic and worked as a nurse before changing career."

He's apparently multi-talented, but it would be frivolous to point this out with Clara still lying on her bed looking shaken. I became less worried about her as soon as he turned up, so he's already made me feel better.

"I'm glad to say there's no sign of concussion," he tells us, and even Clara smiles. "But if you have any dizziness or you just don't feel like yourself, ask Shabeer or one of the staff to send for me."

I now realise that this was the likely outcome. We've squeezed a lot of drama into one day. Any more would have been unrealistic.

Once bow-firing, head-checking Steve retreats with a confident smile, I have some more fun hunting for the television. It's in the ceiling this time, so that's exciting, but when I put on what I thought would be a nostalgic cartoon from our childhood, it doesn't have the effect I wanted. Instead, Clara looks at me like she can't understand what I was thinking, and the comical violence feels insensitive.

She grabs the control from me and the screen turns blue. "Sorry, I'm just not in the mood."

"No, I'm sorry for hijacking the TV." I take her hand in mine. "This is much better."

For a moment, I feel like I'm at home in my bedroom with my best friend. I'm thirteen again, dreaming about three different boys who I'll never date.

"What did you think would happen when you got here?" she asks in as inquisitive a manner as someone can adopt without finishing the sentence with, *hmmmmm?*

"Nice food?" I answer at least half truthfully.

Soft giggles overtake her, and I remember why I've always liked her so much.

"No, I mean it. What did you imagine this would be like?"

"I don't know," I reply as my mind sets to work. "I had a million thoughts about it, and many of them were probably far-fetched. I suppose what I really hoped was that everything would be the way it was when we first met."

"It's not though, is it?"

She sounds a little sad again, and so I try to cheer her up. "Do you remember what it was like the first month we lived together? Back before there was any drama, and we all just got along?"

My dreaminess has spread to her now. "Yeah... yeah, I do."

"I think that was the best time of my life. I know that sounds sad, but it was so exciting living with Ade and Dawn and... well, all of you. Jake was very sweet when we first spent time together. You were finding yourself through your painting, and Ade was full of grand, beautiful ideas. Getting to know him felt like meeting John Lennon or Freddie Mercury when they were just starting out."

"I know exactly what you mean. I woke up every morning thinking I was in a movie." She smiled cautiously. "I was excruciatingly shy when I got to university, but you were all so nice and included me in everything you did. For that whole first year, I felt totally at home."

I thought back to the very beginning. "We used to sit in that ugly, sterile kitchen in our flat and talk for hours. I think we all found our places in the group on the very first night in halls."

"I probably wouldn't have said a word if it weren't for you and Dawn."

An almost silent laugh escapes my lips. "I don't know what good I did, but Dawn couldn't resist organising everyone. From the moment we met, she started planning excursions and activities like a primary school teacher." My voice dies for a moment. "I wish she were here now. It feels wrong without her."

Clara squeezes my hand, and we lie in silence for a second. I almost ask her why Dawn rejected the invitation, but she's more important right now.

"And I wish you'd become really famous for your art. You're so good," I tell her when the quiet gets too much. "It would prove that you don't have to be one of those instantly noticeable extroverts to make it."

She sighs and I realise that I've phrased this all wrong. I should have spoken more sensitively, seeing as Clara had a problem with her course in our second year and didn't finish. She never explained what it was, but I always assumed she was depressed or lonely in London. She was back living at home when the rest of us graduated.

"The truth is..." she replies with great hesitation. "The truth is that I found it all too miserable. When I went back to Chichester, I still wanted to make something of myself. I really believed I was talented enough, but I hadn't met the right people in London and, short of tiny gallery shows near me, there was no way of showing my work to anyone. The whole thing made me feel like a failure – that I'd been wasting my time. And that's why I eventually gave up and found a proper job."

I squeeze her hand a little patronisingly as I watch the digital screensaver on the TV going round and round and morphing through various shapes and colours. "Look at it this way. Of our group of ultra-talented individuals, one of us is unemployed, one of us is a kept woman, and one of us is a day trader with a drinking problem. Jake's been to jail for... some reason, and Ryan says his work in the music industry isn't as interesting as it might sound. You could probably say that Ade compensates for the rest of us, but it doesn't make me feel any better about my non-starter literary career, or the mind-numbing job I've done for the best part of a decade."

"Are you saying that we're all failures, so it doesn't matter?" That giggle of hers ignites once more and I can't help but smile at her.

"I'm saying that we defined success all wrong if the only way for any of us to be happy was if we won an Oscar or the Turner Prize." I pause to think about this and realise that this is exactly what I wish someone had told me many years ago. "I'm saying that failure isn't what it's made out to be."

These words ring around my head, and I study her face again. I always thought it was sad that Clara was so shy. When we were alone together, just like now, she would poke her head out of her shell. She could be funny and silly and wild, but as soon as there were a few people about, she disappeared again. I always assumed she had a weird upbringing, as she's not even unattractive, with her pale skin and striking grey eyes. I'm not saying that looks are everything, but they can still shape our experiences. As she never mentioned her family, I figured that her parents had suffocated her, and she never got over it.

"It's a real shame..." she says, but I don't ask her to elaborate.

There are so many questions I could ask, but I don't. We lie here, both busy with our own thoughts as the boat carries us across the ocean. The time passes serenely, and when my eyes grow heavy, I know I won't open them again for some time.

TEN

I'm woken by the sound of Clara moving so softly around her room that it almost sends me back to sleep again. I lie in a kind of trance and either forget to tell my limbs to move or the signal doesn't reach its destination. It's only when I hear a soft *bong* from a hidden speaker that I fully regain consciousness.

I get the impression that Clara has not been as lazy as me. There's no sign of her bag anymore. She's changed her clothes too, and I'm fairly certain that the noise that woke me was the door to the room opening and closing. Perhaps she's been out to see the others. I have a brief feeling of FOMO before doing my usual positive-thinking routine and shaking it off.

"Clara, I should have already told you something. You see, I stopped writing years ago." These are the first words out of my mouth after I come back to the world. "I really have no excuse. Sometimes I have good ideas, but there is always this invisible obstacle. It isn't just that I find other things to do; I feel completely blocked up. Real writers can get through that. If I could just set a few hundred words down every day, by the end of the year, I'd have a novel."

For the length of time that it takes me to spew this out, she stands frozen before her wardrobe door.

When I finally stop, she shrugs but knows just what to say. "It's like you said, Bridge. No one thinks badly of you because you're not a famous writer."

And then she goes back to her tidying.

I sit with my back against the fifty or so pillows that separate me from the headboard, and I realise that every thought I just expressed was formed in my sleep. I have no concept of how long I slept, but I'm certain that our conversation continued to play out in my brain. Something about this excites me. Perhaps I've been constructing stories in my head all this time. Perhaps there are whole books up there, just waiting to be transcribed.

There's another soft *bong* on the speaker system, and this time it comes with a message. "Hello, shipmates, this is Captain Sasha speaking. We will be convening for dinner in the dining area on the upper deck in fifteen minutes. Please dress for the occasion. Bing bong." She makes these last two sounds herself, then a cackling laugh cuts into the room before her microphone switches off.

I can just see her up at the helm of the ship, flirting with the captain and trying on his hat.

"How are you feeling?" I ask Clara when the drama of the afternoon comes back to me. "How's your head?"

She puts her hand to the wound self-consciously. "It hurts, but I think I was lucky to hit the side when I did and bounce away from the boat. If I'd smashed against it lower down, I'd be dead."

"Well... let's not think about that. When I found you under the water, you weren't unconscious for long."

She walks over and wraps her arms around me. In the almost two years I lived with her, I don't think she ever initiated physical contact, so it comes as something of a surprise.

"Thank you so much, Bridget. I'm trying my best not to think about what happened, but I'm pretty sure you saved my life."

She's so petite that she barely has to bend down even though I'm sitting on the bed and she's standing up. When she pulls away, I find that I'm the shy one.

"I really didn't do anything special. I'm just glad I was there."

Before the emotion hits home, I make an excuse to leave. "I'd better get changed for dinner. I'll see you up there."

She nods in her typically cautious way, and I slip from the room. I must still be tired as the sliding metal door feels heavier than when I went inside. Jake is lurking out in the corridor for some reason. He's leaning against the wall between his room and mine.

"All right, old friend?" he says, as if it's perfectly natural for him to be there. "Are you joining me for dinner?"

I can't help laughing at him. He sounds so silly, and I remember when we were first going out and I thought he was charming. "Are you looking for a date?"

He glances along the corridor with a cheeky grin. "If the answer is yes."

I stare at him from three feet away. "What are you doing, Jake?"

"Me?" He points to the creaseless white shirt he's wearing, and I can tell that he's made an effort. I can smell that he's made an effort too. A deep, musky scent fills the space between us. "I'm just asking a pretty girl out to dinner."

"Uh-uh," I say to cut him off, but this response is too vague, and he keeps trying.

"You do look very pretty, Bridge."

"Did you forget?" I find myself encouraging him.

"Not for a second. So shall we meet back here in ten?"

"Or we could learn the lessons of the past." The silence that follows seems too cruel. Reviving our adolescent affair wasn't high on my list of priorities, but I can't deny that there's a moment of static between us that I haven't felt in a long time.

He moves closer and is about to say something funny or flirtatious or both, when a door opens behind him and Ryan comes out. He's looked uncomfortable all day long and instantly blushes when he sees us.

"Sorry to interrupt." He immediately turns towards the stairs.

"You're not interrupting," I manage to reply before poking Jake in the ribs to suggest that the whole thing was just a joke. "This one was being a prat for old times' sake."

Jake tips his head back and shows that mischievous smile again. There's no fazing a guy like him. He walks away with Ryan as if nothing significant happened.

I go into my cabin to get changed. I brought a grand total of two fancy outfits, so it will be no great challenge to decide what to wear. I even struggle with my dried-up mascara and a slightly scuzzy stick of lipstick to make myself presentable.

When I finish, I stand in front of the mirror and wonder how I look. I am thirty-two years old, but people often think I'm younger. My eyes are the same dark brown as my hair. I may be pretty, but it's not a question that's ever plagued me the way it does some people; I am who I am.

And as I stand there, I feel pretty good about myself. My floor-length silk dress with red roses stamped all over it makes me think of the elegant curtains I once saw in a French palace (on a TV drama). The red heels I wear underneath it are just tall enough to make people notice the difference and, as I turn to leave my cabin, the skirt trails behind me like I'm off to get married.

I admit that I dip my hand into my suitcase before leaving to grab the bottle of vodka I brought with me for Dutch courage – for moments just like this one. I take a long slug, and now I'm ready to go.

ELEVEN

Navigating narrow staircases in precarious heels on a boat should be an Olympic event.

The wind has picked up as we get further away from the land, and I already wish I'd tied my hair back as it whips around me and covers my face. For a moment, I know how Clara must have felt falling head first off the ship. My stomach lurches as the sole of my shoe slides along the step, but there's a handrail for me to grip, and I tell myself that this brief panic will soon be forgotten.

I hear voices above me as I reach the main deck. There's a soft glow reflecting off the ceiling two levels above me. I feel myself flowing towards it like the silk I wear, spiralling up the last two staircases to meet the others.

I suppose it's not a bad entrance. I'm the last to arrive, and I stand with the wind whipping my dress about and my hair whirling like the snakes on Medusa's head as air rushes up the stairs behind me. I didn't mean to be so dramatic, but everyone turns to look.

They cheer for some reason, and it takes me a moment to realise why.

"Our hero!" Ade says, pouring out glasses of something that

looks like wine as if he didn't normally pay someone to do that for him.

Even Clara joins in with the applause. She lifts her hands above her head as I take the closest seat.

"You little star," Jake says, so I guess he hasn't given up on charming me just yet.

Sasha goes a step further than the others; she always has. "What would we have done without you?" She rushes up to my chair and puts her hands on my shoulders.

She's dressed in a long white skirt with a stripy top that fits the maritime feel of the place. I would say that I'd out-dressed her for once, but it won't surprise me if she excuses herself after the starter to break out a new look.

With drinks served, and one shoved in my hand by Ryan in the seat next to mine, we fall quiet to listen to our host.

"I don't want to be too serious or anything, but I have to tell you how glad I am that disaster was averted. If it hadn't been for you, Bridget—"

I have to interrupt him, and it's not just because my built-in British modesty forbids any praise that lasts longer than six seconds. "You mean me and Ryan," I remind him, tipping my glass to the sullen figure at my side.

Ade's expression changes. It seems for a second that he's reluctant to amend his toast, but he eventually gives in. "Right. If it hadn't been for you and Ryan, this dinner would have been a bit of a downer."

Clara puts her hand to her mouth to cover a laugh, and Jake punches Ade on the arm for the understatement.

"I'm joking, I'm joking." He turns to Clara with his glass still raised. "I would be heartbroken if anything had happened to you. I've only just found you again."

His words linger a little too long, and it forces Sasha to lift her glass above everyone else's and say, "To Bridget and Ryan, for being superhuman rescuers."

"To Bridget and Ryan," everyone echoes and, because it seems rude not to, I find myself toasting my own bravery.

There is one person who did not cheer quite so enthusiastically. Tom is sprawled in his seat, glancing around the candlelit table as though he has a bone to pick with each and every last one of us.

Rather than worry about that bubbling volcano, I take in the space around me. The floor, table and chairs are all made of teak, which reminds me that there is no sign of Mick. Half of the sky is covered by the overhanging roof, but I have a clear view of the moon, and the stars are brighter than I've ever seen them in England. I suppose we're far enough away from any islands now to escape the light pollution. The beauty of a clear night is just the kind of thing that makes me cry, so I'm glad that I manage to keep my feelings in check.

Discussion bounces across the table at diagonals as Sasha and Ryan gossip about one of their old lecturers who got a part on a TV soap. Clara laughs at Jake's jokes, and I notice that he's the only one not drinking the wine. Phoebe and a guy I haven't seen before arrive to transport trays from a dumb waiter that is hidden behind a retracting picture frame.

"How many people work on this boat?" I shout to Ade at the other end of the table.

"Normally about thirty, but I've come out with a skeleton crew of twenty this time." He probably realises that this sounds crazy but adds, "I wanted a more intimate experience."

It's at this moment that Tom decides he's had enough. He grabs the empty wine bottle from the waiter as it's about to be taken away and stares at the label.

"Why are we here?" His voice is louder than anyone else's, and it silences the table. "Why did you invite us when we haven't so much as exchanged postcards in years?"

These are the questions we've all wanted to ask but didn't have the nerve – or perhaps no one wanted to wake up from our pleasant dream.

Of course, there's something Tom wants to know even more than this and it absolutely roars out of him. "And why would you only serve non-alcoholic drinks?"

As we're not the type to make a scene, the rest of us mumble half-hearted messages of disapproval.

"That's a bit rude," Jake says, though he presumably still hopes to discover the answer and looks at Ade expectantly.

Even Sasha's rebuke is comparatively mild. "Come on now, Tom. Why spoil this nice evening?"

Because he is a showman, Ade rises from the table. The dancing light from a line of candles shines on him. It banishes the shadows and somehow turns his skin even darker.

"I always planned to tell you tonight," he says in a voice that isn't quite his own. He must have noticed, as he clears his throat before trying again. "I was waiting for the right moment, but I guess the time has come."

He stands before us in his artfully crumpled linen shirt and trousers, with his arms out like a wannabe prophet. I feel that he planned our whole visit for this very moment, but his voice still lets him down.

"The thing is..." It's too quiet, and he comes to a sudden halt. I remember that there was a time when he wasn't as confident as he wanted everyone to believe. There was a time – right back when I first knew him – when he only dreamed of being immortal; he didn't yet believe that he was.

"The thing is..." As he hesitates once more, I can see that he needs us just as much as we need him. He peers up at the natural spotlight shining down on him. "I asked you all here because I'm trying to be better."

Tom slams his fist down on the table and his knife shudders away. "What does that mean? What does anything that comes out of your mouth even mean?"

The two waiters appear with the first course before melting away into the shadows, like children who don't want to get involved in their parents' argument.

No one is scared of Tom. He's a dragon without claws, fangs, or fire. It's Ade we want to hear.

"I have made a lot of mistakes in my life. I've hurt everyone around this table, and I..." As he speaks so cautiously, it's hard to imagine him singing to a crowd of eighty thousand. "I brought you here to make amends."

"What you mean is that you got us out to the middle of the ocean because there's nothing you like better than a captive audience." Tom crushes his pristine white napkin into a ball and then relents and flattens it again. This is in no way a metaphor for his feelings towards Ade. "You knew we'd tell you where to stick your apology if you came to us in Britain, so you thought you'd wow us with your big, fancy boat."

I decide not to point out that he was the most impressed of the lot of us when we arrived, and I wonder what's changed.

When no one else says anything, Jake does. "What were you expecting? Did you think that Ade was bringing you here for financial advice?"

I remember Ade and Tom walking off together after we went swimming, and I think he might be right. Did Tom offer his services only to be knocked back? For a moment, he looks as though he might shout or cry, but nothing more comes.

"Why are you so angry?" Clara asks from across the table. Her voice is as small as it ever was, but something in her tone shows her strength.

"I'm not angry." Tom sits up straighter in his chair as if to suggest that he is the reasonable one. "I just don't appreciate being brought here under false pretences. It's not as if we can hop off the ship and head back to land, is it?"

The anger that he just denied is visible as he clenches his jaw and taps his finger over and over in the same nervous pattern.

"We've gone too far to turn back," comes Ade's response. "Perhaps the helicopter could fly out to us if you are desperate, but it was rented, so I'm not sure if it's available."

"Ha! It isn't even his helicopter!" Tom points to Ade and

laughs as he looks from face to face. To celebrate this small victory, he reaches for his glass before remembering that there is no alcohol in it and becoming frustrated again. "He made that whole big scene, and it's not even his helicopter!"

He's like a malfunctioning robot who, now that his battery is almost dead, can only stare at the substance that will do nothing to power him back up.

It's time for me to feel sorry for Sasha again. She looks down at her lap, and I realise that this is nothing new. Her resigned expression tells me that her husband's public outbursts are a regular occurrence and not something she knows how to handle.

Was it really only a few minutes ago I showed up here looking insanely cool with my hair blowing in the breeze and everyone shouting my name? Ade's announcement has been hijacked and then stabbed to death. Sadly for him, it's easier to maintain control of a multitude of baying fans than a small group of friends.

The waiters sense calm and make a quick dash to present their cloche-covered dishes at the table. It's supposed to look fancy, as the steam wafts out from under the silver covers, but it reminds me of the breakfasts we had in the old-fashioned seaside hotel I used to stay in on holiday with my family. Of course, no one is looking at the gourmet food, which is a shame as, back home, I survive on a diet of beans on toast and freeze-dried noodles.

Ade is doing his best to pretend that nothing out of the ordinary has happened, but we're still looking at him like he's about to do a magic trick. "The plan is to sail all the way to the Maldives," he says, to change to a safer topic. "From there, you can fly back to Mauritius or home to England. It's entirely up to you, and—"

Tom can take it no more. He lurches to his feet and grabs the glass of de-alcoholised grape drink that has been taunting him for so long. He casually launches it over his shoulder, and it goes spinning down to the deck two floors below.

My body braces for the inevitable sound of glass smashing on metal. It's almost a relief when no one cries out in pain.

Ade realises he made a mistake and returns to his previous

announcement. "I'm trying to say sorry for being a bad friend. Through the first two years of uni, we were inseparable. I loved you guys like family, and then Clara left, and Dawn stopped talking to me for a long time, Jake and Bridget split up, and we all fell apart. Or at least, that was the story I told myself, but the truth is that I was to blame as much as anyone. I should have been more—"

Tom has heard enough and backs away from the table. "This isn't the dream holiday I was promised," he moans, like a man about to turn into a werewolf. "It's a nightmare, and I'm already sick of it."

TWELVE

It's not clear what comes next. No one knows how to return us to the carefree atmosphere of that afternoon at the back of the boat or even fifteen minutes earlier.

I really hoped that Ade would continue with what he was saying. I want to hear about that period from his perspective. I want to know about the argument between him and Dawn that meant we didn't move in together in the third year as we'd planned. I want to know why Clara quit her degree, but Ade sits back in his place, and an ugly hush consumes us as we pick at the meal. A single, large ravioli sits looking lonely in a red sea. The flavours are unplaceable, and not the reassuring comfort food that we need at this moment. I would honestly prefer baked beans after all.

I was hoping that Ade's guitar was near and he could play us another of his hits, but before anyone can rescue the conversation, poor Sasha decides she has to unburden herself.

"You probably realise that Tom's drinking is out of control, but you mustn't blame him entirely," she confesses, looking at me over the candles. "He's had a hard year."

"You really don't have to tell us," Jake replies under his breath.

I know why he'd say this. His own story is about as transparent as the teak floor. He's hinted at scandalous details, but he isn't the kind to bare his soul. I don't know why he ever left Ade's band. I can't imagine how he ended up in prison, and I wonder if he really has a kid who was born while we were dating. I still look at him as the kind, complicated boy I loved, but I don't know a thing about him.

"I want to," Sasha counters. "Not just for all of you, but for my sake too." She takes a deep breath and, when that is not enough, she has a gulp of her drink. "You see, I lied to you all."

My skin tingles as the wind kicks up. It's not actually cold, but the sudden sensation – like fingers walking across my body – combines with a brief buzz of excitement that we might finally get some answers.

"Tom isn't some high-flying trader... not anymore, at least. He lost his job a few months ago, and our lives have been pretty close to hell ever since."

When Sasha and I used to talk in private, I could never forget that she was a drama student through and through. Even during her most intimate late-night confessions – when she'd find me in my room after she'd been out on a date with her moneybags boyfriend – even at her most vulnerable, she came across as a girl running her lines for her next play.

I don't get that now.

"It really wasn't his fault..." she begins again and then realises that she is speaking to a group of people who only know fragments of her story. "You see... I quit acting because his job paid so well. I had an agent and had done some TV work, but there was far too much uncertainty for my liking. It was a choice between switching to theatre or being a housewife, and I decided that the latter would require less heartache and rejection."

I look down the table at Clara, whose cautious expression presumably mirrors my own. I have a feeling that this might not be what the Sasha of tomorrow morning wants us to hear, but it would be callous to interrupt.

"I always knew that what I wanted more than anything was to be a mother. I might have told you that I wouldn't be happy in life if I never saw my name in lights, but there was something I needed even more. The idea was that I would pump out the babies while Tom made us rich. He held up his side of the bargain, but my body was having none of it."

Ryan peers down at his now empty plate, and I doubt he'll look up again for some time. He's always had the air of someone who has ended up at a party without being invited. This is only amplified when a pretty girl with perfect skin starts tearfully confessing her every fear and failure. And there *are* tears already. Sasha's dimpled cheeks glimmer with the shine of freshly applied saltwater.

"We tried everything." Her voice breaks, and I wonder which part of this story hurts the most. "We had cycles of artificial insemination, IVF and PGD. I took every kind of supplement, memorised the most ridiculous old wives' tales as if they were scripture and added everything from black garlic to chia seeds to my diet in the hope of solving whatever the problem was. None of it did any good."

I'm suddenly aware of music piping out of a speaker in the floor beneath the table. It's only faint, and the sound is slow and maudlin, but I'm fairly certain it's an ill-chosen piano version of Queen's "Fat Bottomed Girls".

"The worst thing about it was that we never discovered what was wrong. Not one doctor could find a reason for why we hadn't conceived. We'd been trying for years. And I think it's safe to say we'd both given up and settled into a dull, dependable life together when the floor was pulled out from under us." She tips her head back, closes her eyes, and I want to run to comfort her, but I don't move an inch.

"The truth is that trading is a cut-throat world. The companies take people young, then work them dry, and Tom wasn't suited to it from the start. He likes to pretend he's this tough, steady guy, but he has a very soft underside that he spends all his time trying to hide. In his job, there was so much money to be made, and he was supposed to set everything else aside to pursue it."

Another half-sob, another crack in her voice, and I feel it too now. I can see how deep the emotion goes.

"He was never strong enough for that. It's not just that the work takes so much from you. There are a thousand rules to follow and expectations to meet."

She talks of Tom's occupation as though it is her own, but I guess they had to be a partnership for him to do such a demanding job.

"Underperformance can get you fired in weeks, whereas one of his colleagues had a cocaine habit, and no one gave him any trouble because he made the company millions every day. He was a high-functioning addict, and I doubt he was the only one there."

In awkward unison, three of us around the table drink at the same time as she searches for what she's trying to say.

"What Tom did could have happened to anyone. If there's one thing that his company cares about, it's not staff doing lines in the bathroom or after-hours drinking. They honestly couldn't care less about interns getting felt up by senior colleagues so long as no charges are brought against them, but the second that there's a whiff of irregular trading, you're out."

Ryan inhales a bit too loudly, and we all turn to look at him. "Sorry," he mutters, but Jake is bolder than him and asks what we're all wondering.

"You mean he used knowledge that he shouldn't have? He cheated the system?"

Sasha's pace increases as she explains herself better. "No, he would never do that. Not only is it illegal, the risk of getting caught is too high. He was in charge of selling some high-value shares to a colleague in another company. When the transaction didn't go through, he messaged his contact, who turned out to be on holiday and had forgotten to do her job. To stop her from getting in trouble, he messaged her directly, which is against company rules. The terrible thing is that she was the one who told Tom's employer that he'd been communicating with her during a sale. They fired him the same day."

"Is that it?" Jake is rarely the most discreet individual and delivers this remark with an unimpressed huff. "Why would that lead him to drink? He can get another job elsewhere."

"No, he can't. It doesn't matter that he had no intention of breaking any rules, and it was the woman he was trying to help who messed up. Tom is untouchable now. No one will employ him. He'll be lucky to get a job teaching economics, if that's what he wants, because he's broken a fundamental rule. He gave his company years of his life, and then they snipped him off like a deadhead on a rosebush."

"Was that when he started drinking?" my stupid mouth asks without my permission.

Sasha's piercing green eyes flash in my direction. "He's always been a heavy drinker, but before then it was social. We'd go out with his colleagues on a Friday night, and he would blast the week out of his head with ten pints and whisky chasers. Weekends were spent nursing a hangover, and then he'd gear up for the week again."

She pauses, and it's clear that none of this is easy to say. "When he was fired, the weekends bled into the week. As he has no reason to stay sober, he doesn't." She shakes her head, and a tear falls from her cheek into her bowl. "I truly don't think he can stop."

For a moment, I wonder if this is the reason there's no alcohol on the boat. Has Ade been watching over us like a guardian angel? Did he know about Tom's situation and bring him here to go cold turkey?

It falls to Ryan – the outsider, the hanger-on – to comfort her. "That's so difficult, Sash. But we're here for you. We all are." It occurs to me and surely everyone around that table that, until now at least, this simply wasn't true.

The atmosphere never recovers after this. Subdued conversation fills the gaps between silences. The servers return to deliver the fish course, and we eat because there's no other option. I wish with all my might for the meal to be over, but they keep bringing more food.

I don't know how we get through the evening. I am the first up from the table as soon as my dessert bowl is empty. I don't wait around to flirt with Jake or quiz Ade. I run straight to my room and sit on my balcony, feeling grateful for just how vast and lonely the ocean in front of me is. I want to cry for Sasha, but the tears don't come. I want to jump into the water, but I would be left behind and drown, so I decide that there's nothing left to do but go to bed.

I want to drift away on a dream, but I realise that I've left my phone up on deck. The phone which has no coverage, no internet and no real use drags me back to the world against my wishes.

The ship is dead again, and the only people I pass are workers washing down the decks we've barely dirtied. These are new faces I haven't seen before. The night people, who hide away in their dark cabins when the sun's out. I nod to them and scurry past on my way to the upper deck, where there are still candles burning.

"I'd leave him for you. You know that," I hear Sasha say as I reach the top of the stairs. For a moment, as she moves to straddle Ade, I'm a rabbit caught in a car's headlights, unable to back away. Every instinct I have tells me that I shouldn't be here, but it takes me five whole seconds to break from my trance.

Stuff the phone, I think as I dash away down the stairs. I make it to the main deck and around the master suite before crashing straight into someone coming the other way.

"Sorry, Bridget," Tom says with his hands out in front of him. There's none of the gloom or rage that he showed at dinner. He's an entirely different person. "Sasha didn't come back to our room. Have you seen her?"

THIRTEEN

When I wake up the next morning, I spend a few hours alone on the balcony in my room. I take my morning pills and try not to think dark thoughts. I fail, of course. My head is full of old friends and old hurts, the sort of thing that, for a while, haunted me so much I went to see a doctor to get something to make them go away. Right now, I feel simultaneously guilty and disappointed in just about everyone and everything.

I would never have admitted it when we were at uni, but I was always jealous of Sasha and Tom's plush existence. The fact I barely make ends meet doesn't stop me from dreaming of the house they have or the cars they drive. And for all my pearl-clutching over whether I would buy a superyacht if I had a spare fifty mil, I'd still like to face that dilemma for myself.

I lie on my lounger thinking of what I saw in the candlelight. I think of Sasha with her hands on Ade. I think of his expression and wonder what it meant. He looked kind of surprised at what was happening, but that doesn't mean he didn't grab her and kiss her as soon as I left.

In a way, that isn't even the most relevant thing. I remember the tragic story that Sasha told us and all the times I could have been nicer to her and Tom. It's like a switch has been flicked, and

I'm left questioning whether I was the mean one all along. I play through a blooper reel of clips from our friendship. I used to think they were lauding their wealth and success over me, but maybe they were just trying to make me feel included. I think about her invitations to cocktail parties and nights out with the girls – "It's on me, Bridget, I know you can't afford it" – and I wonder if I was a complete and utter cow to her.

I see what good their wealth actually did them, and my guilt hardens within me.

"Bridget, are you in there?" Jake calls through the non-existent keyhole.

I'm still trapped in a thought and, before I can answer him, Ade dances back into my head like he's putting on a show for me. I suddenly need to know whether he's any happier than the rest of us. He's about a thousand times richer than Tom, so if he isn't content in life, who is? The lithe Scandinavian fiancée I imagined him having hasn't appeared and, from what I can see, short of a hairy, drug-addicted drummer, he's on his own out here, floating around the world on a hollow tin can.

"Bridge, can I come in?"

"Okay. Come!" I shout back, a little too dictatorially.

He puts his head around the door, and I realise for the first time that it doesn't have a lock – or perhaps there is one and I don't know how to use it.

"If you're here trying to seduce me again, I think it's a bad idea." Who am I? This sounds terrible, and I wish I'd just waited to see what he wanted like any normal person.

He sneers at me, as he has every right to. "It's not that, and I'm sorry if I was in a silly mood last night. I just…" Thankfully for both of us, he decides not to explain. "I was supposed to meet Mick this morning in the cinema. He's producing a concert film from Ade's last tour and wanted my opinion on it."

"There's a cinema?" I practically yell at him. "Why did no one tell me?"

Admittedly, I knew about the video wall and the various giant

TVs, but I was severely missing cinema-style seating (and popcorn).

Jake looks annoyed and returns to his point. "We were supposed to start half an hour ago, and he hasn't appeared."

"Is that surprising?" I ask, a little bemused that I would be the one he comes to ask about this. "He didn't strike me as the reliable type."

"You don't know Mick like I do. He was pretty keen."

I can see he's nervous and try to sound more accommodating. "Tell me what I can do."

"You're good at this sort of thing." He sighs and walks past the bed to stand beside me. "I just want you to be there when I knock on his door in case, in case... I don't know what."

If yesterday hadn't happened, and I wasn't now worried that I'm a terrible person, I would probably have made a joke of this. I would have laughed aloud and told him not to be such a drama queen. But I don't sigh or roll my eyes as I get up to search for the white cotton kimono that was in my cabin when I got here and will not be after I leave.

"Do you know which cabin is his?" Jake steps outside and I follow him.

I'm about to ask why he would imagine such a thing when I realise that I actually do. "Yeah, it's one of the three big rooms upstairs. It's next to Tom and Sasha's."

We accelerate along the corridor and up to the main deck. He points to the first door we come to and, as if I'm joining in with his mime act, I signal to keep going.

"This one?"

I nod and feel nervous without knowing why.

"Mick, are you in there?" Jake taps ever so softly on the metal door, which really defeats the point of what we've come to do. "Mick?" He calls more loudly this time, and when that doesn't elicit a response, I lean past him to bang on it.

No sound comes back to us, and we look at one another.

"Perhaps we should find Ade," I suggest, but his suite looked dark when I saw it, and I'm afraid that Sasha was in there with him. As far as I'm concerned, the fewer people who know what I saw last night, the better.

Before I can think what to do, Jake pushes his long hair back off his face, knocks once more and then slides the door open. The darkened room beyond smells of cigarettes and sweat and something else I don't want to identify. There's no sign of Mick, and I'm almost grateful. There was one obvious thought in my mind, and I'm so relieved that it hasn't come to pass.

"Is Mick a heroin addict?" I ask when I spot a syringe on the bedside table, and it fits with everything else I know about him.

Jake is looking about the room and hesitates for a moment. "Among other things, yes. Though I haven't hung out with him for years, so I don't know what he's been up to recently."

He runs to look behind the grand piano in the corner of the room. Oh, yeah, there's a grand piano. I should probably have mentioned that. This cabin is pretty much the same as mine, but twice as big and with a giant musical instrument taking up the extra space.

There's another obvious place that we haven't searched, and sadly it has fallen to me to do so. I move slowly towards the door to the bathroom in the hope that Jake will notice and take over. I put my hand on the handle and feel the tension that was bubbling up moments earlier now return. I'm just about to enter when I hear a voice behind me.

"What are you doing in here?"

I want it to be Mick's, but I know that it's not.

"Why are you in here?" Ade demands, and Jake pops up from behind a sofa to explain.

"We were supposed to meet Mick in the cinema, but he didn't come."

"Yeah, he's like that." Ade's face has none of its usual light and magic. He has the look of a man with a hangover that won't leave him, though presumably that's impossible if there really is no booze on board except for my 75cl of vodka.

He doesn't wait for me to answer but muscles me out of the way. He gets straight to it rather than putting off the inevitable, as I was. The door goes swinging away from us and, though the boxed-in shower is empty, there's a glass partition which hides the toilet, and I can see the hazy outline of a figure propped against it.

"No, Mick," Ade says in a low, plaintive tone that reminds me of one of his songs. "Oh, mate. What have you done?"

He hurries forward as Jake runs past me to help, so I just stand there for ten seconds, watching their silhouettes.

Ade kneels down, but Mick still doesn't move. "You bloody idiot. What were you thinking?"

There's no reply. Ade slaps his friend's cheeks, but I can see from the look on Jake's face that it won't help.

"He's dead, Ade. Look at him. His face is literally white."

I can't say why this is the moment I decide to join them, but that's what happens. I walk into the grey-tiled bathroom and, when I stop, there's a dead man in front of me with a needle sticking out of him.

FOURTEEN

"I genuinely don't know what we're supposed to do," Ade says when he gathers us all together in the lounge. We're just metres away from where Mick overdosed, and I keep thinking, *What if? What if? What if?*

What if I'd done the neighbourly thing to my shipmate and called in to see him last night instead of thinking only of the memory-foam super king mattress that was waiting for me? What if I'd asked Ade why Mick hadn't come to dinner or taken the slightest interest in the guy who'd kindly shown me around the ship?

"We'll have to turn back, won't we?" Sasha's tone is unusually innocent. There is normally a worldliness to everything she says, but she seems as lost as the rest of us. Lost or putting on an act because she knows I saw her last night. It's hard to say which.

Standing in front of the dull black TV wall, Ade shakes his head in bewilderment rather than denial. "I don't know what's best. I'm waiting for the captain to decide."

It's easy to think that we are the ones in charge, but it's clear that's not the case. I'd really bought into the idea that this was our playground, and we could do whatever we liked, but there are always adults around to tell us what to do – real adults like teachers and sea captains.

If one nice thing has come out of this tragedy, it's that Tom and Sasha are on better terms than they were last night. Tom has shaved. His clothes are fresh, and he looks smart and in control as he holds his wife close against him. Sasha looks tiny in his arms, but she clearly wants to be protected, and I wish that someone would do the same for me, even if it is just for a few minutes.

"What's the range of the helicopter you *borrowed* yesterday?" Tom is still no saint and can't resist a dig at Ade.

There's a pause before every response. It's almost as if he's being fed the answers through an earpiece and his manager or publicist or whoever has to talk before he can. "I think it's about two hundred and fifty miles. This yacht has a cruising speed of twenty knots, which is about twenty-three miles an hour. We left Mauritius at four yesterday, and it's just gone twelve."

I wait for someone else to work out this equation because my brain isn't in the mood for anything taxing. Actually, it's not that difficult. It's just 20 x 23, which is clearly more than two hundred and fifty.

"That's four hundred and sixty miles," Jake mumbles. He's been quiet since we found Mick. I don't know whether they left the poor guy where he was, as I didn't stick around to watch.

"Wait, are you suggesting that we call a helicopter to pick him up like a courier collecting a package?" Clara makes this sound dreadful, which, of course, it is.

"Well, that was the idea," Tom replies without remorse.

"It's either that or we turn the ship around." I say this despite myself. The idea of doubling back makes me feel even sadder, but I understand it might be necessary.

"Of course we'll have to go back," Ryan says. He has quickly become the conscience of the group. "We're not going to keep going with a body on board. Right?"

"Why not?" I'm surprised to hear Ade respond. He's done a good job of acting like a sympathetic person until now. Not the kind to suggest we ignore the fate of his friend in favour of sunning ourselves a day or two longer on holiday. I know he has a darker side, but he hasn't let it slip.

"I would think it's obvious."

Much as when Ryan had arrived on board the day before, Ade now looks at him with a glimmer of anger. "Who are you to say that?" He waits for an answer that no one will provide. "We're in international waters, and we'll hand over the body to the authorities as soon as we come into port. We're not concealing a death from anyone."

It's strange to hear him refer to Mick as "the body". He's already lost his identity, and it feels wrong that Ade would be the one to set that in motion.

"Come on, mate," Jake pleads. "This is Mick we're talking about."

"He was your friend." Clara is just as indignant as she was at dinner last night. "You've got to do right by him."

"That's what I was trying to do!" he replies in such a cold, harsh voice that I lean back on the sofa to remove myself from the conversation by a few centimetres. "Why do you think I brought him out here with us and made sure there was no drink or drugs for him? I thought I could take him away from his troubles. He promised he wasn't carrying anything. I even checked his bags before he boarded."

I'm not sure I've ever seen Ade so emotional. This is a man who appeared at the Grammys with a tear rolling down either cheek as he performed, but that was for the stage, and whatever is simmering beneath the surface right now is different. I feel that he wants to scream, but he holds it in.

"If we keep going, we're only a couple of days from the Maldives. I don't see that one day or two makes a great deal of difference."

I look at Clara because she's the sensible one among us, but she can only shrug. When no one else presents a valid reason to turn back, Ade nods as though everything is decided.

"I'll talk to the captain. Unless he or the authorities tell me otherwise, we'll keep on."

He puts his arm around Clara to comfort her, and I look at Sasha to see whether she'll react. She does, but only to place her darling husband's hand on her cheek.

As he marches from the room, Ade is soldierlike and perhaps a tiny bit mechanical. You don't get to the level he has without being ruthless. I have to wonder whether this part of his character was always there, and I was blinded by the brightness of his talent.

"That was brutal," Jake whispers to Ryan, but we all hear.

"There's nothing to be gained from being miserable." Oddly, Tom isn't as keen to go home as he was at dinner last night. Perhaps the initial impact of going without booze has worn off. Or perhaps he's just really good at faking it. "I mean, I'm sorry that the guy's dead, but it wasn't our doing."

I wish that Sasha would disagree with him, not because I think it would change his mind or I want to see them argue again, but for the fact that a detached pragmatism has taken over everyone, and I don't like it. The sunspot of Mick's limp, lifeless form remains in my vision.

Sasha says nothing. Tom pulls her into him, and she wiggles her shoulders to and fro, like a baby bird trying to get closer to its mother.

"How many of you even want to keep going?" Jake walks into the centre of the room to ask. "Clara fell overboard, and now Mick is dead. It's hardly conducive to chatting over old times and doing cannonballs off the ship."

"The problem is that nobody is sure how we feel," Clara says quite reasonably. "It's not that we want to be insensitive, but I didn't know Mick very well and can't decide how I should react to any of this."

Jake sends a look across to me, and I know he needs my support, but Ryan answers before I can. "It's pretty clear that what we think won't change anything."

Jake just shakes his head. "This is all wrong. How can any of you think otherwise?" He goes to the bar, which I now see contains a massive selection of soft drinks and alcohol-free spirits. He looks at the bottles, which are illuminated by a forever modulating coloured light. Like a little kid on his first trip to the children's section of a library, he scans the shelf before selecting what he wants. He reaches for a blue glass bottle then sends it spinning through the air to smash against the back of the door.

The muscles in his neck flex as he releases it, and he curls his lips like a dog waiting to attack.

"I'll see you all later, yeah?"

He follows the bottle's path to leave the room, and I watch him go, knowing that I should have said something. I should have fought to find my voice, but it's all too much. New waves of sorrow and distress crash over me, and some instinct from deep within the shady caverns of my brain tells me that we're making a mistake.

FIFTEEN

The fun thing about facing a problem like this on a superyacht is that we're on a superyacht. I am haunted by an image that will never leave me. I can think of very little but the angle at which the syringe was hanging from Mick's arm and the way his head was resting on the seat of the toilet. It's beyond horrible. But I can distract myself with any one of the many entertainment facilities that the *Tanis* offers. So, after five minutes of spiralling discussion, I leave the others to plan their own programme of activities and, after a quick change of clothes, I go looking for the cinema.

The engine of the ship is easy to ignore, but I occasionally hear it – or at least feel it. A slight vibration buzzes through the hull and up through the various decks, and it makes me think of a huge sleepy creature suddenly yawning. It helps remind me that there is another plane below our own. An underworld where a whole community of people must live and sleep and work, with only a few chosen representatives allowed to see the sun before scuttling back there. I imagine myself going all the way down through the decks to meet these affable mole people and becoming their queen. Sadly, the cinema is just below my room, so I don't have to explore any further.

Though I have spent precisely no time whatsoever in direct

sunlight since stepping off the plane, my skin feels refreshed and replenished as I enter that cool chamber to disappear into darkness.

The room is perfectly air-conditioned – fresh but not too cold – and I feel like I'm swimming underwater as my eyes take their time to adjust and I stumble around in search of a light switch.

"No, no, don't do that," a voice says from nowhere, and I come to a complete stop.

Jake sticks his head out of a door that I couldn't see until now. I figure he's found the projectionist's booth before I can, and I wonder for a moment whether we're depriving some poor underworld dweller of their raison d'être. Is there a person on this ship whose sole function is to start a DVD player, just as monarchs from the past had fireworks masters and peacock keepers? Ade said he was operating with a skeleton crew, so presumably not.

Jake is busy setting everything up and a minute passes before he speaks again.

"I've chosen a movie just for you," he says, as if he knew I was coming.

The room is small, but there are three rows of seats and a line of tiny lights in the aisle to guide us to them. There must be a manual of some description in the booth, as he seems very knowledgeable about how it all works. He's even found a key to a cupboard just below the screen from which he now takes two bags of popcorn.

He hands one to me, and I try to hold on to the sadness that had gripped me before the prospect of cinema-sweet refreshment buzzed through my brain.

"I was hoping to watch the concert film Mick made," he says in the right tone of voice for such a statement. "I thought it would be a bit of a tribute to the guy, but there's no sign of it here."

"What have we got instead?" I sit down in the middle seat of the middle row.

"Wait and see."

He dashes back up the aisle, and a minute later a light turns on that does very little to brighten the room. There's a kind of blackness to it, so it must be the projector bulb. I look up at the beam above my head, but then it changes colour and a snow-capped mountain rears up on the screen before me, and my ears are filled with the sound of an orchestra crescendo.

"Too loud! Sorry, too loud!" the warning travels out to me. "Give me a sec."

The volume decreases, and a few moments later Jake bounds back into the room and crashes down beside me, almost sitting on his own bag of popcorn.

"It's lucky they didn't explode and go everywhere," I tell him. "You would have had to beg to share mine." I stick my tongue out, and the white light bouncing off the wall shows me his smile.

I recognise the movie from the second name on the cast list, then feel annoyed that I didn't get it from the first. A bird's eye view of St Peter's Square appears before the words *Roman Holiday* pop up in giant printed letters.

"I introduced you to this film!" I say, excited to see it again after so long.

"I remember!" He copies my chirpy tone, and we fall silent as the credits roll.

It feels good to travel back in time seventy years to when men wore killer suits and women could walk around dressed like Audrey Hepburn. For a very silly moment, I question whether anyone died of overdoses back then, before remembering that *Roman Holiday* was made right around the time that Frida Kahlo died from a lethal dose of opiates.

So much for nostalgia.

And yet, sitting in this darkened room watching a movie with Jake as we did three times a week when we lived in the same building, I can't think of any time in my life when I was happier. We went through lists of the best films ever made, both to find new favourites and feel like we weren't completely ignorant. We swapped recommendations, and while that did mean I had to sit through the action masterpiece *Con Air* more often than I would have liked, it also felt like we were learning to accept each other as we should.

By the time that Gregory Peck shows Audrey the sights of Rome, I keep having to remind myself that Jake and I broke up for a reason. I mean, I can't recall what it was anymore, and so I don't immediately push him away when he finishes the popcorn and puts his hand on the armrest next to mine. But I only put my head on his shoulder because it's the afternoon, and I'm always sleepy at this time – plus we seem to have skipped lunch. With changing time zones, staying up late and everything else that's happened, I haven't the energy to stay awake no matter how charming Audrey and Gregory and Jake might be.

I don't know how much of the end of the movie I catch, but I wake up hours, minutes or seconds after it's finished and find that my ex-ex is still doing a good job as my pillow. I don't wake him. I just settle back into a dream in which I get to wear beautiful clothes and zip around an ancient city on a Vespa (but women, minorities and the poor are simultaneously treated better than they were in the fifties).

By the time I wake up for good, it's late in the afternoon and I'm starving hungry. I listen to Jake's almost musical breathing as he sleeps in the faint glow of the projector's beam. Part of me wants to wake him with a kiss. Part of me wonders whether, now that we're older and hopefully wiser, we could make it work, but I don't bother him with any of this. I put my lips against his forehead and whisper a silent goodbye to the boy that, deep down, I probably still love an awful lot.

SIXTEEN

I find my way back to the corridor and realise that I've hardly been on this deck before. There's a gym, a poorly stocked library and a bunch of cupboards, but nothing to keep me down there, so I return to the main deck. Ryan is standing vaping at the side of the boat, but he doesn't notice me as I pass.

The others are back at the jacuzzi at the front of the ship, and I get the sense that, if nothing had happened to Mick, this is what we'd be doing anyway. The floating island we're on is luxurious and beautiful, yet also rather tedious. Even the best prison in the world is still a prison and, on a long voyage, that's what this place becomes.

As soon as I sit down, the waiter from last night comes to ask what I'd like for my late lunch. The question is so broad that I struggle to answer. Thoughts of cheese soufflés and beef Bourguignon run through my head, but I can't settle on any of the elaborate dishes that come to mind – nor would I really expect the chef to whip one up for me – so I reply in a weedy voice, "I wouldn't mind a cheese sandwich."

Tom sneers at this, and I bet he thinks that such bland, proletarian fare sums me up perfectly. I suppose he'd be right, but when my snack arrives ten minutes later, it's tastier than anything I've eaten in days.

Ade is sitting on a sun lounger at the prow of the ship, staring at the horizon. I don't know whether he's mourning his friend or his plan for the week, but he doesn't say anything. He doesn't even laugh at me when I keep expressing how delicious my meal is.

"Seriously, you should all order some," I insist. "They must use a different kind of cheese than we have at home. Or perhaps it's the bread."

"Well, it would be one of those things, as they're the only ingredients." Tom looks very smug considering his display last night. No matter how good it tastes, I'm tempted to take some cheese out and throw it at him.

He's still not himself. He wades through the immense jacuzzi in circles but occasionally stops and becomes frozen. His mind in these moments is clearly somewhere far away, and I feel that he is not just on edge, but on the edge of his next meltdown.

Clara sits reading a holiday thriller under the parasol. She occasionally looks up and offers a sad smile to whoever's eyes she catches, but she stays quiet, and I decide not to bother her, even to ask whether she'd recommend the book.

"Make the most of the weather," Ade eventually says kind of wistfully. "There are reports of a storm coming, but I doubt it will cause too many problems."

Tom instantly looks petrified. "Isn't that what they said in *Jurassic Park*?"

"It's the tail end of the cyclone season," Ade ignores him to tell us, but this is far from reassuring.

When he says nothing more, the tension remains. Sasha is in a different bikini from yesterday. It is bright green and equally noticeable, but not even her husband gives her the attention she deserves. I notice that Ade never looks at her directly. Does that mean he rebuffed her yesterday? Or they rehashed their old fling and he's trying to keep a low profile? I don't know whether I still feel bad for her, or I'm desperate to have some sense of what I oversaw, but I engage her in conversation.

"I don't miss the acting," she says in the middle of a discussion of her home life. "It's the kind of thing that, as soon as you're away from it, you see all the drawbacks. When you're stuck inside that bubble, you think it's what you need. You think, *If only I could get one amazing part, everything else will come good*. Then you get the part, nothing changes, and you're back to wanting more. It's like gambling. You always believe the next bet will change your luck."

Another bubble, I think but don't say.

I can't quite remember how we got onto this topic, and I struggle to respond, but Sasha's happy to keep talking. "I left all that behind me a long time ago. I've no regrets." She glances at Tom, and I remember her tear-stained confession after dinner. I remember the intensity of her words and the feeling that, if she didn't share her story with someone, she might just implode. Polite, well-spoken women like Sasha are far more prone to implosion than to the noisier alternative.

"When we're back in London, I'll come round to visit," I tell her because I'm not a cruel person, and I feel worse for Sasha with every passing minute. Did she throw herself on Ade like any number of women before, or is he stringing her along? These are the only possibilities I consider. "It's silly that we live in the same city and never see one another."

Sasha lifts her hands out of the water to clap in excitement. I'm amazed to see that, though she's been floating about in the jacuzzi for half an hour, they're not even wrinkly. Is there a special rich person's treatment that pre-emptively removes water wrinklage? Botox for the fingertips, perhaps?

"I'd love that!" she exclaims with another clap. "And now that you've ditched your job, I can coach you into writing the novel that's trapped inside you."

"No, I don't think—"

"There's no such thing as no, Bridget. No is a four-letter word." Even she realises this is nonsense, and she laughs at herself. "We all know how good your writing was at university. You got higher marks than any of us, which empirically proves that you are a better writer than Ade was a musician. And look at him." She does just this, and there's a noticeably lustful curl to her lip.

"You're certainly a better writer than I ever was," Tom mumbles from his new spot in the centre of the jacuzzi. I'm a little surprised he was able to pay attention to our conversation. He looks pale even after a day in the sun, and his eyes have a haunted sheen to them that wasn't there before.

"A dead rabbit could write better than you, Tom," Sasha tells him with no small amount of snark. Whatever calm there was between them after Mick died has surely shattered.

He freezes again and shows no emotion. It's hard to say whether it was her remark that bothered him.

"Say you'll do it," Sasha begs me, as though any change I make will enable her own. "I'll do whatever I can to help."

I don't answer, but I think about her offer. Could this be my turning point? I want to tell her that I have nothing to write about, but maybe that isn't true anymore. Maybe I just needed the next stage of my life to begin.

"All my writing back then was for assignments. Fulfilling a task that a teacher set is hardly proof I'm a good writer. I just did what I'd always done at school and followed the instructions."

Sasha's suddenly more energised. She's the person I met on my first day in London thirteen years ago. "Then I'll give you assignments." She sways with the bubbling current as she explains her plan. "We'll start off small. I'll say, write me a character who is currently unhappy in life but sees a path to change. And then you can put her in the first chapter of a book. One chapter will become two, and so on and so forth until you have a novel. Please say you'll do it."

She's imagining herself as the Ezra Pound to my T.S. Eliot. And because (unlike either of those men) I am a born people-pleaser, I say, "Sure. Why not. I have approximately enough in savings to survive for six months. I'll write a book for you, Sash, and the rest will take care of itself." She laughs at this, but not because of my overly optimistic response. The possibilities of the plan have given her energy, and I'm glad that I didn't reject the idea out of hand. It reminds me that I still care about these people. I actually want us to get along as we once did. And the even stranger thing is that I'm excited too. I want to write the book I've never even started. I want to make my living as an author and never set foot inside an office again. But most of all, I want to believe in myself the way Sasha does.

Ade sits up in his chair and turns to us with his famous smile. It's the same look he wore when he met the Prince of Wales at the Royal Variety Performance after his first album went platinum. I've seen it looking out at me from a hundred magazine covers, and it used to greet me every morning when I rolled out of my room bleary-eyed.

Before he can say anything, there's that same soft *bing* I heard the night before, and he looks up at the dark windows above us. He raises one hand to say, *Sorry, I'll be right back*, and then jogs off to see what the captain wants.

I think I might already know what it is. While I've been sitting here, our smooth ride has become noticeably rockier. The sky is still blue up above, but the horizon is black, and the meteorologist who lives in my head has noticed that the atmosphere is changing. Even the water in the no-longer bubbling jacuzzi is restless as the ship rises and falls more dramatically than before, and I have the definite feeling that a storm is on its way.

SEVENTEEN

The sun sets early around here. By six o'clock, it's already getting dark, and there are clouds sweeping in to block out the twilight. The temperature drops just enough that it's no longer comfortable to be half naked, and we run back to our cabins to change. Wearing long sleeves and trousers once more makes me think that I've put my real skin back on. The *Love Island* reject I've been imitating for the last day wasn't me, and the feel of the fabric gives me an unexpected sense of contentment.

When we reconvene in the dining room, which was previously separated from the lounge by a sliding partition, Jake is back with us. He's shy with me in a way that I don't recognise. Despite the sweet and generous person he has shown himself to be whenever we are alone together, his public face has always been different.

Jake once punched a guy for flirting with his cousin when she came to stay. Jake would get drunk, and I sometimes didn't see him for days as he fell from pub to party and back on a forty-eight-hour trail across London that wouldn't finish until late on Sunday night when there was nothing left to entertain him. Jake has several different personalities, and the cautious, hesitant person who stands in the shadows as Ade addresses us isn't one I recognise.

"We need to start again." Ade walks around the table as he

speaks. "I told you that I invited you all here for a purpose, and that still stands. Mick was one of the main reasons I bought this yacht; I knew how much he needed to get away from everything, and it is eating me up that I failed to protect him."

"How did he get the heroin?" Tom has long forsaken any attempt at charm. "I thought you said you checked his bags."

Ade glares at him, and I wonder if the real reason we're here is so that he and Sasha had an excuse to meet up. If that is the case, why did they invite her husband?

He stretches his guitarist's fingers out on both hands and waits for the instinct to throttle Tom to die back down. "Mick was an addict, and addicts generally find a way. Perhaps he bought it from one of the crew, or he managed to get some brought to him when we were last in port. The point is..."

I get the definite impression that he had a whole speech prepared before Tom set up this roadblock, but he hesitates over it now. "The point is, we're still here together, and you're all very special to me. When I think of the years we shared in London, they seem... perfect."

I know just what he means. As Sasha sits in one of the dining chairs with her husband's hand on her shoulder, and the rest of us lurk out of the way, I think we all do.

"I was happier than at any other time in my life. Money and success don't bring fulfilment," says the rich, successful man, "but you guys did, and I've spent the last I don't know how long wishing we could go back."

I'm tempted to suggest that he should buy the university so that we can cosplay our old lives, but what started out as a hopeful speech has taken a sadder turn. The sorrow that is present in so much of Ade's music is plain to see.

"We haven't exactly disappeared." Sasha delivers this simple truth, and for once she's not trying to impress him. "You could have called us whenever you wanted. You didn't have to do all this."

Ade leans forward with his fists pressed against the long glass table as he replies. "No, I couldn't. I have been in a dark place for a long time. I'm glad to say that I got out of it a couple of years ago, but I feel like it's my fault that Mick never did."

With each new nugget of information, I try to join the dots. The fact that a rock star had a hedonistic lifestyle is not surprising – his wish to rehabilitate almost inevitable – but I fail to imagine how he is to blame for his drummer's death.

"There's another reason I wanted to see you." He pauses and releases a breath he's been holding. "I've always felt like I let each of you down in some way."

He looks at Ryan, which reminds me just how little he fits into any of this. He was never one of the group – he told me himself that he thought Ade barely knew his name. I'm not saying that a relative stranger isn't welcome, but it strikes me as odd that Ade should address this comment to him.

"And so I need to apologise."

Ade stops to look at Clara, and I consider for the first time that I know nothing about their friendship. Even though he was at the centre of our collective universe, he preferred to spend time with one or two people at a time. He always hung out with Jake and me together (and then Jake and me separately). And I vaguely remember him talking to Clara when the rest of us were busy, but I can't imagine why he would feel the need to apologise to her. He had a far better excuse for not staying in touch with her than I did.

For the most part, we listen to his oddly contrite message with quiet respect. Sasha nods gratefully throughout, and Jake doesn't throw any more bottles, which is a massive improvement on our last meeting. In fact, he puts his arm around Clara as if he's so moved by what's happening that he has to share his emotion. I should have known that Tom would screw it up.

"I don't know why you think I deserve an apology. I had very little to do with you, even when we lived together." He keeps blinking as if he's got something stuck in his eye. "As far as I'm concerned, you weren't even that talented. You have to admit there were better bands around who never got to record a duet with Ariana Grande."

I wonder what programme of spiritual realignment Ade has gone through. I can practically hear him repeating a mantra to stay calm.

"I fully accept that I am not the best at anything I do." This response is almost enough to shut Tom up for a while. Almost.

"Either way, I don't need your apology. Keep it for Jake. He's the one you screwed over." He shoots a glance towards our friend in the corner. "Cutting him loose just before you made millions. That's cold, that is. If I were him, I wouldn't have come."

Tom puts his free hand to his head, and I can see that he's trembling. Sasha tries to grab hold of him, but he moves away from her to stand on his own.

"Unless you've brought us here to give him this lovely boat of yours... Is that what's happening? You're giving back what should have been his?"

Ade closes his eyes and stands perfectly still. In his black shirt and trousers, there's something juvenile about him. He looks like a boy going for work experience at his mum's company, praying that he won't make a prat of himself on the first day.

"I thought not." Tom folds his arms and looks proud. "You're not really that sorry after all."

Sasha is caught in the middle. She stares into space, unable to look either at the man I assume she loves or her husband.

"What's got into you?" Weirdly, it falls to me to ask this. "You can see that Ade is making an effort. I know you might have your reasons not to get on, but at least he's trying." It suddenly occurs to me that I might not have been the only one who saw Sasha and Ade together, and I decide I've said enough.

"Yeah, Tom." Jake looks unimpressed. I'm amazed he's stayed quiet for as long as he has. "Learn when to shut up."

Tom is perfectly restless: the muscles in his arms flex in a seemingly random sequence that a genius mathematician might be able to extract some great secret from, but it's lost on me.

When he sees that even Clara is glaring at him, he backs away with a shout of fury and frustration. There's something melodramatic about the way he moves. He is the stooped, limping monster, escaping from a mob of torch-bearing villagers. "You're a bunch of worthless, unfeeling—"

"Oh, come on!" Jake cuts the insult short, his voice now raised. "We went through this last night. How often can you show us how miserable you are and still expect anyone to care?"

"You don't get it, do you?" He sounds so broken and desperate, but his wife can't bear to look at him, and he's lost any sliver of sympathy he might have had from the rest of us. "You never saw me for who I am."

"This isn't you, Tom," Ade tries again. "I've seen it with other friends before. It's your body crying out for alcohol that's making you act this way."

"Then you had no right to take it away from me." Tom points his finger back at him like a gun, but when he tries to shout again, nothing comes out.

He doesn't leave us entirely this time. He collides with the long curving sofa near the door and falters. Instead of running from the room in the hope he'll make us feel guilty for the way we've treated him, he lies down just as the rain starts to fall.

In the space of a few seconds, every drop sounds like a bullet hitting a metal plate, robbing Tom of his dramatic moment. The rest of us hurry to the windows to take in the otherworldly display. We look on in silent wonder, like children excited for the first snow of the year. Thunder carries through the room like a drum roll, and I flinch as the sky lights up.

EIGHTEEN

Boy Phoebe arrives just in time with a trolley full of food for us. Girl Phoebe is not so lucky and appears a minute later already soaked. They set about their task without a word, and we pretend not to notice them. This curious form of hyper-discretion is a two-way street. It is their job not to be intrusive, and it's ours to act as if they don't exist.

I go to stand with Ade. His closeness reminds me of the night we drunkenly kissed in a cupboard, and I still feel weird about it after all this time. He looks down at me and smiles a sad smile. I usually think I'm pretty tall, but Ade makes me feel like a pixie. It was almost as if he was bred in a laboratory so that the people at the back of his concerts could still get a glimpse of his ever-changing hairstyle. Even in the time I've been on the ship with him, the bleached dreads have been arranged in three different formations and none of this is important because, as the thunder thunders and lightning cracks, I feel like none of us will ever find the words to break this uncomfortable silence.

As we stand watching the rain and the dark clouds, I think of the way Mick was slumped against the glass wall by the toilet. I think about the tourniquet on his arm and the tightness of his muscles, which had become discoloured in death. I think about his eyes peeking out from behind lashes and lids as if the last hit he had was the best of all. I try to think of something else, but that just reminds of Sasha and Ade, and I'm so thankful to Phoebe when she clears her throat and in an apprehensive voice declares, "I'm sorry to interrupt, Mr Okojie, but dinner's served."

We sit down to eat, and the sky continues its show for us. As we're so far out in the Indian Ocean, it's possible that we're the only ones lucky enough to see it. The view stretches around the room, and it feels as if the storm is closing in on us from all sides.

The boat rocks so much that whenever someone serves food from the elaborate buffet in the centre of the table, they pause over the bowl and then quickly whip their chosen helping to their plate for fear that it will drop. Jake has been put in charge of carving a leg of Spanish ham, but he occasionally puts the long, savage knife down to avoid slipping and stabbing someone.

Sasha consumes the bare minimum of salad and cold meats and then decides it would be best to take Tom to their suite. He hasn't moved since he lay down on the sofa, but I have the feeling he's still awake. I can picture him staring wild-eyed at the wall, trying to make sense of the world and whatever state his mind and body are in.

When his wife tries to help him to his feet, he makes no attempt to resist. He's as willing as a sleepy child to be taken where he needs to go. Petite Sasha puts his broad arm over her shoulders, and they both make their apologies.

"Really sorry to dampen the fun, guys." Tom sounds like he means it, but this message doesn't fit with anything else he's said tonight. These are the words of a man who has to get up early for work the next morning and is disappointed to miss the end of the dinner, not an alcoholic struggling to cope without a fix.

"Have a nice night," Sasha coos. "We'll see you in the morning."

It's all strangely civil, but their departure plunges us back into silence. There are five of us around the table, and I'm sure we all wish that there was a port in sight or it was at least time for bed.

"It's weird to have been apart for so long and to come back together." Though the quietest and most discreet, Clara is also currently the bravest person here and won't let the fractured evening overwhelm us.

"I kind of feel like I'm crashing the party," Ryan admits, and Ade raises his eyebrows but says nothing.

"Don't be ridiculous," Jake reassures him. "We always saw a lot of you, especially when me, Mick and Ade were gigging in the last year of our course." He pushes his long hair from his eyes, and a truly wicked grin reshapes his face. "Here, Ade, do you remember that night in Camden when—" He evidently realises that whatever sordid tale he was about to share might not be suitable. "Actually, never mind."

Ade doesn't smile. He looks serious and nods, as if trying to decide whether he likes a piece of music he's hearing for the first time.

"You know what?" He glances from face to face, but I for one couldn't possibly guess. "This feels right."

He seems to relax for the first time today. It's like those broad shoulders had a load whisked off them. I suddenly understand that the atmosphere in the room doesn't belong to us. It is entirely dependent on our lodestar, Adesina.

"I remember one night when we were all together..." he starts again. "I mean, even you, Ryan."

Ryan is currently chomping on a slice of chorizo and is unable to respond, but he shows his appreciation at being included by raising his fork in salute.

"The first gig our band played."

"Oh, please don't," Jake puts down his cutlery to cover his face. "We were terrible."

Ade ignores this interruption. "It was in a dingy little pub in Peckham."

"It was the Firkin, and I was standing in the middle of the front row." Now that his mouth is empty, Ryan reels off the information like he wants us to know how proud he is to have been there. "Best gig ever."

"Which shows you have very bad taste." For his trouble, Jake gets a stick of carrot thrown at his head, and Ade keeps talking.

"We'd been practising for months, but I had a sore throat, so I told Jake he had to join me on backing vocals to get me through."

His former guitarist interrupts at this point to prepare us. "Just so you know, his anecdote is about to get a lot more pathetic."

Ade has always loved telling stories and barely breaks off for the interruption. "So we got up on stage and played a really long instrumental intro, not because it was planned, but because neither of us wanted to start singing."

The two have fallen into a neat little double act, just like when I first knew them. Ade used to conduct the conversation, but Jake was always there to chip in asides. "I ended up playing a half-remembered lick from a Frank Zappa song that my dad loved because I could tell that Ade didn't want to get to the first verse."

Ade quickly picks the thread back up again. "And I went along with it because I felt exactly the same way and, as the bassist, it was easy enough for me to pretend I knew what I was doing." The two of them look straight at one another, then laugh like mad things. I can already tell that this tale will be funnier for them than anyone else. "For some stupid reason I've never understood, when we started the song properly, the audience actually enjoyed what we were playing."

"And that's why I instantly fell in love with the music," Ryan says, still waving his fork around to make his point. "I've never seen another new band who got the crowd behind them in seconds. It felt radical and unique."

Clara is happy just to listen to the ping-pong match of a discussion. Her tiny grey eyes flick back and forth around the room with every point that is played. I imagine I look much the same.

"So the crowd is into it, and I finally have the courage to start

THE YACHT PARTY   117

the first verse, but it's been so long since I said anything, and I'm still so nervous, that the first words come out in a high-pitched squeal." He bites his lip and looks up at the teak ceiling. "I can't remember what the line—"

"It was, 'Let me out, I want to see.'"

Ade clicks his fingers three times super-fast and points at Jake. "That's it! That's it! 'Let me out, I want to see.' Which you have to admit, sounds like the most desperate cry for help imaginable, and it was only enhanced by the fact that I sung it like I was a chipmunk someone had stepped on."

"But the crowd spontaneously yelled out in response." Ryan shakes his head. I don't know if he's overjoyed to relive the moment, or still amazed that it happened.

"Be fair. Half the people in that room were already in love with Ade," I have to point out, as nostalgia has infected them. "Do you remember how the girls from Sasha's course followed you about everywhere?"

Perhaps it's the mention of obsessive fans, but Ryan loses some of his enthusiasm and looks gloomily at his plate.

Even Ade calms down a notch. "That's true," he concedes. "But they'd never heard me sing before or play the bass very poorly, and it seemed like every last person in the room was really into it."

Jake raises his hand to interrupt. "I'd just like to remind everyone that I was also on the stage with him."

I copy the gesture because I love teasing them. "And I'd like to point out that there was also a bloke called Ben on drums."

"True again." Ade winks at me, and it really does feel like we've travelled back in time. "But what I'm trying to say is that, if it hadn't been for that gig – and all of you there, spaced out around the room cheering on me and Jake and a bloke called Ben, who quit the band before our first tour so Mick could take over – we'd never have had the confidence to make a go of it, and we'd never have discovered our sound."

"Wait," Clara says when we've all sat considering this for a few moments, "are you saying that it was in that moment you chose to sing the way you do?"

Ade turns to Jake for confirmation.

"It's not fake exactly," he's quick to explain. "We just realised that, when Ade sang like that – occasionally really high but really low the rest of the time – people enjoyed it."

I knew this story already. I was not far from Ryan when it happened. And that was the night—

"And that was the night Bridget finally agreed to go out with me." Jake is shy again. I think he might even be blushing, but his hair hangs down in front of his face, and I can't quite tell.

Clara's fair eyebrows rise higher up her forehead, and her eyes get really big. "I didn't remember any of that."

"You were standing near the back talking to that awful Jonathan guy who claimed he wanted to be a poet." Apparently, it still irks Ade that there were two people in the room who weren't paying attention to his grand debut.

To cut into our conversation, a flash of lightning illuminates the room. The subsequent startled hush is interrupted by a burst of thunder that's so loud it sounds as if it's coming from within the ship. Before we can recover from the shock, the yacht lunges downwards and panic spreads through the group. Clara, Ade and I all grab hold of the dining table as my stomach turns and, just for a moment, it feels as if we've taken to the air. When the ship rights itself, and we realise that we're not headed to the bottom of the ocean, Jake and Ryan have every right to laugh at us.

Jake looks like he's having a great time until Ryan picks this happy moment to raise a difficult question. "Come on, Jake, you have to tell us. Why did you leave the band? You could have had a yacht of your own."

The laughter slowly dies. Ade looks edgy, but he fixes his eyes on his former bandmate and won't shift them until he hears the answer. When it comes, Jake's voice is more fragile than I was expecting, and no one there believes a word he says.

"I was a bad guitarist. The record company didn't want me

because I only knew three chords." Clara looks at him sympathetically, and Jake's leg jogs beneath the table as he switches focus once more. "Anyway, what's for dessert?"

"You can tell them the truth." Ade's response is little more than a begrudging whisper, and Jake turns to stare at him like he's in the mood for a punch-up.

"I have. It's the only truth that matters."

NINETEEN

The problem with revisiting the past is that you see just how little resemblance it bears to what has replaced it. After dinner, someone puts on a playlist from when we were teenagers, and it almost sets us right again. It's all cheesy pop and indie rock, except for the odd clubby track which does nothing for me. Ade and Clara dance like an elderly couple at a wedding, regardless of the soundtrack. Ryan and Jake prove they are music nerds by reeling off facts about each song, and I hang around wondering whether I am the one who should have been left off the guest list.

I go to watch the storm again, and though the lightning appears to be retreating, the movement of the boat is more violent. If there's such a thing as sea legs, then I haven't found mine yet, as every dip and lurch increases the feeling inside me that Mick was the lucky one, and we're all going to drown. I see the *Tanis* lying on the ocean floor and divers searching for our remains. I tell myself it can't happen to a ship like this, but we are so alone out here, and the sea is so wild, that I know we're not truly safe.

Ade must feel sorry for me, as he stops dancing and comes over. I catch a flash of his reflection in the window before he arrives, and the image is so bleak and ghostly that it almost makes me jump.

"Are you all right, Bridge?"

"Me? I'm fantastic." My response sounds uncertain, and I try to recover. "Is this what you had in mind when you mysteriously sent out plane tickets to people you hadn't seen for years?"

He smiles on one side of his mouth, which causes a large dimple to form. "Not exactly like this, but there's plenty of fun still to be had."

"I missed you," I tell him before I can chicken out. As soon as I say it, I realise that this is what's felt so wrong since I've been here. "I missed our friendship."

A bolt of lightning bright enough to light the dim room shines back off one side of his face. "So did I. And that's the apology I owe you. It's really simple in fact; I'm sorry for being a useless friend."

I don't know what to say to this. The overly polite part of me wants to insist that I could have reached out to him, but it's not true. He was removed from my world, and any attempt I made to pull him back into it would have felt like I was trying to jump on his fleet of world-touring bandwagons.

"The last time I saw you..." He pauses and I become aware of Jake and Clara singing along to a dreadful Black Eyed Peas song. "The last time I saw you, I already wasn't myself. It was after our gig in the Astoria."

He doesn't need to remind me. I've been thinking about that night all week. Thinking of the way he looked at me as if he barely knew who I was. The way he laughed when I tried to talk to him as if I meant nothing to him.

"It's okay. You were busy with other friends. I shouldn't have expected you to abandon everything because—"

He takes a deep breath, and I can see how difficult this is for him. "We both know that's not true. I was a stuck-up brat. I'd got it into my head that I was some kind of legend. That's how it felt at the beginning when everyone was calling my name. I felt superhuman, and I had all the arrogance to go with it."

"You don't have to explain," I say in a *why-worry-about-little-old-me* sort of voice that makes me sound all the needier.

"Yes, I do. When I invited you to the concert, I wanted you to be there. You were my best friend, and I wanted you to be proud of what I'd become. But on the night, I was instantly afraid that you'd see what a phony I was."

"I would never—"

"I know." He turns away for a moment to find the right words. "I'm not saying you would be cruel, but I was aware how artificial my life was, and you've never had any time for fakes. I was sure you'd tell me to snap out of it and throw off the leeches. It was exactly what I needed to hear, and it terrified me."

"It's okay, Ade. To be honest, I thought I was the one who messed things up." I put my hand out to take his, and he looks at it as if the very gesture is foreign to him.

He speaks more quickly now. "You mustn't think that. I insulted you in front of everyone. I introduced you to the girl I was with, then made it sound like you were just some nobody who went to my uni. The truth is, I don't even remember what her name was."

I don't know if he wants to feel sorry for himself, but I won't let him. "We all do things we regret."

"But I should have been better. I'm trying to be better." He says this like it's another mantra, and I can see that he means it.

"There are probably other people you should worry about before me," I reply and, when the wretched look remains on his face, I pull him closer. It's pretty difficult to be nurturing when a guy is a foot taller than you. All I can do is place my head against his chest and pat his back in a slightly patronising fashion.

We stand like that for a long time, and when we pull away, the others have all slunk off somewhere. The music still plays, but the dancers have gone. It's half past nine, and the evening is dead, so there's only one thing left to do.

"Thanks, Bridget," he says a little formally when we reach the door. "Thanks for coming and listening to me. That was all I could have hoped for, and you're kind to see it through."

I squeeze his hand again and want to ask what made him like this. I think of talking to him about Dawn or Sasha, but I know he doesn't want me to. He needs to have a similar conversation with every last person here. As much as I'd like to know what triggered his soul-searching, it's not my place to ask. We stand in the doorway for a few moments, then head out into the storm.

When the door opens, it feels like a bubble has been popped and my fear of the furious ocean grips me once more. The storm is far louder than I had imagined. The no doubt triple-glazed glass in the lounge cut us off from the world. Hearing the rain attacking the yacht and the waves crashing against the hull makes me more aware of our endless seesawing. Ade walks off to his cabin, and I head to the deck below, but I have to hold the handrails and pause every few steps to stop from falling over. I'm surprised no one has come to warn us of the danger of being out on deck, but then the crew clearly have their orders to be neither seen nor heard.

I make it back to my cabin and, even though I was under cover for most of the way, I feel like I've just walked through a carwash. My clothes are so drenched I have to wring them out in the sink before I warm up with a shower.

I've had my closure tonight. Ade said the exact thing I wanted to hear, yet it's only made me more worried for him. I've been robbed of the idea that his superstar life was perfect; the reality is far bleaker. He's like Robinson Crusoe out here, and now even his Man Friday has gone. He'll go on tour again before long, but nothing he said made it sound like that's a better option.

There's a lump in the middle of my chest as I lie down and think about the channel of sadness that runs through my friend's life. Ade may well be the most eligible man on the planet, but I get the sense that he can't trust a single person. Maybe that's why he's desperate to relive our student days. Perhaps he feels that people who knew him before all this might understand – the ones who were around before the private helicopters and all that bloody teak. Assuming we don't sink in the night, I will do all I can to help him.

I'm in that happy space, between the waking world and whatever we get a glimpse of in our dreams, when angry knocking pulls me back out again.

"Who is it?" I shout, but they obviously can't hear me as the sound continues.

I force myself to roll out of bed and grab the kimono, as if my blue pyjamas that say *Anyone for a nightcap?* are so revealing that I have to cover up.

The knock, knock, knock has become a bang, bang, bang and, when I open the door, I see Tom's haggard face looking back at me.

"Is she here?" he demands.

His insistent tone hits me as the rain runs from his hair in a seemingly endless stream. "What's the matter? What's happened?"

"It's Sasha. She's gone."

TWENTY

I'm afraid that I know exactly where Sasha is. It occurs to me once more that, for all his humble apologies and need to make amends, Ade may have organised this whole thing to enjoy a fling with a married woman. Of course, I'm not about to tell her husband that. I put on some sensible clothes, then we wake Ryan and Clara, but there's no sign of Jake in his room.

"They'll be together somewhere having a chat," I tell Tom in the corridor as we wait for the others to get changed. I don't necessarily believe what I'm saying. Sasha and Jake were never really friends despite spending two years of their lives at the same address.

Tom doesn't believe me either way. "If that's the case, then where are they?"

"Is there any reason to think the worst?" Ryan asks as he steps from his room, still doing up the belt on his trousers. An efficient crew member has left life jackets on hooks beside our doors. I've already made sure that Tom put his on, and now I do the same for Ryan.

Tom isn't thinking straight. He can't deal with what's happening, so he focuses on Sasha and starts with the basics that he's already told me. "There was a knock on the door to our suite. I think it was twenty minutes ago, but I'm all mixed up in time."

"It's okay, Tom," I promise him, feeling all the sympathy that the man deserves. "Let's just take things slowly. Ryan can go to the bridge and ask the captain what we should do. The rest of us can keep searching for Sasha. If we find any other members of staff, we'll get them to help."

This is a plan. It's not necessarily a great one, but it's clear enough for Tom to follow.

"Look out for Jake too," I tell Ryan, who is already putting it into practice. "You were together when you left the lounge. Do you know where he went?"

He is about to turn off the corridor to head upstairs. "He was in a bad mood and went off on his own."

Clara looked frightened when we woke her and has now gone full mouse. "So we have to worry about him too. I can't take it." I hand her a life jacket, as it's the only thing I can think of to calm her down.

Her panicking has made Tom even more agitated, so I try to get us going again. "Like I said, they're probably just having a drink somewhere and reminiscing. We'll find them."

I take Tom's arm to help him along. His movements are still too slow, and though I'm not a doctor and know little about addiction, it's clear that alcohol withdrawal has left its mark on him.

"The cinema: they could have gone there," I say to give us some hope and, rather than heading to the upper deck, we drop down a floor.

"Sasha loves films," her husband replies in a broken voice. The words are a crutch to help him along, and he walks a little quicker than before.

When we get to the cinema, it doesn't surprise me that there's no film playing and no one inside. It's just as Jake and I found it that afternoon. There's nothing to say anyone has been in there. Even the empty popcorn bags and stray kernels have been cleaned up by a member of the crew.

Back outside, the wind is so fierce and the rain so sharp that Tom has to hold on to the railing and narrow his eyes. "This can't be happening. It can't. I can't do this without her."

Clara puts her arm around him, though I doubt he notices.

"Okay." I've adopted a calm, efficient manner, but it's just an act. "Why don't you two find the staff room downstairs – there's bound to be one, and it isn't so late that they will have gone to sleep. I'll keep looking while you ready the troops!" I have never used this phrase in my life and doubt I ever will again, but the confidence with which it is delivered does the job.

"Thank you, Bridge. You're a good friend." Tom is on the point of crying, though his face is still wet from the storm, and any tears would blend right in.

I shoot Clara a frown to show that I'm sorry for dumping him on her, and we head in opposite directions. I couldn't leave Tom on his own, and I'm not sure that Clara will be the one to scour the ship for our missing friends, so this is the best option.

I circle the deck, trying the gym, the library and a few small lounges, but there's no sign of either of them. I'm fairly certain that Sasha went up to Ade's room when her husband was asleep to relive whatever they got up to last night. How Jake fits into that scenario, I can't tell you.

I walk up to the master suite, wondering whether Sasha and Ade were carrying on behind Tom's back the whole time we knew one another. It suddenly makes sense to me that Dawn wouldn't be here this week if that was the case. She was always Sasha's confidante. Maybe she couldn't stand the thought of seeing them together again.

To add to the drama of secret affairs and two missing passengers, the storm makes my task even more difficult. The rain stings my face as I fight my way up the stairs. I don't dare look at the ocean – the thought of my friends falling overboard sends a jolt of panic through me. The idea that the last time Jake saw me I was cuddling Ade makes it even worse.

I can hear the roaring waves, and a high whistle as the wind attacks one of the spinning turbines at the very highest point of the top deck. I don't have waterproof clothes, but I'm happy I packed so badly because my chunky leather boots don't slide around as I walk. Another conclusion is that Sasha had no such sensible footwear and has slipped silently into the ocean. For this reason, I'd much prefer her to be off bonking one of our friends.

"Ade, we need you now!" I call as I bang on his door. I will him to appear with that guilty look on his face. I know it so well, and I know it will be impossible to hold anything against him when I see it. I think even Tom might forgive Ade for sleeping with his wife when those dimples show up and he looks all coy.

"What's the matter?" he asks as he slides the door across. I can see that the bed is still made and there's no one else there.

"We can't find Sasha or Jake. No one's seen them for half an hour."

The shock of this statement takes some time to reach him – or perhaps that's just what he wants me to think. "The last time I saw them was with you in the lounge."

He is still fully dressed. There are papers on the rollout desk in the corner and, as everything else is so neat in there, I can only assume he has been writing.

"I don't care if she's in here with you." A small burden is removed as I tell him what I saw. "I know you were together last night, but Tom is already half out of his mind. In the state that he's in, he might end up doing something dangerous."

He opens his eyes wider and gazes down at me. "Bridget, I'm telling the truth. She's not in here. And whatever you saw last night wasn't what you thought." I hesitate for a moment, and he quickly adds, "You can come in and look for her if you want."

I don't know whether I believe him, and it would be stupid not to check.

"You don't deny that you slept with her once," I say, to maintain my stern attitude as I look in the wardrobe and under the bed.

"Do we really have to talk about that?" He stands back against the wall, like a criminal trying to show a police officer that he's co-operating.

"I saw you together last night." It feels good to say it, but when he doesn't answer, I find my earlier theory even more credible. "I think it went on longer in London than the rest of us knew and Dawn found out. I'm guessing that was why she didn't want to live with you in the third year."

He looks sorry for himself, but won't reply, and so I concentrate on finding Sasha. The door to the bathroom is closed. I stalk across to it, and once again find myself hoping that she is an adulterer: a living, breathing cheat.

But when I open the door, there's nothing to find but a rolltop bath and a waterfall shower. There's not so much as a pair of knickers or a misplaced shoe there, and whatever hope I'd had retreats.

"I'm sorry," I tell Ade when I return to his room. "I had to be sure. I just..."

There's a brief stillness before he offers some small revelation. "Sasha is very unhappy in her life. I didn't take advantage of her." This doesn't really tell me what happened, but before I can ask anything more, he speaks again. "There are flashlights somewhere. Come with me."

He grabs a waterproof sailor's jacket from his cupboard and throws it on over his sleek black outfit. On stepping outside, I can already hear people calling for Sasha. Her name is so distorted by the wind that it's easy to imagine that sirens are calling her to visit them in the suffocating depths of the ocean.

We loop around to take the stairs up to the bridge deck, which I haven't explored before. There's a cupboard at the top and Ade hands me a coat of my own and one of those gigantic torches that are like portable floodlights. As we stand there, Ryan comes out to speak to us, and it suddenly occurs to me that, though the ship is still rocking about, we're not gliding through the water as we were.

"The chief officer has cut the engines until we decide whether we need to double back."

Ade nods distractedly, then grabs the same supplies for Ryan before turning to descend the stairs. When we reach the wider deck below, we switch on our beams, and Ade directs his down the side of the ship in case... in case the simplest and saddest solution is the right one.

I point mine up at the top decks and instantly spot a figure there. I guess Jake's a secret *Titanic* fan. He's standing on the highest level of the ship with his arm wrapped around a metal cable and the other outstretched like Kate Winslet in the movie.

"You idiot," I shout up to him, even as the relief that he's alive runs through me, "you could fall to your death."

He doesn't hear me at first, so I point the torch right in his face to get his attention. Two-million candle power has its uses after all, and he glares down at me. I've never seen someone look drowned without going underwater before, but the wind and the rain and the still lurching vessel don't seem to bother him.

"Get up here!" His voice sounds like it's coming from miles away. "It's fun!"

Ade has heard and comes to stand next to me. "Jake, stop being so dumb." He highlights the path down with the torch and then waggles it about to show that he's angry.

The yacht's main floodlight clicks on, illuminating a swathe of the sea before us. For a moment, Jake looks like a weary old sailor on a galleon. Still holding onto the rigid cable, he leans further out and makes a face like he's about to fall. Ade mutters something rude, and I release a held breath when Jake finally does the sensible thing and drops down to the level below.

Ryan is further along the deck, helplessly shining his torch into any corner where Sasha might be hiding. There are crew members searching too, and something about the way they move – listlessly, almost resignedly – makes me want to speed up the search.

I jog as fast as I can across the helipad without falling over. I have one thought, one hope that might make things better, and I walk to the very back of the ship with Ade and Jake at my heels.

The stairs here are chained off when the *Tanis* is in motion, but it's simple enough to get down.

I have a vision in my head of Sasha going there to reflect on the events of the last couple of days, but when we point our beams at the dive platform where we'd swum, there's no one to be seen. The picture changes, and I imagine her falling into the water. I see her waving her arms helplessly as we motor away into the night before her panic drags her beneath the waves.

I can't summon the courage to go any further, so Jake ducks under the chain and down the two flights of stairs to look in the beach club just as Clara and Tom arrive alongside me.

"We're still looking," I whisper to her so that Tom doesn't hear.

There's none of his usual smarm or smugness left. He looks like a man who is slowly transforming into a beast. He is part golem, part troll. Though his shoulders are hunched, he seems entirely unaware of the rain that is falling, and his gaze is devoid of hope.

"There's no one here," Jake calls from below, and my heart feels like it wants to give up beating.

TWENTY-ONE

The search continues for some time, but there is little belief that we will succeed. Not really. Sasha had been caring for her sick husband before she disappeared. She would have told him if she was planning to head off to watch a film, have a run on a treadmill or read a book somewhere.

"She's a strong swimmer," Tom keeps saying now that we accept that she won't be found on board. "If she's fallen from the ship, it doesn't mean she's dead." We all want to believe this, but I doubt that anyone does. "I've remembered the time that she left now. It had just gone ten by my clock – two or three minutes past, maybe. Surely the captain can use that to work out where we were and take us back there. Surely there's still hope."

No one disagrees with him and, with a towel draped over my shoulders, I turn to Ade, hoping he'll know what to do.

We've gathered in his suite; it feels safer in here somehow. *The master suite is surely the perfect place to make a master plan*, is my naive thinking, though I question what we can do in a ship in a storm in the middle of the rebellious ocean.

Perhaps the vintage red rotary phone beside Ade's bed has put me in mind of cunning plans and daring solutions. It looks like something from an early James Bond film and, to my amazement, he walks across to it and dials a single number to connect to the bridge.

"Hi, Andy, the missing woman's husband thinks she was last seen just after ten o'clock. Might that help us locate the point where we need to be looking?"

There's silence in the room as he listens to the captain. If this was a cartoon, we'd hear a squeaky response travel over to us, but we can only guess what is said from Ade's pensive expression.

"Thank you. I do appreciate it. And thank you for coming back on duty. I hope you won't have to be up too late." The oddly formal moment over, he puts the phone down and talks to us instead. "He says that he's put out a distress call, though there's nothing to say how quickly any sort of rescue services will arrive. We're away from major shipping lanes here, and there are no nearby vessels. We're as far from land as we can get."

He could have probably found a softer way to break this bad news.

"But we are going back for her, right?" In normal circumstances, Tom would have jumped to his feet and rushed forward to compel Ade to do something. But he only has the strength to perch on the bed and shout his troubled thoughts across the room. "We are going to look for her?"

"The captain is turning the boat around now."

This feels like the official announcement that Sasha is in the water somewhere. The room falls silent, and I'm sure I'm not the only one to see her out in the blackness – to feel her fear as the storm does all it can to drown her. Ryan watches Tom as silent sobs rack his body, and it's clear that he's wondering how our friend fell overboard in the first place.

It's Jake who finally breaks through the uneasy quiet. "We have to be realistic," he begins, before coming to a complete stop and looking uncertain about what he wants to say.

Ade is sitting at his desk, turning from one side to another in his spinning chair. "I think we've been realistic from the beginning."

Is there a note of irritation in this? Perhaps he's worried what will happen when the internet discovers that his drummer OD'd and a woman fell from his yacht. Natalie Wood's death followed her husband around for decades after she drowned off his boat.

"Let me finish." Jake doesn't look up as he says this. He's staring at the floor as though he needs all of his brainpower to work out this equation. "I'm saying that it's extremely unlikely for two people to die so close together for apparently unrelated reasons."

Clara puts her hand to her mouth to cover a gasp, and I realise just how much she has in common with the children from an Enid Blyton novel. She even looks a bit like one, with her neat little hair slide and 1940s bob.

"How could you think that?" Tom's words run together into one long slurred sound. "We have no idea what happened to Sasha yet. How can you be so morbid?"

"Well you said that someone knocked on your door, not that I'm accusing anyone." Keeping his cool, Jake's eyes never leave Tom. "I just think it's worth pointing out that we don't know whether Mick's overdose was self-inflicted. There could have been someone with him when he died. And there's something no one's mentioned..."

I know him well enough to realise that he doesn't want to say any of this. His features are crumpled together, his tone reluctant, but he clearly believes that there's no other choice. "Does no one else think it's odd that Clara toppled off the upper deck into the sea? There was a corridor right behind the spot where she'd been standing. Someone could have sneaked up and pushed her over. Perhaps they did the same with Sasha."

"I don't see how I..." Clara is trembling. She opens her mouth to speak, then shakes her head. It must be hard to contemplate the possibility that someone tried to kill you.

This is all too much for Tom. He looks down at his hands as if checking he still has all his fingers. Is hallucination a symptom of alcohol withdrawal? When he looks at us, does he see monsters with three heads? The horrified look on his face makes me question whether his reality and ours are the same.

When he notices that Jake's eyes are still on him, he struggles for a response. "If you think for one second you're going to push what happened onto me..." He doesn't finish his sentence, but then he doesn't need to. In his condition, it's unlikely he could carry out any threat.

Ryan is looking at me in the same way as when we rescued Clara yesterday afternoon. "Jake's got a point." Like a bad actor in a school play, he steps forward to speak. "We should at least question whether all these things are connected."

Tom cranes his neck to look at him. "'Connected'? You're not Inspector Morse, mate!" He tries to sit up but his head rolls about his shoulders for a moment. "Who even invited you?"

"Forget I said anything."

"No, come on. Tell me." Tom won't let it go. He puts his hands behind him on the bed and pushes himself up to standing. For a moment, he reminds me of my grandfather when he had a bad back. "What are you doing here? I barely remember you existing when we lived in New Cross. So why do you think you have any right to comment on *my* wife or *my* friends?"

His face is sweating. He's a shaking, nervous mess, and I'm glad he isn't any closer to Ryan or he might try to punch him.

"I said I'm sorry."

"Who did invite you here, Ryan?" a voice from the corner asks, and I turn to see Ade directing his furious gaze at our unlikely companion.

"What do you—" Ryan puts his hand to his chest and clears his throat. "I mean, you sent me a plane ticket. You wrote me a letter."

"No, I didn't."

The temperature in the room suddenly drops thirty degrees. It's as if a dumper truck has flooded the place with ice. Ryan looks around in search of support, but he has no allies here. Sasha was the only one of us who really knew him, and she's gone.

"I sent six invitations." Ade holds his fingers up to drive the message home. "Six tickets. Clara, Sasha, Tom, Jake, Bridget and Dawn were supposed to come. Dawn told me she couldn't make it, but when my man went to collect Clara and Jake from the airport, there you were."

Ryan has no obvious response to this – no real explanation – so he starts to ramble. "I'm not saying that I didn't think it was weird. After all, you and I never knew each other very well. But I know about the trouble you've had over the last few years, and I wondered—"

"Oh, do you?" Ade launches himself from his chair, which goes rolling into the desk behind him. "Then how do you know that, when my people have done everything in their power to keep my business out of the press?"

Ryan looks petrified, but he keeps talking. "Because I work in the music industry, and there were rumours. There are always rumours. I thought you wanted to make it up to me."

Ade's immense muscular frame is suddenly more noticeable through his T-shirt, and he shouts at Ryan from two feet away. "Make up for what?"

I can't stand to see people being bullied. The sight of an unstable Tom and an enraged Ade ganging up on the slightly chubby fanboy is too much to bear.

"We all need to calm down," I tell them, because I see where this is heading. Without Sasha, there's too big an imbalance – too much unnecessary testosterone slopping about – and this lot might end up ripping someone's head off. "You're not thinking straight. Why would Ryan want to hurt Mick? Or Sasha, for that matter?"

The force of my words seem to have the desired effect on Ade, and Tom is already making such an effort to stay on his feet that he doesn't have the energy to continue his attack. Unhappily, there's someone else here to do it for him.

"You're right, Bridget." Jake sounds unexpectedly mature. "But he still hasn't explained what he's doing here if he wasn't invited."

"Yes, I have." Ryan shakes his hands out nervously and walks to the other side of the room to put some space between himself and the panel of judges. "The letter came in the post. There was a ticket. I sent an email to the address provided to confirm I was coming."

"There was no email from you," Ade snaps, but anyone could open an account in his name, so that doesn't prove anything.

"Did you notice the postmark?" I ask, because that was the first thing that occurred to me when Ade's letter came.

"The postmark?" Ryan's voice has gone higher, and even if I'm trying to help him, he still sounds defensive. "Why would I? Is that even a thing these days?"

"What about airmail stickers?" I try again. "Did it look like it had been sent from the Middle East? Mine was."

"Mine too," Jake says.

"No... No, I don't think so. It looked like any letter I get for work."

"So, it was sent from within the UK." I sound like Nancy Drew.

When this gets us nowhere, Jake grabs hold of the discussion once more. "Okay, so you received the ticket in the post. It's hugely unlikely but theoretically possible that someone heard about what was happening and decided to mess with Ade. Now tell us what he did to you that warranted an apology."

"I don't want to be here anymore," the one person who had stayed out of the argument suddenly cries out. Clara is sitting on the floor with her arms wrapped around her legs and a look of something approaching terror on her face. "Do you hear me? I can't deal with this. We don't even know that Sasha is dead, and you're already turning against each other. I can't stand it."

Her words leave a hollow ring behind. The macho idiots who had been trying to out-posture one another look sorry for all of five seconds, and it's up to me to make it better. I cross the room to sit down beside her, and I know that whatever anxiety and anguish she went through all those years ago is playing out in her head again as the boys ignore her suffering and continue to push Ryan for answers.

"You still haven't told us the whole story." Even as Jake says this, he glances across at Ade, and I wonder what he's thinking. "Why should we trust you when you haven't told us what Ade did?"

TWENTY-TWO

Ryan waits for permission to answer, even though the ungrateful rock star was just screaming in his face and accusing him of murder.

When Ade turns away in apparent resignation, Ryan begins. "I used to run an Adesina fansite and, because of that, I ended up writing a piece for a newspaper about the band's fanbase. His manager messaged me through the website to offer to set up an interview, and it was a dream come true. I'd met Ade loads of times when the band were starting out, but not since he'd blown up. There was a secret gig at Shepherd's Bush Empire, so they gave me a backstage pass."

"And we did the interview and got on very well." Ade still won't look at anyone. "There's really very little else to say."

The pendulum swings, and now Ryan is the indignant one. "But there is. Because after that, we went for a drink across town. We talked about the music we both loved and what inspired us. I left the pub on an absolute high. You had to make a call, and I ended up waiting for a taxi as a gang of drunk lads came over and started pushing and jabbing and calling me gay. I mean, we were in Soho, so it wasn't exactly a stretch of the imagination that I might be. They got nastier and more violent, and just when I was really starting to worry, you appeared, and I thought everything would be okay."

Ade's lips are shaking as he breathes in and out. He clamps them together, but he can't hide his emotion entirely. "I admit... I should have done more, and there's no excuse." He looks across at the man he let down. "That scummy little bunch of ratboys recognised me. When I stepped in to help Ryan, one of them whipped his phone out and filmed everything. His mate got right up in my face and went, 'Are you like him too? Is this your little boyfriend?'"

He breathes slowly in and back out again. "And because I was a total coward, I backed away and said, 'Nah, mate,' trying to sound cool like that. 'Nah, mate. I barely know him.' I watched as they pushed Ryan to the ground. If the bouncers hadn't run over from the club across the road, it could have got really nasty, but I still wouldn't have done anything to stop it because I cared more about the damage it could do to my reputation than I did for Ryan."

I can't say what hearing this does to the man who lay frightened on the pavement, because he tamps down all the emotion and stares resolutely back at his former hero.

This isn't enough for Ade; he needs to suffer his punishment a little more. "The bouncers sent the boys packing. Ryan got into a taxi, and we didn't see each other again until yesterday. And afterwards, instead of trying to make it up to him in some way, I acted as if it had never happened." He turns to look at the rest of us. "It was the same with all of you. I could have been your friend. I could have held on to the people who mattered, but I did what was easiest and pretended not to care."

Tom falls back onto the bed again. This isn't his moment, and he'll have to wait his turn.

Clara holds me tighter, like she's praying for calm, and just when it seems that the discussion will die down, Jake returns to an earlier topic.

"That still doesn't explain what you were thinking, Ade." He keeps his voice low, but there's a persistence to him that is out of character. "You haven't told us why you let Ryan get on that helicopter if he wasn't invited."

"I would have thought that was obvious," Ade replies. "I remembered exactly what I did to Ryan, and when the driver called to tell me who had turned up at the airport, I thought it was fated. I thought he'd been sent here to help wash my slate clean. But there's a difference between wanting to make amends and actually doing it."

"That's you all over, Okojie. You're selfish." Tom is a yapping dog. He will make a lot of noise but achieve very little. "You brought us out here for your own sake, and now people are dead. It wasn't to give us little folk a holiday. It was to make us so grateful that we'd have to forgive all the obnoxious stuff you've ever done."

This is when the whole thing falls apart. It's unclear who's accusing who of what, or whether anyone seriously believes that there's a killer among us, but every man in that room is suddenly shouting as Clara puts her head in her hands.

"What you don't understand..." Ade begins.

"This is the kind of..." Tom says at the exact same time.

"I never wanted..." Ryan complains as he turns away.

Jake is taking this seriously and wants us to know that "no one is paying attention to the most—"

"Enough!" I scream, because I suddenly hate every last one of them. "Sasha is missing, and Mick is dead; his body is just a few rooms away. So what good is arguing going to do us?"

I don't know why, but this is what makes me start crying. "Don't attack one another when things are already bad enough." I'm aware that I sound terribly preachy, but then I've shut my mouth rather than stand up for my beliefs my whole life. "Ade, we forgive you. We all forgive you. Now get over yourself and be a better person by using your millions to save the planet or looking for a cure for cancer instead of buying ridiculous toys like the monstrosity we're floating on."

I sit here sobbing, which serves to make a bad situation just plain awkward. Everyone looks at me with pity in their eyes. Even poor little Clara looks sorry for me, when all I wanted was for people to stop shouting.

Jake still won't give up on whatever he wanted to say. "Mick's death could have triggered everything else, even if it was just an overdose."

Tom huffs like a grumpy boar. "A minute ago, you said he might have been murdered. So now you're suggesting that Sasha simply fell off the boat in the storm?"

My well-meaning ex-boyfriend closes his eyes for a moment and shakes his head. "No, I'm saying that, if you wanted to get rid of her, this was the perfect moment to do it."

A roar goes up, and I have a feeling that Jake is about to get punched. I don't stay to find out what happens next. I launch myself straight at the door. My eyes still blurry, I've forgotten that it slides open, and I almost bang straight into it. I doubt that any dramatic exit in my life has gone to plan, so this hardly surprises me.

Outside, the wind bats me about to bring me back to my senses. The air on deck feels like it's laced with some exquisite fragrance. Perhaps it's the smell of the sea or the rain, but I breathe it in and feel more human. I'm relieved to have escaped from all that anger, but the storm doesn't want me to remain outside. The front of the boat tips up at an unsettling angle and then drops dramatically down again. I wipe a combination of saltwaters from my eyes and take the hint to chart the now familiar path back to my cabin.

My sobs sound louder inside my bedroom. They echo off the walls as if to taunt me, and I half consider pressing the button that opens up the wall onto the balcony. The thought of lying on my bed with a front-row seat of the surging sea is both tempting and terrifying, but I have no desire to go sliding off the balcony to join Sasha on the ocean floor.

I also have no wish to be murdered, and consider going to sleep in the locked bathroom, but I figure it'll be more bearable to put the mattress against the door. At least that way, if there is a killer stalking about the place and they try to come in, I'll hear and be able to retreat. It weighs a ton, and I almost give up a couple of times, but I finally manage it. Then I'm free to lie down on all the cushions and covers on the floor, like a kid having a sleepover.

I lie there, unable to believe the nightmare we're in, but I know I won't sleep, so I take the bottle of vodka from my bedside table and swallow all I can in four long chugs. I never normally drink alone, but the oblivion it offers is too tempting. It burns as it goes down, and it doesn't taste how I was expecting, but it feels better than what came before. I take my bedtime pills like a good girl, and that's when I'm sure that something's wrong.

The pain isn't just in my throat but throughout my body. I'm desperate for sleep, but it won't come. Instead, my heart feels like it's running the hundred-metre sprint. I swear it's twice as fast as normal and, when I tell myself to get up and do something about it, my muscles don't react. My body is slow, but my brain is busier than ever.

I'm scared in a way I'm not used to. I miss everyone I love. I miss Clara and Ade, and my mum back at home. And somehow, most of all, I miss the boy that a major part of me still loves. Jake's only fifty metres away, but I can't go to him. My limbs feel impossibly heavy, and there's nothing I can do to move them. I spent the last ten years thinking that there was nothing good in my life, but now that I know I'm dying, I even miss my stupid job and my ugly office. I miss the view from my window of the car park outside my flat.

I want to claw at my skin and thump my heart to make it work as it should, but all the synapses in my body have been disconnected. I try to call Jake's name, but I can't make a sound. I see him rushing through the door to save me, and for a half-second, I fail to realise that it's only a fantasy. My head swims, and for one heart-stopping moment, I'm Sasha fighting against the storm. I can't hold on to my thoughts long enough to know how I feel about them. I see image after image – a flashing reel of incongruous scenes from my life before my eyes finally close and whatever I've just drunk does its worst.

No one is coming. No one knows I'm about to die. So I lie on the floor until the lights inside my head turn off one by one.

PART 2
JAKE

TWENTY-THREE

When I met Bridget, I knew that I was in love from the very first moment. I could see that she was too nice for me, but I would have done anything to be with her.

I knew that I couldn't be Jake, the guy who gets drunk and angry and starts fights for absolutely no reason. I'd be Jacob, who's into arty movies and long books and is open to the idea that pop music is actually bearable. I got better at the guitar, joined a band, wore smarter clothes, and it was all for Bridget. And okay, 'Jacob' never quite stuck, but for a little while, the rest of that persona felt like a good fit for me.

When I saw her on the day we moved into our flat in Loring Hall, I couldn't quite believe that the girl of my dreams would be living in the room next door. Sasha was the bold, flashy one. She walked straight over like she expected me to fall at her feet. Dawn was outgoing, and Clara was sweet and kind, but there was magic in Bridget's eyes. It was like she had a secret and, if I was my very best self, she might share it with me.

It took me months to convince her that I wasn't a moron. It didn't help that, even in my nice new clothes and with my hair grown out like I thought I was Kurt Cobain, I still looked like a neanderthal. I realised at an early age that my neck and hands and shoulders are just too big and broad for anyone to take me seriously. When I was at school, teachers took one look and decided I was trouble: so that's what I became. If they'd given out end-of-school prizes, I'd have been voted boy most likely to do a spell in prison. And they'd have been right.

Bridget made me want to change. And to be fair to him, Ade did all he could to help. The three of us were inseparable back then. Most men would have been intimidated by a pretty boy like him, but we were always mates, and I doubt Bridget would ever have gone out with me if it weren't for my best friend.

It wasn't just that he used to talk me up to her. No, he let me be in his band when I had no real right to be there. I mean, I wasn't a terrible guitarist, but if I hadn't stood on a stage with a man who would become a legend, it's unlikely that Bridget would have rushed up after our first gig and planted her lips on mine. She fell in love with me because of the energy in that back room in a crappy pub in Peckham. She saw something in me that was never supposed to be there.

Eighteen months later, she told me I wasn't the same person she'd fallen in love with. It sounds stupid to say that fame had gone to my head, seeing as I wasn't the slightest bit famous, but being in a band meant that my mask had started to slip. I guess that I'd forgotten to show so much of my softer side. I would go out all weekend without replying to her messages, and we spent much less time together than before. When I realised what an idiot I'd been, it was already too late. I asked her to move in with me, and she said that it would be better if we broke up.

I'm not so arrogant that I think the boy I pretended to be back then was the real me. When I was supposedly heartbroken over Bridget refusing to go out with me in our first term, I slept with a girl off Sasha's course. To be fair, I didn't know that I'd got her pregnant, but when she wrote to me seven months later and told me that I was about to become a father, I replied telling her she was a liar. So that was eight years of my daughter's life that I wasn't there for. And to be totally honest, it may not even be the worst thing I've done. I've recently come around to the idea that, for much of my life, I really haven't been the nicest guy. I couldn't even hold on to the girl I loved.

Bridget and I broke up at the same time as the band got signed. Those two overwhelming events split me down the middle. On the one hand, I was ecstatic over the idea that the kid my teachers had looked down on could become a rock star, but that night when I went back to my flat, I felt like jumping out of a window or smashing my head against the wall. Instead, I went out to a bar, started a fight with the first guy I could find who looked like he would punch me back and spent a night in hospital as a result.

A month went by, and Bridget stopped hanging out with me entirely. All I could talk about when we were together was how much I loved her and how miserable my life was, so it was natural that she cut the cord. I scraped through university, but all I cared about was the tour I was about to do with Ade. I built it up to be my salvation, but in the end all it offered was the chance to get drunk, do drugs and sleep with girls who really wanted to sleep with Ade but settled for approximately second best.

Bridget wouldn't respond to my emails anymore. I sent her postcards wherever we went because I thought she'd get a kick out of that, but who needs a photo of Leeds Town Hall from their long-distance stalker?

The last time I saw her before this week was at our homecoming gig a few months after we graduated. I knew she was going to be there, and I built it up to be the turning point it never could be. There was a party at Ade's swish new flat after the show, and loads of our old friends came. I played it cool with Bridget. I made small talk and didn't give away that I was still crazy about her (or crazy in general). I went to talk to other people to give her space, and I was building up to having a real heart-to-heart when I noticed her chatting to Ade.

I guess they were both drunk. I mean, I've held on to that idea, and it certainly didn't lead to anything long-term. But when I saw them slinking off towards the coat cupboard by the front door –

hands entwined, guilty looks on their faces – I wanted to smash up that irritatingly modern flat. I wanted to splash paint all over the walls and rip down the neon-blue curtains.

Instead, I plotted revenge. I'm not saying that the plan I came up with was any good, but I made the decision through the fog of heartbreak and jealousy.

We were heading into a big London studio to cut our first demo a week after the party. We'd been playing the songs we wanted to record for the best part of two years, but I decided to sabotage the whole thing. I told Ade that we couldn't play the songs that I'd helped write unless we shared lead vocal duties. Now, I'm a terrible singer, so I knew he'd never accept this. The label tried to talk me down, and Ade stayed out of it altogether. I doubt he even knew why I was so upset.

Perhaps if he'd realised, we'd have been able to talk it through. He would have told me that he and Bridget were just friends who'd had too much to drink. And it wasn't even as if she was my girlfriend anymore. Obviously, if that had happened, I would have punched him with my big dumb fists. But after that, I would probably have seen sense and gone into the studio with him.

The fact that he couldn't put the pieces together drove me crazy. I needed him to apologise for something he had no idea I knew about. He was admittedly a bit thick not to join the dots, but the day came for us to head to the studio, and I simply stayed away. Ade was a better guitarist than me anyway, so he took over my job, and the label found a new bassist, who would go on to be a permanent member of the band. That lucky guy would become richer than everyone I know from my normal life combined, but I kept my battered pride – which really is the worst consolation prize in the history of idiots.

They only used a few of the songs I'd worked on because it turned out that Ade was overflowing with ideas. He came up with "Promises" in fifteen minutes while the others went to buy kebabs. Or at least that's how the official story goes.

He got his own back by claiming that he'd written every last song on his own. I didn't have any money or the knowledge to go about suing him. I also didn't have a scrap of proof. There'd only been two of us in the room when we wrote the songs, and we both had guitars. He was so good at building up my confidence that it's more than possible he had the ideas and made me believe it was the other way around.

Ade came out of the womb with talent. He was born into a big family of second-generation British Nigerians, and every one of his siblings ended up being incredible in whatever they devoted themselves to. One is a high-court barrister, another a concert pianist. His parents had given them the support that they needed to excel. When I told my mum I wanted to study a degree in popular music, she told me she wouldn't speak to me if I did. Dad was there for me, but she stuck to her word.

And so Ade became famous, and I self-destructed. Instead of getting a job and scraping together a living, I tried to form another band, convinced of my own brilliance. Hardly anyone turned up to our first gig. The label sent a guy to listen, but he didn't stay till the end. Inevitably, there was a lot of screaming and anger, and I was on lead vocals. It was all very clichéd.

I'd got it into my head that I was a rock star and carried on down that well-trodden path to excess. A year after I last saw Ade, I was living in a squat in an abandoned pub in Croydon. I had devolved way beyond the status of hard-done-by mess to something far nastier.

And then one day I went to a cash machine to raid the bank account where Dad sent me a hundred quid a month because that was all he could afford to waste on keeping me alive. I punched in my pin number, and the little blue screen told me I had a balance of £36,000 (and a hundred from my dad).

I remember peering around me to check whether I was being pranked. The old gent standing behind me, with a bow tie and hair pomade, didn't look like a character from a candid camera show, so I withdrew £500 and stuffed it into my pocket. I didn't go into the bank to find out how the money had got there. I was convinced it was an error in my favour, and I had to make the most of it while I could.

A week later, after filling that time with headache-inducing alcohol and plenty of other substances I no longer remember, the money ran out, and I had to go back for more. £35,600, the statement on the screen revealed this time. I was feeling sore from my bender and would probably have died if I'd jumped back on that particular train, so I did something I hadn't planned when I arrived there. I entered the bank.

Dirt and grease don't bother you so much when you're plagued by them daily. But walking into the Lloyds Bank on the high street, I became aware of just how out of place I was. Feeling more self-conscious than I had since that first day at university, I went up to the counter and handed over my card to the presentable young lady who, in any other situation, would have looked offended by my very presence.

"How can I help you, sir?" she had been trained to say.

I put on my most polite voice, smiled and tried to sound like a human being. "I need to send some money to my dad. He's always so good to me and doesn't have much. So I thought I'd send him £1200."

She nodded efficiently and took the bait. I don't know if I did this because I wanted her to think well of me. I'd like to believe that my love for my generous father made me want to give something back while I could. More realistically, this was part of the camouflage I needed to take out another ten grand. When she handed over this windfall, I slipped it into the inside pocket of my leather trench coat and was about to leave when curiosity got the better of me.

"Is there anything else I can help you with today, sir?" the girl in the blue uniform had been trained to ask.

"There is one more thing. I was wondering if you could tell me who the last deposit in my account was from?"

"I can provide a printout of your recent statement if you'd like me to."

She didn't wait but got to work clicking. As she did so, she must have caught the name at the top of the list as she suddenly looked at me differently.

I'd seen it happen countless times before.

"You know Adesina Okojie?" girls used to ask in amazement, as though they'd discovered I was the heir to a small oil-rich kingdom.

I didn't need to see what was printed on the statement, but I looked anyway.

15.04: Transfer – £36,000.00 – A. Okojie.

TWENTY-FOUR

Ade had decided that the value of my contribution to his career was nine grand per song. He was already massive by that time. "Promises" had spent months in the charts, and he was now touring America with Mick and the new bassist, so it's not like he couldn't afford more. He'd used the guitar parts I'd written for four songs and sent me 36k accordingly.

I felt very little gratitude to him at the time, but whatever else happened, that money changed my life. I took a while to decide how to use it, but I knew I couldn't continue as I was. The paint was peeling off the walls of the windowless room where I slept. It was always cold in there, and mould was starting to form in one corner. If I hadn't been doing an excellent job of making myself ill, that room would have had a shot at it.

The other lads I lived with suddenly repulsed me, even though they were probably much better people than I'd ever been. I don't know if it was the fact that I finally had some real money, but I felt out of place with them, and the pull of another drinking session no longer had the shine it had previously possessed.

I'd always had the idea of moving abroad, so two days later, I flew to Barcelona. I didn't speak any Spanish or have anywhere to live, but that's not as scary as you might think when you're running away. I'd bought new clothes from a charity shop and left pretty much all my old possessions at the squat. I didn't tell anyone in London I was leaving. I just walked out of my life and into a new one.

I stayed in a cheap hostel for a few weeks, resisting the temptation to go to bars. I knew that if I went out drinking, within forty-five minutes at most, someone would have offered me cocaine or a spliff. There's a quality about me that makes people think I must be a junkie. It's the same thing that turned off my schoolteachers when I was a kid. Even in the daytime, just walking down Las Ramblas, the beer sellers would run over to me and whisper synonyms in my ear. "Charlie, coke, pasta?"

If I started drinking, then the drugs would follow, and I'd wake up a few months later with no money left. I couldn't let that happen. I booked myself onto a course to become an English teacher. I had a flat lined up for the end of the month and, until that time, I spent all day long on the beach, or in a library teaching myself Spanish, or reading the kind of books I hadn't read for the last two years because I was hooked on drink or fame or Bridget.

My head was clear, and I felt free. I did the TEFL course to the best of my ability. I made friends with the Americans, Canadians and South Africans who qualified alongside me. I started playing tennis, of all things, and I liked my life.

It'll come as no surprise that this didn't last. The reality of staying sober for a short time in order to achieve a simple goal is different from taking a job and knowing that you will have to do it day in, day out for months or even years when the only reward is a low salary and a bit more free time than other professions offer. I wasn't a dreadful teacher, and I really did like my students, but by the end of the first term, I needed something more exciting to look forward to. I convinced myself I could go out in town and not have a problem.

The first time I went out was a Friday night; I didn't go home again until Tuesday. I never messaged my friends or parents in that time, and I failed to turn up to my job on Monday. I can't remember where I went or what I did. All I know is that it wasn't good.

My bosses were surprised and sympathetic and knew I wasn't the kind of guy to let them down, so they gave me another chance. By the fifth time, they kindly "let me go".

I still had half of the money from Ade, and I could probably have found another job teaching which might have lasted a month or two, but that was just kicking the can down the road. And when things were starting to look black, I met a bright light in the city.

Charlie had nicely groomed hair and well-cut suits. No one wears a suit on a Saturday night in Barcelona, but he did. He was from Cambridge or Winchester or somewhere posh, and he flashed the cash around like he was a sheikh.

We met in a tacky Irish pub where he was buying everyone drinks, so we soon ended up talking. There was something about the way he smiled – as if he wanted me to know that we were in the same club now, and we could do anything together – it reminded me of those first days getting to know Ade.

Charlie worked in an office and earned 5k a month. I'd never known anyone who made that kind of money, and I decided I wanted to be just like him. If he'd told me that there was a job cleaning up after the elephants in a circus, I would have done whatever it took to get it. To be perfectly honest, that would have been a much better outcome, because Charlie was a conman.

That's not how he phrased it, of course. A few weeks after we first met, he broke it down like this: "My company offers people the opportunity to invest in something that could make them a fortune."

I mean, this should have been enough to tell me that the only ones making serious money were Charlie and his bosses, but as you've probably already worked out, I wasn't the smartest kid in the world.

"It's actually quite beautiful in a way." He held his hands up like a movie producer laying out his vision. "All you have to do is call people up who are already looking for investments and convince them that we're the right fit."

Charlie took me out that afternoon to buy a better suit, and I turned up at his work the following Monday already sold on a dream.

I was given a script and made to learn it. Everyone I worked with massaged my ego into thinking I was a natural, and perhaps I was. I would ring up fifty people a day, and I would get 30 per cent of them to chat to me, which was apparently pretty good going.

It required a series of calls that went back and forth between myself and a colleague, but it set the mark off guard. We didn't ask for anything at first, so it didn't feel like we were out to get them, and people fell for it.

"Hi there, my name's Jake, and I'm calling from RP&B. I believe my colleague was in touch with you a month back to discuss the opportunities we're seeing with a particular tech start-up in America right now?"

The upshot was that, after the penultimate phone call, if everything went to plan, I would send them a portfolio for a new company with a generic name and a fancy website. They would look it over at their leisure and, when I rang the next time, the British pensioner who I was trying to rob would confirm that a bank transfer had been made, and we both celebrated the imminent dividends we would enjoy.

It wasn't long before I realised that we weren't just sweet-talking gullible old people into trusting us with their money; it was straight-up fraud. The stocks we were selling were in companies that didn't exist. I still had principles, and this wasn't what I wanted to do with my life, but the hourly rate, the commission on top and the constant compliments were just too good to give up. I felt like one of the boys in a way I never had before, but my conscience was loud and throbbing, and I had to do something to shut it up.

At RP&B, or whatever the company was called that month, you didn't lose your job if you failed to turn up one morning.

Charlie knew what he was doing when he chose me. He was a master of spotting vulnerable idiots who cared more about money than other people.

I kept telling myself, *Do this for one more month to save up and then show them who you really are.* But the months rolled on, and I grew richer because other people were growing poorer. I was a reverse Robin Hood, so I bludgeoned my brain every night to numb the pain and rolled into the office the next morning to repeat the process.

I've never added it up, but I must have stolen millions of pounds. Everyone there was loaded, and the big bosses hardly ever showed their faces in the office because they were paying us to distance them from their shame. And I really do believe that they all felt it. Even criminals know the line between right and wrong. I saw it whenever someone like me boasted about ripping off an old granny. Charlie and his boss were all smiles, but I could see that it didn't sit well with them. I knew that, deep down inside, they wanted to believe they were still good eggs.

This may have continued for ever if it weren't for my parents. I was twenty-three by now, and I'd been promising that they could visit ever since I moved to Spain. I kept putting it off because I didn't want them to see the person I'd become, but then one day my dad called up to say that Mum, of all people – who'd practically disowned me because I wanted to play the guitar for a living – had booked tickets and they were coming that month.

I freaked out, tried to clean up my act, failed, tried again and, by the time they arrived in Spain, I at least looked like a functioning person. I put on my best suit and took them out to a nice restaurant overlooking Barcelona.

Dad was clearly proud of me. Mum pretended she wasn't there, and I acted as though I was a big success. I took a day off work to show them the city I'd fallen in love with and try to make them believe I was a decent person. By the end of the day, even Mum was beginning to enjoy herself. When we sat down for dinner, she smiled at me for the first time in years.

At work the next day, it took me about seven seconds to realise that my parents were just like the people I was ripping off. I spent the day in a slump, longing for the clock to tick faster so that I could see my folks and feel clean again. By the end of my shift, I felt so bad that I called them to cancel. I stayed at home and got drunk, called in sick the following day, lost track of time and found I'd slept through twenty no doubt terrified calls from my parents.

When I was finally lucid enough to see them, they could tell that something was wrong. I showed up at their hotel, and my mum's stern expression said, *I always knew that this would happen. That's what you get when you study music!*

"Your mother thinks there's something up with you, Jacob," Dad said in his heartbreakingly sympathetic voice, which made me feel like I was six years old. "I'm afraid I'm inclined to agree."

And because I felt as though I was made out of paper that had been ripped up and glued back together, I didn't lie and promise them that everything was fine. I told the truth.

I started crying and shaking. My face turned red, my nose ran, and I wanted to hide under the bed. No matter what we'd been through, they were still my parents. I cried, and Dad held me, and Mum spoke to me for the first time in years.

"My poor boy, why didn't you just tell us?"

TWENTY-FIVE

I moved back home again. I did very little, and my parents watched over me like jailers. I tried to be grateful for small mercies. I was alive, for one thing. I'd never got involved in more dangerous substances. I hadn't got arrested and ended up in a Spanish prison. I was no longer plotting to swindle people out of their retirement funds.

I eventually got a job in a musical instrument shop in my little town in Surrey. It was safe and undemanding. Years passed. I got older but couldn't bring myself to try dating or going out again because I knew what would happen. I really didn't want to mess up. I couldn't stand to do it to my folks, if no one else. I lived my life knowing that potential disaster was just around the corner and that the solution was to keep things simple.

I watched Ade go from big to bigger to stratospheric. He outsold The Weeknd and then Coldplay and then, one year, Beyoncé. I don't know whether I felt jealous or angry. To be honest, I doubt I was capable of any great complexity of emotion. I was simply aware of the difference between our two lives and uncertain whether mine would ever start again.

The narrative that my mother did her best to believe was that

I'd had a hard time but was getting back on my feet. Whenever she talked to friends and family on the phone, she'd say that I was saving for a place of my own. The poor woman needed something to hang on to.

By the time I'd been at home for four years, I'd come to believe that was what I wanted too. I rented a flat in the neighbouring town, so as not to be too far from my parents' civilising influence. But nothing else changed. I had the same empty life and the same poorly paid job. I played my guitar when no one else could hear me, but I no longer thought of myself as a musician.

And through it all, I thought of Bridget and the two years we'd spent together. Perhaps I'd idealised everything from back then. Perhaps Ade and the others weren't the best friends I could ever have. Perhaps Bridget wasn't even the best girlfriend, but none of that mattered. I loved thinking about that time and trying to play back the conversations we'd had around the chipped dinner table in the ugly brown lounge of our second-year maisonette.

I forgot the bad times. I could even overlook what Ade had done, because I was living my life as a tribute act to my late adolescence. Working in a music shop is the perfect job for a daydreamer, and so that's what I became. Whether I was taking inventory, unpacking boxes or waiting for customers to appear, my head was permanently somewhere else.

The problem with living in the past like that is that you forget you have a present. I was so lonely in the flat I never wanted, with Sundays at my folks' house the only break from the routine. There was no way things could go on as they were. I suppose that, by ignoring all the mistakes I'd made, I forgot what a mess I'd become. I forgot about the mouldy squat in Croydon and finding myself alone at four in the morning on the beach in Barcelona without knowing how I'd got there.

And if the truth be told, I never thought of myself as an addict. I hadn't been through rehab or followed any kind of programme. I thought I'd be fine to start drinking again as long as I was careful. That went pretty well for a week or two. I proved to myself that I could take things slowly, that I didn't have to worry too much, and so off I went once more, out with school friends who'd been saying we should meet up again after all those years.

The very first night I went up to London, I got blackout drunk. I don't know what else happened because my brain helpfully erased the details, but I woke up in a police station, and they certainly hadn't taken me there for my own safety.

Once I'd sobered up enough to sign my name, they charged me with trying to throttle a guy I'd hated when I was at school. In a street in Holborn outside an All Bar One, the rage I'd been storing up for years had flooded through my hands and into poor Wayne's neck. My sweet, kind father had to come to pick me up, and I almost cried at the sight of him. I knew right then that this wouldn't lead to the kind of slap on the wrist I'd had whenever I'd got in trouble as a kid. 'Life-changing injuries' was how the local paper described what I'd inflicted.

A court date was set, and I was actually relieved. I thought that I'd been waiting all those years to get my life back on track, but the truth is that I was awaiting my sentence.

I saw myself as a potential killer. That's certainly how the judge painted me, and I refused to weasel out of it. My solicitor wanted to talk about my issues with mental health, the fact that I had no previous convictions, and my general good behaviour since a minor run-in with the police when I was eighteen. I wouldn't allow him to put forward any mitigating circumstances.

I deserved what was coming. I'd robbed people blind and never been punished, and I was so out of it that I could have killed Wayne. I had to plead guilty because I wanted to admit what I'd done, but if I'd lied and said that I was innocent, I would have got a heavier sentence. I was given twelve months in prison. I thought I deserved more, and I told the flabbergasted judge just that.

My parents were horrified, but they came to the court, and they stuck by me. Even Mum was painfully nice about the whole thing. To be honest, I revelled in the thought of my punishment. When I walked through the prison gates, I thought my suffering was unique, but there were blokes inside whose lives made mine look like a trip to feed the ducks. Some of them frightened me, some of them terrified me, but quite a few of them talked to me, and it wasn't difficult to see that I was the lucky one.

There were drugs in there, just like everywhere else I'd been for the last ten years, but I knew what they did to people, and I found it in myself to resist. I selfishly used every last haggard face as a mirror, every sad story to inspire a course correction of my own. I served four months because they needed the space for someone else. It'll sound like another cliché but, at the end of it, I came out a better person.

I engaged with rehab. I found a group that suited me, rather than sticking with the first I tried. I told my parents everything I'd done throughout my life, right down to putting pins on the teacher's chair when I was nine years old and getting that girl pregnant at uni. That was the first thing they made me face up to. We tracked the mother down, and suddenly I had a daughter. And even though I missed all those years of Heather's life, I've tried to make it up to her since. And I am honestly thankful every single day that she was willing to let me try.

I see her every other weekend, and we go up to London together to museums and parks. I'd like to say that I show her the city that has meant so much to me. The reality is that I get to see everything through her eyes now, and it's incredible. She is bright and brilliant and beautiful, and though it breaks my heart to think of the time I wasted, I love every moment that I get to spend with my daughter.

I've never touched another drop of drink. I don't spend time in places where I'm likely to be tempted by drugs, and I don't feel sorry for myself like I used to. I could have given up and given in. I could have counted my sorrows instead of my blessings, but I wanted to build my life back properly this time. I wanted to be there for Heather, after I'd gone missing for so long. So I became boring, and I love it. I have a nice, easy, boring life. I will never become famous – never write a hit song or perform at Wembley Stadium.

Aside from my daughter, my greatest achievement by far was when the rock star Adesina Okojie sent me a ticket to Mauritius to spend time on his yacht, and I thought, *Meh. Can I really be bothered?*

TWENTY-SIX

It was the thought of seeing Bridget again that swung it, of course. I didn't imagine us falling in love and getting married. I just wanted to see her. I wanted to watch films with her like we did when we lived down the hall from one another. I wanted to talk for hours through the night until one of us realised that the sun had come up.

The moment I see her again is just as I hoped it would be. The group doesn't feel the way it used to, and Clara almost dying doesn't help, but when I get to spend the day with the girl that I instantly realise I've never stopped loving, it's easy to overlook those comparatively minor problems. Especially when Bridget comes up to dinner, and we toast her for saving Clara's life. The wind whips her dress around, and she is breathtaking. I think that even Ryan and Tom look at her differently, whereas Ade pretends that he hasn't noticed.

Her eyes lock on to mine down the table and – though it's probably egotistical, chauvinistic and deranged – I let myself believe that I'm the one she's come here to see. I know it's too good to be true, so when Tom makes a scene, and we have to sit listening to Sasha's genuinely sad tale, I think, *Yep! This is pretty much how I expected my big night to go.*

As sorry as I am for them, another part of me wants to diminish

Tom's suffering. A much more selfish part of me says that he's a tourist. He's not an alcoholic after a few months of daily drinking. He still has his money from ten years in the City and a rich family to fall back on if his investments don't pan out. That very mean instinct within me insists that he isn't an addict until he's woken up on a dirty mattress in a lightless squat (preferably in Croydon).

As if to underline this point, when I wake up the next morning, we find Mick dead in his bathroom. It all feels so inevitable. The plane ticket in the post, a yacht that would take me a thousand lifetimes to save up for, Bridget: all of it was stacked up to show that people like me and Mick are not allowed nice things.

It's clear from the beginning that Ade won't turn the boat around for the sake of a dead junkie. He bites his lip as though he's struggling with his emotions, but no matter how much he cared for his friend, he's never going to change his plans.

"That's why there was no booze on board, right?" I say as I take Mick's legs and we move him onto the bed. "You were trying to save him from himself."

"Well, that's part of it, yeah," he replies, and I wonder whether he knew everything about us before we came.

Was Ade following me while I was following him? He couldn't buy a copy of *Rolling Stone* or go to the *NME*'s website to find out what I was up to, but there would have been ways to check. He could have called my parents as a concerned friend when I was at my worst. Perhaps that's why he sent the money when he did.

It happened a second time, just after I got out of jail and needed to piece my life back together. He didn't put it in my bank that time. I had a letter from his lawyers saying that, because of a court case that had uncovered copyright infringement relating to the band's early musical output, I was due £10k in compensation.

Ade always loved being the leader. Whether it was of the band or our group of friends, he called the shots. We could turn back to Mauritius right now to ensure that Mick's body is dealt with faster, but that would mean giving up on whatever entertainment he's organised for us.

Perhaps I'm being unfair. Perhaps he really does want to do right by Mick, but we've started on a journey, and he obviously feels we need to see it through. Either way, I should handle it better. When we meet back up with the others to talk things over, I hate that I lose my cool and storm off like... well, like Tom, I suppose.

I go down to the cinema and root through the library of movies to save myself from jumping overboard. I'm just about to put on the action masterpiece *Con Air* when I hear the door open and there she is. I watch Bridget through the glass for a moment and, even in the dimly lit cinema, I'm hypnotised.

"I've chosen a movie just for you," I lie, then hurry to find something she'll like.

And somehow, it works. We sit right next to one another in the cinema and, when I put my hand on the armrest between us, she takes it in hers.

My body burns, and I know that I haven't felt this way in years. Isn't it insane that there are states we can only experience in such specific circumstances? The best food in the world couldn't make me feel this way, nor could all the money in Ade's bank. The physical manifestation of love as it fizzes through you is something that many people will never enjoy, and others will spend their lives chasing. It is unique and addictive, and I would fly around the world any number of times to find it – to find her.

She puts her head on my shoulder and, as reluctant as I am to move my hand from hers, I stretch my arm out around her. Eighteen-year-old Jake would have messed this up. He would have desperately tried to move things on and made a fool of himself but, if nothing else, I've learnt to take my time. She drifts off into a pretty dream, and I sit watching her. I can only see about half of her face, but it's worth any level of discomfort to be so close.

I barely notice that the film is on, though my thoughts of Bridget and me bleed into 1950s Rome. For a moment, I'm the suave older journalist and she's the nymphlike princess. We look at one another lovingly over café tables and run away from our responsibilities together. For a moment, life is a fairy tale. I desperately want to hold on to it, but I know that my eyes are drooping, and it won't be long before they close altogether.

The feeling of waking up without her is agony. I want the day to pass quicker so that dinner comes around again. I go back to sleep to make it happen. When I finally leave the cinema, I can feel a change in the air. The sea that surrounds us – that was pretending to be our friend until now – has been whipped up by the wind. The rain will soon fall. There's a nip of cold hidden in the warm breeze, and a storm is coming.

I shouldn't have wished my day away. When dinner does arrive, Tom makes sure to ruin it again, and even the joy of jumping about to old music with my friends can't pick me up again when I see Ade and Bridget cuddling up to one another. I'm back at that party in Ade's flat when I was twenty-one. My throat feels like it's closing in on itself, my brain has apparently stopped working, and I can't even quit the band in protest this time because I already did that a decade ago.

Before I can spiral into the darker realms of my imagination, Ryan suggests that we leave them to it. I grab a fake beer and, once we're outside in the lashing rain, I tell them to go to their cabins without me. I can see that Clara's concerned I'll do something stupid, but I tell her not to worry, and then I go off to do something stupid.

I go back to where I was happiest on board. I climb the stairs to the upper deck where we had dinner last night, but it's not the same. The chairs are tied down to prevent them from sliding about, and sitting on the table doesn't look too appealing. Perhaps it's the illusion of drunkenness that sucking on a beer bottle provides, but I feel no fear as I move one level higher despite the constant rocking of the ship.

Why I decide to pull myself up to the highest point to stare death in the face, I can't say. But for a few minutes, I don't think about my daughter or Mum and Dad and how they would feel if I fell to my death in the endless black ocean. I feel the spray and the rain on my face and, for a short time, there are no consequences to my actions.

I stand up there with my arms wrapped around a steel cable and feel like a surfer riding a wave. It's less exciting when I realise that I have surprisingly good balance and I'm not in any danger, but I don't go back down because I feel strong up here. I feel like I'm in control for the first time in my life, but when I finally hear the musical strains of Bridget's voice, she says, "You idiot, you could fall to your death."

I pretend not to hear and take a slug from the beer that is now 50 per cent rainwater. She shines her torch in my face to make sure I pay attention, but it's only when the ship's captain turns on a gigantic xenon searchlight that I know something's wrong and climb down.

In the light of a torch beam, I can see Bridget's panic even through the rain. I've had plenty of chances to feel stupid this week, but this is the worst so far. All my selfish thoughts fly from my head, and I feel like I'm to blame for the storm, Ade's sad expression and whatever else has gone wrong.

I manage to get to the main deck without dying, and he grabs hold of me to whisper something so that Bridget doesn't hear.

"It's Sasha. We can't find her."

His words hit me harder than I would have expected. The last five years of my life have been centred around calm and stability, and it's impossible to imagine anything so dramatic coming to pass. I need to get my head around the idea that he isn't talking about someone on TV, but our friend. Our well-meaning, kind-hearted friend, who came across as a bit spoilt sometimes but always tried to make people happy.

It's all too much to process. I don't feel steady on my feet anymore, and the constant tilting and correcting of the ship only makes that worse. I press on after Bridget all the same. I want to keep her within sight to make sure nothing bad can happen, to make certain that she won't meet whatever fate Sasha has, but someone has to go to down to the beach club, and so I squeeze her shoulder and duck under the chain at the top of the stairs.

There's no one to find down there and, as I return to the platform, I predict the look of distress on Bridget's face almost to the muscle. She stares down at me, Clara close at her side, and I struggle to produce a word.

"There's no one here."

My voice doesn't sound like my own. It's hollow and tinged with anger. As if the psychodrama of this reunion wasn't bad enough, we have a dead body and a woman overboard. The rain runs off Tom's face as he grips the railing on the floor above me. I climb back up to the main deck, sure I'm not the only one who remembers that the last time we saw Sasha alive was when she went off with her husband.

Ryan pulls me away from the others as we continue the search. "I keep thinking about what happened to Clara."

"Clara?" I parrot him. If there's one person I haven't worried about this evening, it's her.

"When she fell overboard," he explains, but that feels so long ago that it might as well have happened when we were at university.

I realise that we're standing out in the rain, so I take a few steps towards the overhanging roof behind the main suites. "What's that got to do with Sasha?"

"With Sasha and Mick," he says. "Don't you think it's strange that Clara should spontaneously fall overboard? It seems to me that a death, a disappearance and an attempted murder are too much of a coincidence."

"It's a bit early to talk about murder, isn't it?"

"Maybe." He pauses, clearly distressed. "And I don't know that he was responsible, but when I got to the spot where Clara had fallen from the ship, Ade was standing nearby."

TWENTY-SEVEN

Ryan says this as though he's revealed a great secret, and the screen is about to fade to black. But we're still here – still standing on the deck in the rain – and I prompt him for more.

"What are you saying? That he should have done more to help?"

"I don't know exactly, but there was a corridor just behind where he was standing, and I thought perhaps..." He looks at the crashing ocean beyond me, searching for the right words. "It's hard to describe the expression on his face, but his eyes were fixed on the water, and he didn't look up at me as I arrived. I started yelling at him to throw down a life ring, and he finally snapped out of it."

"So you think that Ade pushed two of our friends off the ship and helped Mick to overdose? What possible reason would he have?"

These questions pull him back to reality. "I haven't thought that far." He touches the thinning hair on the top of his egg-shaped head. "But you must admit that it's strange."

"Yeah," I say as I turn to go. "Strange."

Despite my scepticism, Ryan's questions stay with me. We walk back across the deck as my brain whirs. If there is a murderer among us, surely a more obvious explanation is that

Tom saw his opportunity to get rid of the wife who clearly no longer loved him. He could have pushed her overboard and waited to tell anyone that she was missing. But then the even more likely solution is that she slipped on the wet deck in the storm.

Once we've gone through every deck on the ship and talked to the crew, we head up to Ade's suite, and he hands out towels to help us dry off. I haven't felt cold until now, but the warmth of the towel, fresh from a heated cupboard, sends a shiver through me, as if my body now remembers what temperature it's supposed to be.

Ade gets the captain to turn the boat around, and then the arguments inevitably begin. Suspicion veers between Ade and Ryan, who was never meant to be here in the first place. In the end, as keeps happening, the weight of suspicion tips back to Tom.

"... if you wanted to get rid of her," I tell him, "this was the perfect moment to do it."

As soon as the words are out of my mouth, Tom explodes, and Bridget rushes off in tears. I don't know what to do. I feel myself being torn apart, and I want to make sure that she's okay, but Tom keeps shouting at me and I can't think anymore.

"I would never hurt my wife." Something about the way he pronounces these last two words makes me doubt this is true. He doesn't use Sasha's name and makes her sound like a prize possession rather than a person. "I've never touched her."

He grabs me by the T-shirt and pushes me up against a shelf. He wants to hit me and I kind of wish he would. That familiar thirst for violence is back. I'm desperate for any excuse to punch his head in and, even though I haven't had a drop of alcohol, the very memory of it makes me light-headed.

Ade is there to make sure this doesn't happen. He forces himself between us, and I'm happy to step back.

"This is getting us nowhere." He has a level of authority that the rest of us lack. And even though I was just questioning whether he could be the killer, I find his presence reassuring. "You need to calm down and stop behaving like idiots."

Tom grits his teeth as I lean against the bookshelf behind me. I can still feel where he pushed me against it.

"Ade's right; we're supposed to be friends." Clara is the last girl left with us. She stands beside the desk looking like she'd rather be hiding under it.

"Exactly," Tom says, and he pauses to breathe in slowly through his nostrils. "We're supposed to be friends, and that's why this is all so hard to believe."

He sits down on Ade's unnecessarily large bed and goes back to feeling sorry for himself.

The fragile peace holds for a short while, and I feel that this is the moment when everything can change. We can calm down and try to concentrate on what lies ahead. We can come together, but I think we all know how unlikely that is.

"We are friends," Tom whispers to himself and the rest of us relax just long enough to regret it. "But I know there was a knock on the door. I know Sasha spoke to someone before she left the room. She thought I was sleeping, but I heard her talking in a low voice, and then the door closed behind her."

"And what, Tom?" Ade asks when no one makes a sound. "What do you think that means?"

Ryan looks like he wants to raise his hand and say, *Sorry, folks. This has got nothing to do with me. I think I walked into the wrong room.* His whole time here has been a mistake in some way, but he's too polite to make his presence known and goes to sit beside Clara in solidarity.

"It means..." Tom's eyes catch the light of a weird tentacled lamp on the ceiling. "It means we're not alone here, and we've been stupid to overlook the fact."

Ade doesn't need to respond. His face is the picture dictionary entry for *confused*.

"I'm saying that there are any number of crew on board this boat. It could have been one of them who came knocking for Sasha. She was more likely to go off with someone in authority than one of you when she was looking after her sick husband."

"You're just guessing now, Tom," Clara tells him, in the same pleading tone as before.

"No, I'm seeing things clearly at last. How could we have been so stupid?" He claps his hands together then balls them into fists. "One of them must be behind this."

"Why would you think that?" Even as he drops his voice, Ade still looks disgusted by the man in front of him.

Tom sneers as if he knows something we are too dumb to realise. "It's jealousy. Ever since I was a kid, people have treated me differently because I come from money. They say it's about equality and fairness, but the reality is that everyone wants what they haven't got."

He sounds like a Victorian industrialist, peering down on the little people, and I can't hold my tongue any longer.

"So you think someone here is picking us off one by one because they hate the rich?"

"Think about it!" He gives me a second to do so. "First, they failed with Clara, then Mick died, and now Sasha has vanished. This isn't just cold-blooded murder. It's class war."

Is it terrible that the only response I can produce is laughter?

Ade is currently more reasonable than me. "I really don't think that any of the crew would hurt someone."

"Because you interviewed each of them personally, did you?" Tom can't direct as much fury sitting down, so he gets to his feet again. "I suppose you've got to know them all intimately during your time on board."

Ade has no response to this and glances across at me.

"Come on, tell us." Tom juts out his jaw and looks like a football hooligan spoiling for a fight. "How long have you owned this ship? And how many of the people who work on it do you actually know?"

"A yacht is a boat not a ship," Ade snaps, as if that makes any difference right now. "I bought it at the end of last year, and I'm not a prince or a recluse. I talk to my staff."

"Yeah, but you can't know them all. You said yourself there's normally thirty people working on here."

Tom evidently feels that this is the answer. None of us can prove that the crew weren't involved in Sasha's disappearance, and so he is the smart one. The obvious conclusion is that he's making so much fuss because he doesn't want us to think about his involvement, but we're beyond that now. He moves off towards the door, and the others wait to see whether anyone has the energy to object.

"If there is a killer out there, why would you risk bumping into him?" I almost regret the masculine pronoun. *Women can be killers too*, I tell myself, but it probably isn't the time for political correctness.

"Because I have to do something!"

He turns to slide the door open, and when I try to stop him, he spins back around and punches me in the shoulder. It's not the obvious way to hurt someone, but that doesn't change the fact that my collarbone immediately feels like it's broken. I think that even he's surprised by his strength, as he looks at his fist and mutters an unconvincing warning.

"You don't want to do that, Jake."

It's all very macho, and all very fake, but no one is going to change his mind. We just watch as he disappears into the darkness, and I can't help wondering whether we'll ever see him again.

TWENTY-EIGHT

This is just the beginning of the exodus. Ryan is next. "I'd better go with him. He might punch someone. There's no bad blood between us, so he's less likely to have a go at me. Will you come, Clara?"

She looks startled, as though she's surprised to hear her own name. "Fine, but we should check on Bridget too."

"Press nineteen and then hash on any phone to tell us she's okay," Ade mutters without looking at them.

Clara nods before stepping outside after the others. Without them, the room is quiet. Ade goes back to his desk and tidies up the papers. He takes a sheet from the top of a pile, folds it away into an envelope and drops it into a drawer.

"Don't you think we should go too?" I ask when I realise that we've left them to fend for themselves.

Ade just shrugs and puts his fountain pen away in its case.

Until now, I felt that there was safety in numbers. I didn't consider the crew and figured that Bridget was okay so long as the rest of us were together. I would have noticed someone slipping off to kill her, but things have changed. The group has dispersed, and I don't know what to do next.

"Don't you think we're acting like children?" He makes a sound which I suppose might be described as a laugh, but it's too short and bitter to convey any humour. "Sasha falls off the boat in the storm, so we start an amateur murder investigation. We're trapped in an episode of *Scooby-Doo*."

"Don't be so flippant." I still can't say that I trust him entirely after what Ryan said. "It's better than allowing ourselves to be picked off like sorority girls in a horror film."

He doesn't move for the count of five, and I find it quite out of character. "You're not the same person I used to know, are you?"

"What does that mean?"

"It's not a criticism, but you've changed more than anyone else." He falls still again, and I copy him. "When we were at Goldsmiths, all you cared about was making people laugh. You know, impressing them with a gag or a one-liner."

"So you're saying I'm not funny anymore?"

"No, I'm saying you've learnt not to care. That's a real talent, that is."

I sit down in the exact same spot on the bed where Tom was hunched over ten minutes ago. "Except for my daughter, who is almost too old to care, I don't have anyone to impress."

He puts his elbows behind him on the desk to support his weight. "That sounds heavenly. I envy you."

It occurs to me that this is the first time we've spoken on our own since the band started touring. I know that might sound unlikely, but we were never alone then. There was always a girlfriend, a groupie or a drummer there with us. I can only imagine what his life has been like ever since.

"Do you want me to feel sorry for you?" I ask as I look about his plush suite. "Is that why you brought us out here? So that we'd all show our sympathy for the poor little rich boy?"

We're on the verge of speaking honestly to one another, and it's kind of frightening.

"I don't need your sympathy, Jake. I already told you. I'd like your forgiveness."

I want to ask him why, but we're not there yet, and so I let him talk.

"You might not have realised it, but I've never been a junkie. I'm not an alcoholic or a relationship addict or any of those rock star clichés."

I admit this surprises me, and I lean forward, eager to know more. "Ryan said that he'd heard rumours about you in the industry."

"He did, but not the obvious kind." He takes a deep breath, and I get the sense that he still likes me more than I ever imagined – or perhaps that's what he wants me to think. "I got depressed. I mean, seriously miserable for months on end. The last five years have been a procession of lows. The more money I made and the more famous I became, the lonelier I was. I had girlfriends and even got engaged once, but whenever I found happiness, it turned dark soon after."

My mother's love of celebrity gossip comes rising to the surface, and I have to resist asking him whether it was true that he slept with Cristiano Ronaldo's ex and was secretly married to a French actress on Richard Branson's island.

"I developed a reputation for being difficult to handle. Maybe some people mistook me for an addict. I can't say. All I know is that whenever the record company obliged me to make another record, the people I'd worked with on the last one were unlikely to return my calls. Mick was the only person who stuck around, and he was even less reliable than me."

I can hear the rain crashing down on the balcony above. It's a little less intense than an hour ago, but it's still there: a constant soundtrack to the night.

"So what changed?" I ask when he doesn't volunteer anything more.

"You mean, how did I move on with my life?" I shrug and he continues. "Well, I spent a small fortune on therapy. That definitely helped, but I think the biggest thing was that I've come to look at my work as just that. Like an accountant or a butcher – or a day trader for all I know – I turn up at the right time, I do what's expected of me, and then I clock out."

"The rock 'n' roll dream," I tease, and he points across at me.

"That's the thing. Why should it be a prerequisite to party like crazy if you want to be in a band? Brian May from Queen has a PhD in astrophysics. Charlie Watts from the Rolling Stones collected American Civil War weaponry, bred Arabian horses and largely hated touring."

I would tell him that neither of them was a frontman, but he's speaking more rapidly now, and I can't get a word in.

"I spent so long trying to be the person that everyone expected me to be that I lost sense of myself. Perhaps I *was* an addict, but it was the feeling of approval that I craved more than anything. I wanted people to say I was as original as Bowie and as talented as Hendrix, even when I was releasing a single called 'Luv Me, Luv Me (Oh Yeah, Baby)'. You know, I never listen to any of my own music except for a few amateur CDs from the time we were at uni?"

"With me playing?" I ask in surprise. "I didn't even realise they still existed."

"You can find anything on the internet." He tuts to himself and turns away. "I genuinely envy you, Jake. You were lucky to get out when you did."

I don't know whether to laugh or scream, and so I whisper instead. "Incredible. You're almost as clueless as Tom."

He raises his long fingers in the air. "No, wait. I'm not explaining this well. I'm trying to make you understand that none of this was worth it."

"Fine, I'll take it off your hands."

He has something to tell me, and my responses barely matter. "You're still not listening," he insists, which I find a bit rich. "I'm not saying I can turn my back on it. This is who I am now. I am a monster, and as easy as you might think it is to give everything away, that would come with such shame that it would destroy me entirely. I am nothing without stardom – without my fans. I hate that I need them so much, but I do."

"You could at least try," I hear myself say, but these aren't my words. They're Bridget's. Her sense of justice has taken over. "You could find a middle ground between gross excess and barefoot charity. You could sell half of the property you own and invest the money in good causes, which would then produce more money that you could feed back into society."

He stands up from his chair and brings his hands together to beg understanding. "It's not about the money, Jake. It was never about the money."

"You have a funny way of showing it." I almost leave it at this, but I can't let him get away with lying to himself. "The mysterious letter summoning us, the first-class flight, the helicopter ride to your own portable city: what was all that for if not to show off your wealth?"

He shakes his head and turns away from me. "I just needed to get you here."

"And why was that? You keep dropping hints to keep us interested, but I don't feel we've got the whole story out of you."

"You know most of it." He is desperate for me to understand him – for me to believe, but something still doesn't click. "I admit I have a secondary motive but, most of all, I need you to know that I'm not as bad as you might think."

I'm tempted to walk away, but there's this niggling worry at the back of my head that I might end up being stabbed to death or shot with one of those crossbows he has, and so I stay right where I am.

"I don't think anything of you. How do you like that?"

He shrugs as if to say, *That's a decent start*.

"I had to learn to stop caring about this stuff, and now I'm finally in a position where none of it matters." I wait to see whether this is enough for him, but when it clearly isn't, I keep talking. "I have a kid, Ade. I have a daughter I've done my best to build a relationship with because, for years of her childhood, I simply ignored her existence. Of all the people I've known in the world, even if I see your face on aftershave commercials three times a day, you no longer rank very highly."

When the various inputs I've fed into his very expensive system don't compute, he repeats a simple sentiment, "I just need you to know that I'm sorry."

"What for?" I finally shout. "For stealing my songs and paying me off with a fraction of the money they generated? Or for kissing the woman I have loved since the very first moment I met her?"

I finally said it. There's no taking it back now, and even though I have to wait half an eternity for him to react, it was worth it.

"So you knew," he mumbles as he walks over to a cupboard in the corner of the room, takes a key from on top of it and unlocks the upper cabinet.

"And you didn't." I feel like laughing but don't make a sound.

I tune into the rain again and the crashing waves in the background as he removes a bottle of whisky and a single glass. He places it on the desk and pours it half full, then realises he's being a poor host and fetches me one.

He's about to pour again when he stops himself. "Oh, I forgot. You don't drink."

I can cross another question off my list. He has been checking up on us. He knows about my private life, while I only know about his very public one.

"You didn't answer my question," I say when he sits back down to take a steadying gulp.

"I'm sorry for just about everything," he replies, which I reckon is a cop-out, and so I tell him just that.

"Nope, I didn't come all this way to hear your platitudes. Tell me why you chose me to come here and not that annoying guy Jonathan, who you punched after a gig, or the girl who followed you everywhere. What was her name?"

He looks a little crumpled now – no longer belligerent or exhilarated – and he sighs as he answers. "Sally."

"Right, that was it. Sally." I think back to the three-month period when she was everywhere. "That girl was obsessed with you, and you treated her like she was less than human. So why isn't she here?"

"I'm not trying to be a saint, Jake. I want to make it up to the people I care about. You and Bridget are the best friends I've ever had. I strung Sasha along the whole time we lived together. Tom is only here because Sasha wouldn't have come otherwise. Clara was always special to me, and we would never have formed a band if Dawn hadn't encouraged us. I owe my thanks and apologies to all of you, because you were good to me, and I threw you over."

"Wait, that doesn't explain why you fell out with Dawn," I say because I've always wondered what happened between them. "We were all set to stay in the same house together for our third year, then she said she wouldn't live with you, and it fell apart."

"I don't know what happened." I show my scepticism at this, and he instantly tries to persuade me. "I'm serious. I even asked her when we spoke on the phone last week, and she said it should stay in the past."

"Fine, but that still doesn't explain why you couldn't just fly to England to see us there."

He hesitates then tells the truth. "Tom was right. I got you out here because I knew that, once we'd set sail, there would be no backing out. I mean, a four-day voyage from one set of beautiful islands to another is pretty pointless. If I'd wanted to show you tropical wonders, we could have stayed around Mauritius."

"Do you know what, Ade?" Even though this is a rhetorical question, almost by its nature, I wait several seconds before revealing the answer. "I like you better when you tell the truth. Was it really that hard?"

He runs his hands back through the short, bright dreadlocks at the top of his head. "Yes, actually, it was. I'm surprised you haven't worked that out yet. The thing none of you—"

He doesn't finish that sentence because the Batphone starts ringing. It somehow suits Ade that I haven't seen him with a mobile since I got here, and the only way to communicate on the ship is by a phone that looks like it was made in the 1960s.

"Okay..." he replies to whoever is at the other end of the line. "Yeah, I understand... Go somewhere safe."

He puts the phone down and remains staring at it for a while without saying anything. When he finally turns to me, he simply says, "Tom," and I know it's time to leave.

TWENTY-NINE

He pulls on a thick, rubberised jacket and looks in a wardrobe for one for me before we head outside. The rain isn't as fierce as before, but the boat is still unsteady, and the waves are immense.

"That was Clara on the phone," Ade says, but he's ahead of me and I can barely hear him. "They tried to look in on Bridget. There's a mattress up against the door, so she must be asleep inside."

This calms the little voice in my head that reminds me that I left her to fend for herself, but there are other questions still bothering me. "Where did they go after that?"

"Ryan's still with Tom, but Clara left to get help."

We drop down a floor, clinging to the railing as we go, and for a moment, I think that Ade will twist and fall overboard as the back of the boat suddenly dips.

He steadies himself and makes out that it was no big deal. "She said he was acting crazy, which is really no news, but she sounded scared."

We cut into the centre of the boat to find a metal switchback staircase, which is far more utilitarian than anything I've seen on the higher decks. I guess this should already tell me that we're heading to the underbelly of the *Tanis*, where only workers reside.

With this thought in mind, it's not actually as bad down here as I imagined. Though less plush than upstairs, there's plenty to entertain the crew, who make this place their home for months on end. I notice another gym, a reading room and even a less luxurious cinema.

More important right now is the sound of voices carrying down the metal corridor to us.

"How long are we going to have this conversation?" I hear Tom demand. He is the drunkest sober man I have ever met, and I reflect again on what must be happening to his body as it seeks out the alcohol it has been denied.

"Long enough for you to change your mind!" Ryan shouts back, his voice tinny as it bounces off the walls.

We pass storerooms, the laundry, and a large kitchen before turning a corner to get a glimpse of what's happening. Tom is standing in front of the door at the end of the passageway. He has a metal bar in his hand and is shaking it at Ryan as he steps closer.

"That's the crew mess," Ade mutters as he increases his pace to intervene. "What the hell are you doing?"

"This idiot called all the staff together in that room and locked them inside."

"It's the only safe option!" To say Tom is wild-eyed would be an understatement. They are red and somehow puffy, and he looks as though he's been mainlining bleach. "Until we can say which of them hurt my Sasha, this is where they belong."

"They have jobs to do," Ade replies, which isn't the argument I would have chosen. "How do you think this boat stays looking the way it does? Half the crew works at night."

"I don't care. Let it look normal instead of pristine for a day. All I care about is not having my throat slit when I go to sleep." Tom swings the bar through the air to remind us that he's lost his mind.

"Come on, mate, we must be close to the point where Sasha went into the water," I say to focus on something he might actually care about. "We'll need the crew's help to look for her."

"I'm telling you; I don't trust them. Skulking away down here like ants. It dehumanises people. That's what caused all this."

Ryan and I look at Ade in the hope he might know what to say. He doesn't, but he gives it a go.

"You're holding these people against their will."

Tom straightens up a fraction and, smoothing his slick hair with his hand, says two words very proudly. "International... waters!"

We all stare back at him to show that this means nothing.

"No one has jurisdiction here. You can't be prosecuted!"

Ryan's laughter bursts along the corridor before coming to an abrupt stop. "You genuinely think you can commit any crime you like so long as you're far enough from land?"

Tom looks away, as if we're the ones spouting nonsense. "No one's coming past me."

As he says this, I feel the boat slowing down and the sound of the motor changing.

"We can't leave them in there." My voice is coloured by my disbelief. "Surely you know that?"

"They've got food and water. I'm only suggesting we lock them up until the rescue boats arrive."

"Do you really think that anyone is coming for us in this storm?" Ryan normally seems pretty unshakable, but Tom's twisted understanding of the world has changed that. "It could be days before anyone gets here."

I can see that Ade is torn between doing what's right and what's easy, and I get a sense of what he'll opt for even before he replies.

"Okay." He shrugs, and the resistance drains from him. "Let's go upstairs and concentrate on finding Sasha."

Tom nods and breathes in deeply. I feel that he's come back to his senses, just a little, but then he turns at the last second and uses the thick metal bar to smash the handle off the door. I don't know what this achieves. He presumably already has the key, but he seems happy with the gesture and walks towards us with a satisfied smile.

He shoulder-barges past me, which is a bit much as I was the one trying to sound reasonable. Once he's turned the corner, I assume that Ade will rescue his crew, but he goes straight after the madman. I hear pounding from the mess, and a hand appears in the porthole, like in the after-credit sequence of a scary movie. I should probably stop comparing everything to horror films, but if there is one moment in my life that deserves it, this is it.

"Ade!" I yell after him.

I don't have anything to open the locked, broken door, and the look on Ryan's face suggests he's given up too.

"Tom has seriously gone insane," he tells me. "He called all the crew together very calmly, saying he wanted to talk to them about the rescue efforts, and then he flew into a rage and started waving that iron bar around. He made them stand at one end of the room and told us to get out. Clara ran off terrified, and to be honest, I felt the same."

We walk a little faster to catch up with the others, and I try to put this into the perspective of a shockingly bad day. "You know, it is possible that he's locked them up down here because he doesn't want anyone to find Sasha. Maybe she was alive when she went into the water. Maybe he's the one who pushed her, and he realises that the more people there are on deck, the greater the chance we'll find her."

Ryan doesn't respond. The pumping muscle in his neck suggests that the experience has left his brain fried. All he can do is shake his head and mouth words, which I don't catch but fully understand.

As we reach the helipad, the captain shouts down to Ade from the bridge. Clearly Tom's master plan to cut us off from everyone has already failed, and I have to wonder whether there are other crew members about the place that he didn't round up.

We take the big flashlights, and space out around the ship. We each cover one side with Ade at the front and Ryan at the back. I have zero hope of finding Sasha, but every few minutes the torch beam catches something in the bursting waves and, for the briefest moment, I imagine that I've spotted her. The sea rolls and roils. It transforms itself with every shifting second as the spray turns into the shape of an arm or a leg only to disappear again, back into the depths.

The wind stings my face, and it feels as if the rain is actively trying to torment me, but I keep my eyes ahead. My torch beam glides from side to side so that it covers a perfect semi-circle over the water. I keep trying because there's nothing else to do.

I've lost track of what time it is, and the night sky tells me nothing. The stars are blotted out by cotton-wool clouds that have been dirtied by the sweat and tears and mascara of a big night out. I don't have a phone with me, and I don't remember when I last saw a clock. This ship is a casino – a timeless black hole.

I barely felt the cold when I was standing on the top deck, but now it infects me. It runs through my body like an illness, and I shiver more with every passing minute. At some point, Ade shouts a string of wind-stolen words to me and walks along the side of the boat. I don't see him for some time, and it's tempting to head somewhere warm, but I stay at my post. It feels as if another hour has passed when he reappears and gives me permission to abandon the search.

"It's impossible without the right kind of rescue equipment. We have dinghies and a tender, but leaving the *Tanis* would put us in too much danger. There was only ever a slim hope that we would find her. The captain will keep an eye out, but I think it's time to stop."

He drums his fingers on the ship's wall. It's not the most mournful gesture, especially as we're looking for a woman we had considered a friend. I suppose we both have the feeling that she's not coming back, and as we've already spent a decade mourning our lost friendships, it's hard to feel Sasha's absence as we should.

"Where's Tom?" I ask when the sound of the wind and waves becomes unbearable.

"I couldn't find him when I looked just now. Perhaps he walked around the boat as he searched."

The unspoken understanding is that we'll have to track him down again, so we move off to do just that. Even though I've been staring at it for some time, I now realise that the sea has calmed a little. It's gone from stomach-churning to merely unpleasant, and I wonder if the storm is moving away from us, or we've sailed right through it. It also makes me question whether the captain chose the best course earlier in the evening when the weather got bad. I suddenly have a picture of Tom in court, suing Ade and the crew for his wife's death. That seems like the kind of thing he'd do.

Ade and I split up to cover the two parallel corridors. I think of knocking on Bridget's door, but I don't want to disturb her if she's sleeping, and the thought of Tom roaming the ship drives me on. We haven't seen Clara since she left Ade's suite, and her room is dark, so I have to hope she's hidden away safely somewhere.

I'm guessing from Ade's silence that he hasn't found Tom on his side, either, and we meet back up at the chained-off staircase that leads down to the beach club. It feels so similar to the scene that played out earlier that I don't question whether I will be the one to go down there. I duck beneath the barrier and hurry to the open platform. The ship tips, as it does whenever there is an opportune moment to scare its passengers, and I go sprawling forward. I'm centimetres from falling into the ocean when the black anti-slip surface slows me down just enough to grab the railing at the edge.

"Are you all right?" Ade shouts to me, and I finally wonder why I'm the one down here and not him.

"Approximately."

I pull myself up, first to my knees and then to standing. Even though my jeans are soaking wet, I brush my clothes off, as if this will make the slightest difference. I raise one hand to show Ade that I'm okay and then move towards the beach club.

The sliding door opens easily, and it's dark inside. I search for a light, but when I finally find the switch, it turns on everything in the room. Jaunty tropical house music starts up, and two fluorescent flamingos on either side of the bar illuminate to give the place a seedy glow. There's no one sitting on the long cream cushions that cover the benches, but the last time I was here, they were spotless. There are dirty red stains on them now, which are made all the more lurid by that unnatural light.

I move more tentatively, afraid of what might be in there with me. I see a huddled form in the shadows at the foot of the bar, but it turns out to be a footstool with an abandoned towel on top of it. My movements are limited by the fear that travels through me. I step forward with my right leg then bring the left in line with it – drawing out what could have been a five-second journey so that it lasts and lasts.

My heart is faster than any drum roll Mick used to play. It's like a drill in my ear and, laid on top of it, my breath sounds unusually loud and ragged. They are two instruments in a tightly knit band, and my heavy footsteps round out the trio. When I get to the bar, I hesitate to go any further. I can see more stains on the floor, but I don't know whether I have the courage to take the final step. I'm terrified that it's Bridget or Clara lying there, and it suddenly feels as if I spent too long in the jacuzzi and the skin across my body has shrunk.

There's a crash as a wave breaks over the dive platform, and it spurs me into life. I only need to move a few more inches to get a glimpse of the body, but it's the hardest step I will ever take. When I finally manage it, the face I see is bleached with neon pink to complement the pool of red around it.

Poor Ryan, I think. *He should never have been here in the first place.*

THIRTY

This is only my second dead body, and the stillness is frightening. It was different with Mick. He was the focus of a typical junkie tableau that I'd seen plenty of times before. Ryan looks so out of place, lying behind the bar, staring up at nothing. Even without the knife that's sticking out of his chest, his presence here would be proof that something's gone badly wrong.

I try to imagine how the killer lured him down here – how he felt in his last moments – but it turns my stomach, and I close my eyes instead. The now irrefutable knowledge that there's a killer on board the ship colours every thought in my head. I find the same images looping through my brain. The same feelings recur like the peaks and falls on a rollercoaster that goes round and round on a track that never ends. The fact there's an obvious culprit does little to slow it down.

When I can move again, I call to Ade to come.

"It could be suicide," he says a minute later in a last, desperate attempt to ignore the truth. "He was kind of a sad guy."

"Stop looking for easy solutions. Do you really think that Mick had an overdose, Sasha accidentally slipped overboard and Ryan couldn't take it any longer and stabbed himself in the heart?"

He doesn't answer the question. He just points to the handle sticking from Ryan's chest and says, "That's the ham knife from dinner."

Why this would be the detail he latches on to, I can't say. The line isn't delivered with any great feeling, and it reminds me of the clips I saw on the internet from the bad film he made. I think about the weapons and combat training he would have had for it, and I'm very aware that he had just as much chance to kill Sasha and Ryan as anyone else. Of course, I have no desire to confront him without witnesses present.

"We need to find Tom." Ade pulls on my arm, as I've become frozen once more. "We'll lock him away somewhere safe so that he can't hurt anyone again, and then we can wait until the coastguard or whoever comes. No one else needs to die."

"Do you think that...?" I try to keep the steady tone in my voice, but it's all too much now.

"It's probably safest for everyone if we leave the staff where they are for the moment, even if Ryan's murder comes close to proving they weren't involved in anything that's happened." He pauses a moment, then asks, "Are you all right, Jake?"

"That's not important," I tell him. "Let's just find the others and shelter together."

It's not that I've recovered from the bloody sight we've just witnessed – when I saw the corpse, it made it feel as if the blood in my veins had been replaced with concrete. I don't know how long I took between stepping around the bar and leaving to fetch Ade, but I did what I had to do, and I'm trying to keep my head.

The problem is that we don't know where Tom could be, and I'm not desperate to find him if he has another weapon. I look about for something to grab as we leave the bar, but there's no handy ice pick or a safety axe. There's no heavy ornament or conveniently placed Kalashnikov.

"The crossbows," Ade says before my brain makes the obvious jump, and presumably his thoughts have followed a similar pattern to mine.

We walk back out to the platform, but I've learnt my lesson and grip the railing while Ade opens the store cupboard that's set into the wall. He hands out a bunch of arrows, and part of me thinks, *I knew this would happen as soon as I saw there were unnecessarily dangerous weapons on board.* I feel like a total idiot stashing the projectiles in the big pockets of my oversized yellow waterproof, but then he hands the crossbow to me, and it doesn't matter so much.

The image comes back to me of Tom standing with the two weapons in his hands when we were swimming here yesterday. You could see the thought enter his mind that he was now officially dangerous. Perhaps that was when he decided to kill his wife and do whatever it took to cover it up. Was that why Ryan was murdered? To make it look as though something more complex was happening? When we didn't buy into the idea that Mick and Sasha's deaths were both accidents, Tom went full serial killer.

"There's one missing," Ade sticks his head out of the cupboard to tell me. "There were two yesterday. Even if the crew had taken it to be fixed, it would end up back here."

I flex my fingers as I adjust to the idea that someone may be hunting us. "You know how to handle a bow, though, right?"

We carefully mount the stairs, Ade with his bow and arrow, and me with my medieval upgrade. It feels like the end of a *Predator* movie when all the big weapons have been depleted, and the scrappy hero is left to fight a supreme killer with little more than sticks and stones (and perhaps a big hole covered with leaves).

It's hard to know whether we should split up or stay together, but Ade makes the decision for us. In full commando mode, he points me along the right-hand corridor with two fingers, just like he did in that bad film of his. If I do have to be trapped in my own private action movie, I'm glad there's someone alongside me who has a little experience.

We rule out the lower deck, peeking through each door we come to before moving up a floor. We find no sign of Tom, but there's an obvious explanation we haven't considered. This time I'm the one making military hand signals as, using all the training I received playing *Call of Duty*, I strafe up the stairs to the main deck. I already know which one is Tom's suite, but I'm not so dumb as to pull the door open and take a crossbow bolt to the face. I signal to Ade to cover me, then lie down on the floor with my weapon poised.

I thought I was afraid when I crept into the beach club, but that was nothing. I never imagined there was a killer lying in wait for me there – never pictured myself being cut in two by an arrow, but that's a far more likely outcome now. As I ready myself, I realise that, if by some miracle I survive, I am going to cry and laugh so much at the idea of what we're trying to do that I will need therapy for the rest of my life.

I take a deep breath and motion for Ade to push the sliding door aside. He nods, flicks it open, then stands away from the door-frame with his back to the wall. I have to admit that he's pretty good at this.

My finger is on the trigger, my breath suspended. Nothing comes shooting out of the darkness at head height, and so I point to Ade to tell him he's up.

Me? he mouths, and he's suddenly not so much of a hero after all.

I shrug back, as there's no particular reason for him to go first.

He puts his finger to his lips, and we listen. It takes me a moment to separate the waves breaking against the hull from the soft sound of breathing, but then I hear a noise that's more like a snort, and it sounds like Tom is asleep in there.

My brain does a short calculation to work out the possibility that, if he's faking it and waiting for us to come in, he'll have thought to cover the ground. There's little light in front of the door, so I cross my fingers that he won't notice me slithering inside. I wonder if real soldiers ever feel a bit silly doing this sort of thing as they carry out a mission. Perhaps that's what their years of training are really all about: gaining the ability to take themselves seriously.

Elbow in front of elbow, I pull myself forward while trying to make sure I don't accidentally fire the crossbow. It's more difficult than I imagined, and as soon as I'm inside, my fear goes shooting higher. I wish I knew a mantra to keep myself calm. *I hope I don't get murdered. I hope I don't get murdered. I hope I don't get murdered*, doesn't quite cut it.

Hidden in the shadows a few feet from the bed, I stop to listen again. I'm glad that the killer under the covers doesn't stir, but I should have told Ade to flick on the light switch on my signal so that we could get a good sense of Tom's position when he wasn't expecting it. I can make out a shape rising and falling under the duvet, but my eyes haven't adjusted to the darkness, and it's hard to know whether I'm just seeing what I want to.

There's no such thing as silence on a diesel-powered yacht, but between each breath, it comes pretty close.

"Ade, light!" I bark as I jump to my feet and prepare to fire.

With the room bathed in a warm amber glow, Tom is curled up on his side beneath the quilted cover and barely stirs.

Ade waits a few seconds before peeking around the doorframe. He steps inside with his bow pointed at the lump under the duvet. I'm still not convinced that we're safe, and so I walk to the opposite side of the bed and tug the blankets off in a magician's reveal. There is no hidden weapon there: no crossbow or knife stashed for an attack, but it does wake the sleeping beast.

"What do you think you're doing?" Tom turns to grab the duvet back, then notices what I'm holding. "No, Jake, don't do this. Please."

His voice is high and, guilty or not, he's clearly terrified.

"Did you kill Ryan?" Ade demands, and Tom turns to discover that there's more than one weapon trained on him.

"Ryan?" He pushes himself up to sitting, and I can tell that he's still barely awake. "Ryan's dead?"

Ade doesn't glance across at me or doubt himself. He fires off another question and inhabits the role of a vengeful Robin Hood that, were he to be cast as such in a film, would seriously irritate massive swathes of the internet.

"What are you doing in here?"

"I was sleeping!" Tom tries to shout, but the words emerge as a self-pitying moan. "I couldn't stand out in the rain any longer. I tried to find Sasha and failed. I let her down as I always do, so I came back here and cried like a pathetic little kid."

"Why should we believe you?" I try, but there's no real answer to this, so he continues what he was saying.

"I wanted to believe that she was still alive..." Before he can finish this sentence, the tears return, and his voice becomes chopped and indistinct. "I already miss her so much."

He looks from one to the other of us, and I lower the crossbow as his pleading gaze reaches me.

"Fine." Ade follows suit. "Get up. The only thing left to do is stay together in one place and wait until someone comes to rescue us. At least that way the killer can't get us alone." He sounds perfectly miserable, but the tension has drained away, and I can relax just a little. It feels as if I'm breathing normally for the first time in hours, but we're not out of danger yet.

"Where's Clara?" Tom reluctantly swings his feet off the bed and onto the floor. "I haven't seen her since she left the staff dining room."

"She said on the phone that she was going to hide somewhere safe," Ade responds, but he sounds less sure of himself now.

"I'll try her room again. You look around upstairs," I tell them from the doorway. "Whatever you do, stay together. If one of you killed Ryan, I have no desire to be next."

I expect them to say the same thing back to me, but they're oddly meek for once and trundle off to do as instructed. I watch them go and realise that my doubt has returned. If Tom didn't kill Ryan, then Ade could be to blame. He was gone long enough to have run to the end of the boat and stabbed his former fan to death. But then Clara could just as easily be scuttling about the place murdering our friends out of some secret grudge she's never revealed.

As if I've woken from a dream, I realise there's something even more important that I've been neglecting for the last hour. I reach the corridor where we have our rooms and turn to the door before mine. It slides across just fine, but the ridiculously heavy mattress is blocking the way. It's wedged in at an awkward angle, which makes it difficult to get past, but I eventually manage to push the top forward just enough to squeeze my body through the gap.

I tell myself that this would have prevented the killer from taking Bridget by surprise, but my hope doesn't last long. She is laid out on her side with an empty bottle of vodka and a popped pack of pills right beside her. Everything inside me starts to scream. From the voice in my head to the muscles in the soles of my feet, my body is suddenly in pain and mourning at the same time. And as I drop to my knees, my breathing sounds as if it is coming from somewhere else – from someone else.

I doubt I've felt true panic before, not like this. I have no control over my body, nor the will to move ever again. I fall to my knees, and a pitiful moan escapes my lips. My arm extends of its own volition, but I can do nothing else.

I want to go to her. I want to save the girl I've always loved, but she's not breathing. I can see from the way she's lying there that I came too late. The one person here I would have given my life to protect is gone.

THIRTY-ONE

Everything is happening too quickly now. Mick and Sasha at least died a day apart, but discovering Bridget like this makes me feel like I've skipped forward in time. I sit and watch her motionless body from across the room. Her mouth has traces of white, and there's a stain on the chequered carpet in front of her, but I can't bring myself to go any closer. Through my tear-blurred vision, she still looks perfect.

My joyful life-loving Bridget would never have killed herself. The killer clearly wanted us to believe it was a suicide, but we're way past that now. Images of how it could have happened flash through my mind, but I try to block them out.

I'm waiting for the news that Clara is dead in a stairwell somewhere. That would complete my shame. A full set of people I failed to do anything to help because I was on that stupid macho mission.

I need a spark to bring me back to life, and the soft electronic chime over the speaker system provides it.

"Jake..." Ade mutters in the same hurt, frightened tone as when we found Ryan's body. He takes ages to say anything more, as if he's hoping I'll respond. "Jake... we found Clara..." At first, I don't understand why he's taking so long, then I realise that someone must be talking to him in the background whenever he lets go of the button. "Jake, Clara's safe. She was sheltering with the captain. Meet us back in the main lounge."

My deep, almost physical relief manifests itself as a melancholy wail. It sounds as if a previously silent monster has emerged from the depths of my ribcage. It takes the rest of my strength to move the mattress out of the way, and I stop in the doorway, unable to look back at Bridget.

My head is full of her laughter. I remember when we were last happy together. I remember sitting in the cinema with her head on my shoulder and her hand in mine. I remember her nineteenth birthday when I brought her roses, and she took one from the bouquet to hit me with it for being soppy and then kissed me so sweetly I thought I could die happy right there and then. I remember only the good times that we shared and none of the bad, and then I force myself out into the corridor with a crossbow still in my hand.

My sorrow turns to anger, and I know I have to keep going. I have a clear understanding that, if I make it through the night, I'll be okay. It's almost as if the light of morning will save me, but first I have to find whoever hurt Bridget and stop the chain of violence.

When I finally make it to the lounge, I try to slide the door across, but it won't open. I bang my fist against it, and I catch the sound of muffled footsteps before Ade appears. I hurry inside, and he locks it again by pressing a smooth metal panel on the wall. Clara is sitting on the floor by the sofa with her knees pulled up to her chin, and Tom is at the dining table with his head in his hands. I can't think about them yet as I'm suddenly furious again.

"The doors have locks?" I practically scream at our billionaire companion.

Ade's mouth goes down on one side. "Yeah, of course."

"Why didn't you tell us?" I half consider shooting him with the crossbow. "She might still be alive if you'd told us."

He steps away from me, evidently aware of the murderous

glint in my eye. "Shabeer gave you the tour, didn't he? He knows to explain that sort of thing."

"No, Mick did it." Tom doesn't look up, but his gravelly voice travels over to us. "You were locked away in your suite, being all mysterious."

Ade at least looks repentant as he turns back to me. "I'm sorry, Jake. I really am, but I don't think it would have changed much."

The image of Bridget lying dead is still with me, and all the hate I've ever felt for Ade comes surging back. I feel it in every muscle in my body, and for about five seconds I wonder if I should grab him around the neck and strangle him. Before I can decide whether this is an excellent idea or just a very good one, a little voice interrupts.

"Who's dead?" Clara's bottom lip shakes between sentences. "You said she'd still be alive if we could have locked the doors. You can't be talking about Sasha. So who did you mean?"

I hold on to the crossbow but drop my coat to the floor before replying.

"Bridget." Just saying this feels like I've been hit with a sledgehammer. It's not exactly Schrödinger's Cat, but speaking her name out loud seems to confirm that she's gone. "I forced my way into the room, and she was lying there with a bottle of vodka and a bunch of pills. It could have happened hours ago – back when we didn't know whether the first deaths were a coincidence. Finding Ryan in the beach club with a knife through his heart pretty much rules out suicide, though."

Clara puts her hand out to touch me, then pulls it away again. Perhaps she's scared that I'm to blame. I referred to the killer as some hazy, abstract force, but there's a 99 per cent chance that it's one of us. I doubt the captain is secretly bumping off his passengers while also piloting the boat, and we've seen no evidence of there being anyone else here.

"I'm so sorry, Jake." Ade's voice is tinged with his unique brand of soulful empathy. "I know how much she means to you. I can't begin..."

What I can't say is which of us is faking it. We were arts students, so hardly the most unpretentious sorts, but I wouldn't be able to sit here and say pretty things if I'd just murdered four people. But then, for all the mistakes I've made, I'm not the sort to kill someone in the first place.

"Poor Bridget," Tom says from the far side of the room beyond the half-closed partition. "She was nice. Why did one of you have to kill her?"

I've never liked Tom. He has the air of a man who thinks that people should be impressed by him for no reason whatsoever. We've never really argued or traded insults, but we lived together for two years and I can't think of a single happy memory we shared. This makes it all the weirder that he should sound like the rational, caring one among us.

It doesn't last.

"I'm serious." His voice is immediately louder, his tone more aggressive. "Tell me which of you did it and why!"

I came here to ask that very question. "I'm the one holding the crossbow," I remind them, but that sounds like I'm confessing, so I repeat Tom's question. "Which of you did it?"

"This is ridiculous." Ade perches on a cabinet on the other side of the door, so that we are spaced out on three points of the compass.

"Why is it ridiculous?" Tom's reply shoots from him like a bullet. "We need to know who killed my Sasha. Who killed any of them?"

Ade glances at Clara to check that she's noticed they're the only sane ones remaining.

"Answer the question!" I repeat, the weapon still clutched tightly in my hand – the love of my life still dead downstairs.

"How can I?" He opens his eyes wider to show his frustration. "If I knew who killed our friends, I would tell you."

Something about his unflappable self-confidence offends me. I look at Tom, who we all suspected from the beginning, and I wonder if he is just a scapegoat. I look at Clara and see the terrified girl she always was. Ade's the one who knows the ship best. He is the one who wanted us all here. So I concentrate on him for the first time.

"Every time we've discussed it, I've gone along with the idea that you didn't have any reason to hurt our friends, but that's just not true."

He crosses his arms and looks unimpressed. "Oh, so you're going to do a Tom now, are you? Come on then. Let's get it over with."

I ignore him as the pieces fall into place. "You had plenty of reasons to hate Ryan. I didn't put it together at first, but when I saw you standing over his body, it came back to me." I point one finger in place of the crossbow. "He mentioned that he got into trouble for selling bootlegs of our band from the early days. I got a cheque for compensation, and you told me just tonight that you had copies of them. Were you the one who set your lawyers on him? Maybe you couldn't stand the idea of your supposed superfan ripping you off. Was that why you brought him out here?"

"That was Ryan?" His jaw hangs open for a moment before he says anything more. "I had nothing to do with the trial. I didn't even know it was him."

"Which is what you would say if you were the killer," Tom helpfully shouts over.

"There's something else." Alarm bells have been ringing in my head all night, and I'm finally listening to them. "Ryan said that you were nearby when he got to the spot where Clara had fallen overboard. He said that it was beside a corridor, and you could have crept out to push her."

"What are you talking about?" Ade pulls his shoulders back and suddenly looks less patient. He's always been stronger than me, but I finally see just how dangerous he is. "Clara wasn't pushed. She felt a bit dizzy and fell. Stop trying to twist what happened."

Tom and I look at the girl who has tried to stay out of arguments all night. Her eyes flick between us, and I can tell she doesn't want to say anything, but there's no choice.

"I don't know what happened," she mutters with her eyes half closed. "I couldn't comprehend it at the time, but the sensation of falling was so strong that it did almost feel as if someone had pushed me. The bang to my head made it impossible to be—" Her voice breaks as she looks at Ade. "I'm sorry. I'm not saying it was you, but..."

"And then there's Sasha," I say when her voice tails off, and I rediscover my own.

"What about her?" It's clear from the way Tom sways as he stares at me that his ghosts are still tormenting him. He climbs to his feet with all the composure of a barfly at the end of a heavy night, and it looks like he wants to confront Ade, but the effort is too much. He drags a chair over from the table. Like everything on board, it looks well-made and expensive, but he practically tosses it into the centre of the room to sit before us. "Tell me what he did to my wife."

"Jake..." Ade says with a laugh in his voice. He's trying to remind me that, beneath it all, we're still friends.

Tom's response tears out of him. "Tell me!"

"It was years ago," I reply when Ade won't. Now that the time has come to reveal their secret, I can't do it. I'm sick with rage for everything that has happened here, but I don't know that Ade's to blame, and I'm already starting to back down. "Ade told me that it meant nothing to either of them."

Clara sends a disapproving glance up to me, nonetheless. "None of this is going to explain why people died." She pulls her legs underneath her, and her voice takes on a desperate tone. "Please don't go any further."

Tom won't listen. "Jake, what were you just saying?" His voice has changed. It's harsher, more working class, as if he wants to convince us that he's tougher than he really is. "Just tell me."

Ade must realise that the moment of reckoning he told us he wanted has finally arrived as he answers for me. "It wasn't long after you and Sasha got together." He speaks in the candid, slightly noble manner of so many celebrity interviews. "We always used to flirt, but there was nothing to it at first. One Friday night in March, you went out with your rugby mates, and the rest of us had too much to drink. Jake and Bridget disappeared off together. Clara fell asleep, which only left Sasha and me in the kitchen. We were still drinking, still being silly, and at some point..."

"It's not true." Tom can only say this in a whisper, but he soon repeats it with more conviction. "It can't be true because Sasha would never have done that to me."

I'd always assumed that he'd worked out what happened, so it's hard to say whether his reaction is genuine. He and Sasha argued for weeks after that night and seemed close to breaking up. It was only when he asked her to go travelling in the summer that they were suddenly solid again.

"She loved me!" He's screaming now – sucking in air to propel it back out again with the force of both lungs. "You're a liar, Ade. You're lying now because you killed her. You killed my Sasha, and Bridget and Ryan too for all I know."

This statement is as much a plea as an accusation. He desperately wants to feel as if he's come to the right conclusion, because the uncertainty is killing him. It's not Tom's behaviour that most alarms me, though. It's Ade's.

He opens his mouth but doesn't say anything in just the same way he did years earlier. Just before he told me what happened between him and Sasha, he paused as if he'd changed his mind. This time, he stays quiet, and I know there's something he can't bring himself to admit.

THIRTY-TWO

Tom's gaze travels over to the crossbow, but he's in no state to grab it from me. He may be strong, but he lacks the composure to challenge anyone.

"Tell me, Ade!" He scans the room like he needs to check where the exits are. "You brought us here because you were jealous of what Sasha and I had. Is that it? You thought you could break us up, like you failed to all those years ago."

Ade is silent and won't respond. All Tom has is his bravado, but if he can't force an answer from us, what's left?

"Tell me the truth. Tell me why you killed them." His words have no resonance. They're absorbed by the paisley-patterned carpet and soon forgotten.

"We all did silly things when we were kids," Clara tries to reason with him, her button nose scrunching up compassionately. "That doesn't make Ade a killer."

I'm torn between pursuing the idea that the hit singer of "Stardawn" and "Love Goes On" really is a psychopath and trying to calm everyone back down. When I can't think of an explanation for why Ade would have faked Mick's overdose or wanted to hurt Bridget, the anger that had driven me recedes.

"It doesn't make any sense," I finally say. "Why would the two of them hooking up way back then make Ade want to kill Sasha?"

With this easy solution denied to him, Tom turns on the rest of us. "You all knew about it! My supposed friends knew that the woman I loved was cheating on me, and you said nothing."

"We were never your friends." Ade's response may be honest, but it's far from wise. "We put up with your presence because we liked Sasha. I could never understand why she went out with you."

Tom closes his eyes, and I can hear his laboured breathing. "I know you're trying to get under my skin. You're desperate to show everyone what a maniac I am so that you can push all this onto me, but it won't work."

I'm still holding on to the idea that he really is to blame. I want the one truly unlikable person on board the *Tanis* to be guilty, because the alternative is too painful. Sadly, I doubt that Thomas Ledger would be able to invent any of this. I read some of his creative writing from the seminar he had with Bridget, and his dialogue sounded like it had been lifted from a poorly dubbed advert.

He sits in the middle of the room, still swaying slightly as he recalls the life he shared with the woman he loved. I don't think it's too much of a leap to say that he's either a far better actor than Sasha was, or he's telling the truth.

"Tell us the rest," Tom says in little more than a breathy murmur as he looks back up at our host. "Tell us what you did to Jake all that time ago."

Ade is unmoved by the performance. He crosses his legs at the ankles and leans back against the wall. "How has what went on between Jake and me got anything to do with today?"

Tom swallows slowly, and I can see that he's trying to piece everything together as best he can. "I don't know. I'm just some drunk who couldn't even keep the job that my dad pulled a bunch of strings to get me."

Ade's about to offer a no doubt pithy reply when Tom keeps

talking. "But I have an idea." His eyes glimmer, as though someone's just turned on a light. "You dragged us all out here because we'd moved on with our lives and you couldn't stand to be forgotten. You killed Sasha because you threw yourself at her, and she didn't want to be with you." He leans forward but will go no closer. "This whole thing isn't about forgiveness. You hated us for forgetting about you."

"You're talking absolute rubbish." Ade has to force himself to control his temper. "If I wanted to kill someone, do you think I'd bring them to my own property to do so?"

A great smile carves up Tom's face. "You feed off adoration just like your dead buddy hoovered up heroin. It wasn't enough to have every idiot teen in the world listening to your music. You needed us to love you too."

Ade puffs out his lips in exhaustion. "You've got me, Tom. You've summed me up perfectly. I'm an addict for fame. My reputation is more important to me than any of you are. But don't you reckon that, with all my resources, I might be able to find a cleaner way to murder my friends?"

Tom is beginning to enjoy his role. "You'll have some way of worming out of it when the police arrive. *Oh, officer! This unfortunate drunk man lost his mind and murdered everyone. I only survived because he was such a mess that he never caught me.*"

It's not an obvious impression of Ade. If anything, it sounds like a bad Keith Richards.

Ade shakes his head, and his tightly knotted locks flick out in all directions. "I don't know what you want me to say, Tom. I really don't."

"I want you to answer my question. Why did Jake leave the band?"

I'm already tired of this. I'm tired of everything that the two of them are saying. I'm so tired that I end up telling the truth. "He made out with Bridget over a year after we broke up. They were drunk at a party and, from what I know, it didn't go any further. I very much doubt he'd kill me because of it."

It's obvious just how confusing this is to Tom, but he won't let it go. "There must be more. You wouldn't pass up the chance to be rich and famous just for that." There's desperation in every word he utters. He needs me to help him, but I can't.

When I offer no answer, Ade finds his voice. "I stole his songs too. I used the guitar parts that Jake wrote, and I told the label he'd had nothing to do with them. I've waited far too long to apologise. He was my friend, and I betrayed him."

"Then why didn't you do something about it, Jake?" Clara asks, and I can see that, in her own quiet way, she's trying to work out the same thing as Tom. "Why didn't you take him to court or tell the press? Why do we let this stuff linger?"

I realise that this will be difficult to say, as I haven't had to explain it to anyone for some time. "If it happened now, I'd fight back. But I was a total mess. I was an addict like Tom and Mick and probably Ade too in a way. Not so deep down, I still am one."

I wish I didn't have to explain myself, but just as Ade wanted us here to unburden the guilt he's had for years, I feel the same urge. "I understand how you're feeling, Tom. I really do. I know that everything keeps phasing between total clarity and total confusion, but I don't think that Ade had any reason to bring me here other than the friendship we shared. I really don't think he's hurt anyone."

Tom looks like a lost little boy in a supermarket at the moment he realises that his mother is missing. "That's not enough. It's not. One of you must have hurt my Sasha!"

Clara turns to Ade, but her usual sympathetic expression has vanished. Perhaps hearing that he's more human than she previously realised has robbed him of his charm. Or perhaps she's afraid that there are more revelations still to come.

"What about her?" It takes Tom another five seconds to find the energy to extend his arm in Clara's direction, and her previously blank expression is replaced by a far more hesitant one.

"Didn't you listen to me?" I ask to protect my friend. "Don't you realise that none of this will do any good? We should just sit here until help comes and then let the police work it out."

He doesn't pay me the least attention. "Tell me why you flew this forgettable little girl halfway across the world when she barely said a word to anyone back at uni."

There's something that I couldn't have predicted. For the first time this week, it looks like Tom has really got to Ade. The words penetrate not just his skin but deep within him.

"For goodness' sake, Tom," I butt in once more. "Would you go easy?"

Ade won't answer him, so with uncharacteristic strength and a look of determination on her face, Clara rises to her feet and walks towards her interrogator. "I'll tell you all the reasons why I might have killed our friends." She's so small standing before him that I'm worried what he'll do. "I had a crush on Ade the whole way through university. I was jealous of Bridget and Sasha because they could be fun and cheeky with him, while I was a shy little mouse who barely even squeaked."

I imagine that Tom's silent amazement is mirrored on my face.

"You don't have to say anything more," Ade tells her, but he offers no other solution.

Clara grits her teeth and keeps talking. "I knew Sasha had slept with Ade. Perhaps I was the one who knocked on her door and then pushed her into the sea. After Mick's supposed overdose, which I could have engineered, it would be difficult for the police to work out the motive for the first two killings. I knew from Dawn that Bridget and Ade hooked up at that party, so she had to go too, and maybe I killed Ryan because he realised what I was doing."

The silence has held. Even Ade looks uncertain what to believe, and he sends a momentary glance in my direction before I realise something and the tension breaks.

"That doesn't make any sense. Why would you kill the two girls just because they hooked up with Ade a decade ago?"

"Fine, but you can't say for certain that I'm innocent." She's not trying to convince us of her guilt so much as the impossibility of our task. "We don't know who the killer is, and I'm just as likely to have done it as one of you."

"Did you?" Tom would love this to be true.

"No!" Clara's voice jumps higher, and her amazement that he could be so simple-minded is clear. "There's no easy solution for why someone would kill Mick, then Sasha and now Ryan and Bridget. None of it makes any sense."

Even if Tom were twenty years sober, he'd struggle to solve this puzzle. As it is, he looks perfectly unhinged in his dining chair in the middle of the room, like he's hallucinating a dinner party.

"So we're back to my previous question," he says, returning to his favourite suspect. "Why did you fly Clara out here, Ade? Why do you owe her an apology?"

"You don't have to answer." Clara must realise how little her intervention achieved. She returns to her position beside me and crashes down on the floor.

"I think I do." Ade's voice has changed again. There's no arrogance left in him. No swank or swagger. He is calm, and I find that more frightening than Tom's rage.

He wanders over to the bar and pulls a bottle down off the shelf without looking at what it is. He takes the top off and swigs from it. This would have looked cool if I hadn't known that every drink there was either a syrup, a soda or a fruit juice.

As we're watching him, waiting for another secret to fall from his lips, Tom makes his move. He's far swifter than I'd imagined, and it catches me off guard. His chair tips back. Eyes wild, he lunges forward and grabs the crossbow in both hands before I can pull it away.

THIRTY-THREE

Tom doesn't have the co-ordination to attack and speak at the same time, and so an anguished string of sounds emerges from his lips as we fight for control. The weapon between us stops him raining down punches on me, and he doesn't quite get the grip on the awkwardly shaped device that he needs in order to wrench it away.

"Shoot him!" Ade says, and I can honestly say that this hadn't entered my mind until now. The crossbow was just a prop. I hadn't considered firing it.

"Do not shoot him!" Clara instantly disagrees.

With Tom's eyes still on mine, I can see how afraid he is. I could end his life with a squeeze of the trigger, but I wouldn't be able to live with myself afterwards. And anyway, I have a much better idea.

Instead of pulling the crossbow towards me as I have been, I move it closer to Tom. The sudden switch disconcerts him and gives me just enough space to point the weapon at the floor and fire. The bolt lodges itself in the ugly carpet between my feet and, as far as he knows, it's no longer of any use.

My mismatched opponent instantly lets go of the unloaded weapon and falls to his knees. I wait until I'm certain that he won't try anything more before fishing another bolt from my coat on the floor and pulling back the string.

I go to stand by Clara again but keep the crossbow pointed at Tom and Ade. "No one comes any closer. I will shoot next time if I have to." This isn't my voice. That idiot who thought he could raid Tom's bedroom is speaking through me.

"That's enough!" Ade puts his hands up to show that he's not looking for an argument so much as a reset. "I'll tell you whatever you want to know, Tom. I came here to admit my mistakes. I'm not a killer, but I have done some terrible things. And Clara suffered more than most."

"You don't have to do this," she says again, but this time the words barely escape her lips. "Please don't do this."

"The stupid thing is, I instantly liked her. When we met at the flat for the first time, I watched as she chatted to everyone else, and I could see that she was the opposite of me. She was shy and kind and conscientious."

The girl in question won't look at him. She shakes her head, and I wish I was strong enough to stop him, but my mouth stays firmly shut.

"I was never..." Ade struggles with these three words and, leaning back against the brightly coloured bar, his eyes fix on a spot in the middle of the room. "I believed in my own legend before anyone else had even heard it. There was no doubt in my mind that I was too popular for someone like her. So I dated other girls who I didn't like nearly as much, and I felt numb."

I put one hand on Clara's shoulder as she cries silent tears.

"It might sound like I'm rewriting history by saying this, but I swear it's true." Ade's briefly monotonous voice is like a drone in an industrial symphony. "I used to talk to Clara in secret. When Sasha wasn't there to flirt with, and Bridget and Jake were off on their own. We would talk about every topic under the sun, and she made me laugh like no one else. She made me see the world in a different light, and it was beautiful."

He talks about Clara as if she isn't there in front of him. This should all be directed to the girl who's sobbing on the floor, but he doesn't even look at her.

"One Saturday night, when we were invited to a party across town, Clara didn't want to go, so I stayed home with her, knowing that my chance had come. I bought a fancy bottle of wine – well, fancy by student standards – and we spent the night drinking and talking. I needed the alcohol to give me the courage to tell her how I really felt."

He has been speaking at double speed but suddenly stops and slows down. "When I was pretending to be a rock star, I had all the confidence in the world. Girls would fall over themselves to bag me as a prize." I never said that Ade didn't have a high opinion of himself. "But with Clara, I felt like the fumbling teenager I really was. When the moment came, she must have felt my hands shaking. I placed one on her cheek, and she put hers on top of it to steady me. We looked at each other for a whole minute, and they may have been the most exquisite sixty seconds of my life. The excitement and anticipation – the silent thoughts that passed between us – it couldn't have been more romantic. And when I leaned in to kiss her, I hoped it was just the beginning."

He is away with dreamlike thoughts. He is nineteen years old in the tatty kitchen of a tatty maisonette in South London and, for a moment, I bet he can feel Clara's lips on his for the first time.

"We spent the night together, and in the morning, I messed it all up. It was bright outside when I heard you coming home from the party, and I slunk off to my room so that none of you would know what happened. I abandoned the girl I was half in love with because I still thought that – somehow, for some unfathomable reason – I was better than her."

No one says anything. Although Tom's still clearly seething with hate for Ade, even he has fallen quiet. Clara lets out a high, startled sob, but she won't look up and she won't speak.

"We never held hands in public. I never put my arm around her as we wandered about the city together. I never even took her out for dinner. And then a few weeks later, the term ended, and Clara never came back."

"Mate, I'm pretty sure you've done worse things than that," I tell him, but even as I say it, I know I've jumped the gun.

He continues in the same cold, flat voice. "After we finished our exams and went home for the summer – after our first tour with the band started – I got a letter from Clara saying that she was pregnant."

Her sobs have been steadily increasing in volume and frequency, and this draws a jagged gasp from her. "Don't!" she finally screams. "Don't say anything more."

"I have to," he replies without any thought for her feelings, which makes the whole apology worthless. "I'm doing this for your sake just as much as mine." He takes a deep breath to steel himself for the final revelations. "She told me that her parents had found a pregnancy test and there was no question about her having an abortion, so I shouldn't try to convince her. She said we were going to have a little girl."

Clara is shaking, and I finally slide off the sofa to put my arm around her.

"But then a month later, we were up in Glasgow, and my mum forwarded a letter on to me. All it said was, 'I lost the baby'. I can't tell you how that destroyed me. The whole time I was away, I'd been imagining holding our daughter. I'd dreamed that we could be a family and, as soon as I got back to London, I was going to visit Clara and make things right. I'd tried calling and messaging, but I never got any replies. I'd missed her every single day and, when I got that second letter, my world disintegrated in an instant."

I can see the emotion that's running through him, but that doesn't mean it's warranted. I pull Clara's head against my shoulder and move my body around to shelter her. I should do more. I should tell him to think of her and not himself, but I'm just as selfish as he is, and I let him talk.

"The whole thing affected me more than I can say." If he'd told us it had affected him more than the woman whose baby died within her, I really would have murdered him. "When I went back to Goldsmiths in September, Clara wasn't there. I still thought we could make a go of it together, but it wasn't possible because I never saw her again until this week. And I promise that I've thought about our little girl every day since then. I even gave her a name."

In the half-second before he says another word, I realise what he's going to say, and I want to tell him to shut his stupid mouth.

"It's Tanis. I named this ship after the child we never got to meet."

No one moves. No one makes a sound. I look across at Tom to see how he will react to having his moment stolen away from him. I don't know whether he's used up every last milligram of energy, but he just sits there looking shocked. Thankfully, he isn't the one to respond to this dark confession. That's Clara's job.

"You don't get to do that," she says, looking up at Ade. "One fumble under the sheets isn't enough to secure naming rights to a baby like you're sponsoring a football team."

Ade looks hurt and strangely innocent. "It's an anagram of Saint." His eyebrows arch in confusion. "I thought she deserved a heavenly name like that. I thought she deserved to—"

"How could you?" She pushes my arm away and clambers to her feet. "How could you think that any of this was a good idea?" She keeps walking closer to him and, from where I'm sitting, he's a giant standing over her. "You say you wanted to wipe the slate clean – but that is the most egotistical thing I've ever heard."

She looks away, and I wonder for a second whether she'll come back for the crossbow to shoot him through the heart, but that's not Clara's style. She raises her hand to the silver panel on the wall but doesn't unlock the door.

"You know what? I would really like to be alone right now, but I have no desire to be murdered!" She doesn't turn around for ten seconds and, when she does, she won't look at any of us directly. She hurries back to the sofa and curls up on top of it, some distance away from me. Her eyes remain open, but they fix on nothing in particular.

Ade leans against the bar, but he has no new revelations for us. Clara looks more scared than ever – the last girl in a movie, trapped by a pack of potential killers. A few seconds of claustrophobic silence settle over us, and I can't imagine what will fill the void – though it's kind of obvious actually.

"So that's your argument, Okojie?" I'd hoped that he was defeated, but Tom won't give up. "You think the fact you got a girl pregnant and abandoned her is proof you're not a killer?"

"That's not what I said."

"You told us last night what a bad person you are. I think it's time you went all the way and admitted what you've really done. Admit that you killed my wife."

"No chance."

"Admit it, Ade!"

"Listen to yourself. You're saying I pushed Sasha overboard to cover up an affair that I literally just acknowledged."

"It has to be you." Tom grabs his incongruous chair and hurls it across the room. Ade ducks out of the way just in time, and it hits the wall of bottles so that the great glass sheet behind it cracks in six near-even pieces. There's something surreal about the result, and the cacophony of breaking glass and falling shelves leaves Tom stunned.

"This is over," Ade says, but I've rarely seen a person look so hungry for blood. He raises his fists, ready for the fight that the whole week has been leading up to.

I no longer care who the killer is. I just want to get out of this room alive and go home to my family. I realise that if I stick around any longer, I might never see my daughter again. So before it can go any further, I move to open the door with the crossbow trained on them. As Ade shoves Tom back and the two continue shouting at one another, I hold out my free hand to Clara.

"Come with me. We can lock ourselves in my room and be

safe." Even as I say this, Tom pushes his adversary away from him, and I have no desire to see the outcome. "Now, Clara, quick!"

I should have realised that she has no more reason to trust me than the others.

"I..." She's too polite to say it, so I nod to show that she doesn't have to worry anymore.

I step backwards through the door, and the cool air on my skin makes me want to smile. The rain has turned into a fine mist; the boat isn't rocking nearly as much as it once was. It feels like we've almost made it through the storm, but that means less to me than the fact I'm finally free. My head is full of memories. Of meeting my daughter for the first time and kissing Bridget after our gig.

The fresh air has unlocked something inside me, but the exhilaration doesn't last. Bridget is still dead in her room, and even if I'm away from the others, I can't escape the situation entirely. At some point, the rescue services will arrive. I will be treated as a murder suspect, and someone will have to make sense of everything that has happened.

By the time I get down to the lower cabins, all my energy has drained away. I miss my beautiful Bridget even though I hadn't seen her for a decade – even though she's not really mine. I miss the life we briefly shared, and I wish that I could not only travel back in time to relive it, but that I'd learnt enough since then not to mess things up a second time.

I stop in the corridor outside her room. It would be so easy to go in there and lie down next to her, but I'm not quite that weird. I close my eyes and think of her one last time before opening my door.

There's a pleasant twang. The crossbow the killer set there is triggered. The bolt buries itself in my chest. And as I lie dying, I think, *Jake, you total idiot. How could you be so stupid?*

PART 3
CLARA

THIRTY-FOUR

I'll never forget falling in love with Ade Okojie.

It wasn't in the very first moment we met – as he worked his way around the rooms in the apartment in our student-hall, charming each and every person there. I actually thought he was arrogant, kind of pretentious, and far too good-looking to take seriously. No, I fell for him a month later.

We were all supposed to be going out... somewhere. I honestly don't remember where or what we were going to do. A gallery opening? A nightclub I didn't want to go to anyway? Dawn organised it, and Sasha made sure that we all agreed to go. I really was planning to until I got sick and couldn't. Everyone looked sad and supportive, but I knew they would head off into the London night all the same.

I mean, it was only a cold, so I didn't expect anything more, to be honest, but after a thrilling montage of the girls getting dolled up and the boys making the minimum possible effort to prepare, Ade went to the corridor to say, "I won't be going out tonight, sorry. Someone needs to look after Clara."

I doubt I was the only one who was shocked, but they didn't try to convince him otherwise. Not even Sasha worked her persuasive magic – she and Tom hadn't been together for long, so I suppose she was distracted. But the real reason that this was so readily accepted was that, even if he never organised our social calendar or rounded up the troops, Ade was our leader.

The music we listened to together was his kind of music. We all cooked dishes that he'd mentioned – even if he didn't know the difference between a stick of celery and a balloon whisk. On Wednesday nights we watched films that we knew he would like, because we wanted him to like us in much the same way; we wanted our names to be the ones he reeled off when asked about his best friends – just as he said *Blue Velvet*, *Days of Heaven* and *Before Sunrise* when listing his favourite movies.

So the others went out, and he brought me hot drinks all night and read me poems. He was so warm and caring. It was a side of his personality that the wider world rarely got to see, and I felt privileged to catch a glimpse of it. We fell asleep on my bed, me under the covers and him on top. And when I woke up in the middle of the night, with a record still spinning on my dad's old turntable and the glow from my fish tank lighting up the room, I knew that I was in love.

He got sick himself two days later, which only made it sweeter that he'd spent so much time with me. And I admit that I held out hope he might have feelings for me, but I didn't really imagine we could ever be together.

From the very beginning, Ade made his ambitions clear. He told us that he wasn't sure whether he'd actually finish his degree because he expected to be famous before then. It wasn't exactly arrogant – I mean, it would have been if anyone else had said it – but Ade knew this to be the case and was neither proud nor embarrassed by his imminent success.

I was just happy to have found my place in the group. I was the quiet one – obviously – the one the others came to when they had a problem. I wasn't the type to date a burgeoning rock star. So I shouldn't have hoped for anything more when, in our second term, Ade told me he had a secret.

My cheeks grew hotter. It was the afternoon, and everyone else was in lectures, but I still felt proud that he would confide in me. I admit that the words "I love you, Clara" were in my head. I'm sure I was willing him to utter them, but instead he said, "I slept with Sasha when she was annoyed at Tom for going out and getting drunk with his brainless mates."

That was when I knew he would never accept me as a girlfriend. And sure, my heart broke just the tiniest bit, and I called myself an idiot for contemplating the possibility he would allow himself to be seen in public with me. But I was a mackerel who'd fallen in love with a dolphin, and I should never have expected anything more.

It wasn't until the second year of my course that anything changed – after we left halls and moved into a maisonette together near New Cross. Perhaps it was because Sasha and Tom and then Bridget and Jake had coupled up. Ade suddenly started spending more time with me. He would sit and watch me paint or just read in my room when there was no one else about.

I honestly didn't think anything of it, other than that I was lucky to look at the prettiest man I'd ever known. He sang me his new songs, and I pretended that they were about me. We ate dinner together and listened to audiobooks of long, worthy novels that I would never have got around to reading otherwise.

It was familiar. It was friendly. It was nice.

One night towards the end of the year, after Ade had broken the hearts of countless other girls across the city, we found ourselves alone in the house. He sang a new song called "Promises", and hearing it for the first time, it cut through me. I can't say whether he knew the effect it would have, but for the rest of the night, I was hypnotised by him.

He talked about the first time we'd stayed at home together, as if it was just as important to him as it was to me, and I felt myself melting. He was obviously more experienced in love than I was, and he must have known just how much power he had. Perhaps he was bored and fancied shooting mackerel in a barrel, or perhaps he really did like me. It's hard to say at what point things changed for him, but he suddenly seemed nervous. His hand was shaking as he placed it against my cheek. I wondered for a moment whether it was an act he put on to get girls to like him, but then he kissed me and I no longer cared.

The rest of that night passed in a blur. I do know that we woke up to the sound of our flatmates coming home. I doubt he realised I was awake as he grabbed his clothes and sprinted back to his own room, but I was. I watched the man I'd loved for so long running away from me, and it was almost as overpowering a sensation as when he'd touched me for the first time.

Things were different after that. I wondered whether he regretted what had happened or worried about how I'd reacted to it. He never sought me out on my own anymore, and I came to realise that he didn't want to have to spell it out that I was just a one-night stand.

The term ended, and we said goodbye. I didn't know I was pregnant for ages because it simply never occurred to me that it was a possibility. I know that sounds ridiculous, and it's not as if I was unaware that the two things are connected, but I didn't imagine it happening to a girl like me. Which makes me sound like a true moron, but I was one of those women who never had the excruciating periods that the health education teacher at school had prepared us for. It was never at the top of my mind and so, when it finally occurred to me to take a test, I felt as if someone had planted a carving knife in my brain.

I had no clue what to do next. All I knew was that I couldn't tell anyone. But then I did the most careless thing imaginable and left the evidence there in the bin in my family bathroom for my mother to find.

She rang the university to delay my final year. She talked about how we would raise the baby, and while she was supportive throughout, I never felt that she was particularly interested in how I felt or what I wanted to do. I wrote to Ade because she told me it was important, and when all that she had planned for me went out the window, I wrote to him again to let him off the hook.

It's a strange thing to love and hate a man at the same time. It leaves you feeling like two separate people. I knew I couldn't go back to university when the summer was over, even if there was no baby to stop me. I doubted whether I would ever finish my degree, and the longer I spent away from London, the worse I felt. I doubted that I would ever fall in love or have children. It seemed that my value to the world had already dropped to zero.

Back in my childhood bedroom, my dreams of being an artist felt as immature as the frilly yellow curtains and the framed picture of my first cat that was still on the shelf beside the door. Whatever depression I had endured on losing my baby and losing touch with my friends was nothing compared to the depths I now descended into. I was lost for years.

I would wake up in the morning and feel as though I'd left an important part of my brain somewhere. I felt as though I was wandering around an endless forest with no breadcrumbs to guide me home. My mother really did try to help this time. She took me to the doctor, and I was offered all the antidepressants that I could ever need. They made me feel more stable but numb. The bad thoughts were still there in my head, but they no longer had the stinging emotions to go with them. I spent time in hospital. I went to three different kinds of therapy. I saw a little crack of light above me and tried to reach it, but it was never easy.

I felt that same sense of disconnection when I crashed beneath the water yesterday. I thought that the best thing for everyone would be if I simply kept sinking lower. Bridget swam out to save me, but I can't say what pulled me back to the surface all those years ago.

I eventually began to feel like myself once more, so perhaps time really does heal all wounds. It helped that I still had Dawn as a friend. She stayed in touch throughout and treated me exactly as she had when we'd first met. She never really changed, and she made me believe that I hadn't either.

I started painting again and volunteered at the home where my grandmother lived. I ran art classes there and sat listening to anyone who needed some company. Eventually, it turned into a paying job, and that's pretty much my life up to now. I stuck to my simple routine because the thought of deviating from it and having to start again was just too much.

When Ade sent me the invitation, I thought it had to be a joke. For years, every time I turned on my mobile phone, I imagined there being a missed call from him. Every time I picked up the post from my front door mat, I pictured my name in his handwriting. And then one day, there it was. It was only ever going to happen once I'd given up entirely.

I couldn't decide whether to come at first. The thought of him brought back so many emotions, most of which weren't particularly healthy. But I sat thinking about what to do and, after an hour alone in my room, I wrote the email to confirm my attendance at whatever it was I'd been invited to.

I didn't care about the first-class tickets or the helicopter. None of that was why I'd fallen in love with him. What mattered was the moment on the yacht when we saw one another again for the first time in eleven years. He went round the group greeting our friends, just as he had when we were moving into halls. I sometimes imagine what my life would have been like if another flat had been allocated to me, but I have a sneaking suspicion that we would have found one another all the same. Our stars were crossed, even if we lacked the romance of similarly doomed couples who'd come before us.

I watched as he shook Tom by the hand, kissed Sasha on both cheeks, and hugged Bridget. Once he'd charmed the rest of them, it was my turn. He looked me dead in the eyes and I thought I might cry. It was probably a good thing that he pulled me in for a hug; it gave me time to calm down. His cologne smelt just as expensive as I imagine it is, and his linen suit was soft against my cheek, just as his hand had once been.

I tried to get reacquainted with everyone, though it didn't feel the way it used to. We were too cautious and tentative for that, but it was still special. I was happy just listening to their conversations.

Sasha and Tom were trying not to bicker. Jake did his very best not to stare at the girl he loved and probably still does. Ade monitored everything, just as I did, but he knew how to keep everyone entertained and entranced, even when Tom lost his temper.

It couldn't last. I fell or jumped or was pushed off the side of the yacht. Mick the drummer, who had no real connection to this intimate reunion, was found dead in his bathroom. Sasha disappeared entirely. Ryan was stabbed to death. Jake came to tell us that he'd found Bridget murdered in her bedroom, and then he left me alone with Tom and Ade as they tried to kill one another.

THIRTY-FIVE

I'm both jealous of Jake for getting away and a little shocked that he would leave me. I consider running down to the lower decks to hide with the crew, but the door is presumably still broken. The thought of being alone is unbearable, so I just lie here: half-comatose, curled up like an armadillo, awaiting violence.

"Three girls in a flat, and you managed to have your way with all of them." I'm so tired of Tom's smug voice, even if he does occasionally speak the truth. "You must be very proud of yourself. Did you make out with Bridget to have the full set?"

Why he thinks he has any chance of hurting Ade, I can't imagine. The two remain a few feet apart, moving side to side like boxers. Even through the thin sweater he's wearing, I can see just how muscular Ade is. I can see how much damage he can inflict if he really wants to.

"You don't know anything, Tom. You've gone through your life being patted on your head and told how well you're doing. You've failed upwards and been bailed out whenever you made a mess of things."

"Which shows how little you know about me." These are petty claims considering what has happened over the last twenty-four hours, but they're both trying to delay the inevitable.

I don't know why I keep watching. I could at least close my eyes, but that's not my role here. I'm a witness. Tom hunches his shoulders and raises his fists in case Ade starts things in earnest. He's pretending that he knows how to handle himself, but it's clear that he's more scared than I am, and I'm the little girl who's been caught in the storm.

"You stole the one thing that meant anything to me." Tom takes a half-step closer as Ade moves around him. He throws a soft punch, but it gets nowhere near its intended target, and the dance continues.

"You don't know what you're saying," Ade tells him. "You've had your supply cut off, and it's left you in this state. Can you even say for certain that you weren't the one who killed her?"

"I wouldn't do that," Tom swears. "No matter what state I was in, I would never hurt Sasha."

Instead of using this as a distraction to come forward, Ade steps away from him. There's something about his expression that tells me he's beyond the point of caring what he says now. Whatever he's been holding in all day is about to come out, and the intensity in his eyes is frightening.

"You saw us together, didn't you?"

Tom doesn't reply. He's stopped bobbing and weaving or whatever he was attempting to do and can only stare back blankly at Ade.

"When Sasha stayed behind after dinner last night and confessed that she wanted to leave you – you were there."

Tom turns his head at an angle as if he wants to unhear what Ade just said.

"You saw us together! Your wife offered herself to me, and it broke you apart."

"I don't know what you're talking about," Tom snaps, but this must be a lie or he would have answered the first time.

"Yes, you do. You were there when she tried to kiss me and I said no. That's why you've been so angry all day, and why you pushed her into the sea. You killed the others to hide the fact that this whole thing was about her."

"She didn't love me anymore." Tom spits on the floor to show his disdain and, for a moment, Ade can't believe he's finally got to the truth.

"I've been trying to keep it a secret all this time so that you wouldn't stab me to death, but you already knew."

Tom doesn't answer this time, but he comes forward to take another swing and almost makes contact. Maybe he's more up for this than he looks. I've heard of white-collar boxers – stockbrokers and City traders who spend their Friday nights pounding one another in boxing rings for fun. Maybe Tom is one of them and he's just getting his eye in.

Ade smiles at him, his unnaturally white teeth flashing in the dim light. "Is that why you locked up my crew in the mess? So that there wouldn't be any witnesses?"

"That's enough!"

"You're a killer. You don't even know what you've done."

I see the blood go to Tom's head as Ade pushes his buttons. He lunges forward, determined to cause pain, and to everyone's surprise, his swinging right hook connects with Ade's jaw. It stuns him, but he doesn't fall down, and so Tom immediately moves to the body and lands blow after blow.

It looks effective, but it's soon clear that he's made a mistake. This is not a boxing match that will play out over twelve rounds. The aim is not to wear down his opponent but knock him out. Even as Tom pummels him, there's a monstrous glint in Ade's eyes. I've seen that look once before, right after our first kiss. It's a flash of primal lust that hints at something darker.

Ade's left fist swings around in a perfect quarter circle and, as it meets Tom's cheek, there's a resounding click. The defeated fighter falls sideways, straight to the floor.

Tom's facing away from me, and I can't tell how badly hurt he is, but I can see that he isn't moving. He lies right where he is, so Ade edges closer to see if he's okay.

"Tom?"

My heart is racing, and I can only imagine how Ade feels. I watch as the fear comes over him and he considers the possibility that he's killed a man with one punch.

"Mate, are you all right? I never meant to—"

Just as he reaches the laid-out flop, Tom surges to his feet and catches Ade with an uppercut to the chin.

"You cheat," Ade complains, and I once again marvel that this should be the thing that bothers him. "You'll regret that."

He stumbles backwards against the bar, which gives him the space he needs to recover. He must have hit the remote control there, as a wailing sound suddenly fires up, and the TV wall illuminates. Punishing rock music blares across the room. It's all crunching guitars and endless drum fills and, on the screen, quick cuts show an intense, athletic band plying their trade.

Tom hasn't learnt his lesson. He should have made more of his advantage. There's only one way that this fight will go now, and I imagine that even he can see that. There's such sadness on his face as Ade steps forward and, with one ripped, rangy arm, moves to bludgeon him. Tom's neck snaps back and liquid flies from his mouth, but I can't say whether it's blood or saliva.

Instead of continuing the mauling that Ade obviously has it in him to provide, he grabs his opponent by the neck. The look of surprise on Tom's face is painful to witness. He's clearly frightened of what comes next, but there's something more in his panicked gaze. I imagine every regret he's had in his life coming back to him – every poor decision, from the one that got him into this unwinnable fight back through his career, his marriage and his upbringing. I have no way of proving it, but I feel quite certain that he's remembering all his disappointments and embarrassments, and the sorry way everything will now end.

"No, Ade..." Tom tries, but even these words are hard to decipher, and he gives up entirely.

"Don't do it. Don't hurt him," I finally shout, my voice high and shrill, but Ade won't listen. His lust has returned.

He shows his hyena-like teeth as he squeezes the life out of poor, stupid Tom. He pushes his prey up against the TV wall, and one of the panels cracks. A few million pixels die, but the band plays on. There's no doubt in my mind that this is what Ade wants. He's savouring the chance to watch a man die.

I consider trying to stop him, but it's too late for that. The stifled sound of Tom's pain is too much and, as I force myself off the sofa, it feels as if I haven't used my legs in a year. They are unsteady beneath me, but I persist. Tom's gurgling cries are drowned out by another furious crescendo of cymbals and drums, and I launch myself from the room before Ade can turn his attention to me.

THIRTY-SIX

I should probably have gone to the closest cabin, but I want to get far away from the terrible noise that is still ringing in my ears, so I race downstairs to lock myself away in my own room.

I'm just as fired up by adrenaline as Tom and Ade were, but I'm not prepared for the sight of Jake, lying face down in a pool of blood, with his legs sticking out of his room. I let out a scream when I see him there, but I don't want to end up like that, so I carefully slide the door open before ducking into my cabin.

I put my hand to the panel to lock it after me and then sit against the door. I try to slow my breathing back down, but the violence of the last two days keeps flashing through my head. I see Mick collapsed against the toilet and Sasha fighting against the waves as the yacht disappears off into the distance. I imagine Bridget taking her last breath alone in her bedroom and Jake's shock as he fell bleeding to the floor. I see the neon glint of the blade that killed Ryan, and I want to be sick.

I try to steady myself. I stare down at the hideous camouflaged carpet that probably cost more than most people earn in a year. I've learnt this week that having an undepletable amount of money does not guarantee good taste, and the swirling beige and khaki design only makes me dizzier.

It reminds me of lying in my parents' bed, looking up at the psychedelic 1970s wallpaper when I was a child. I would stay there for ever, getting lost in the pattern, so that I would eventually feel seasick and have to close my eyes. I was always a nervous little girl, and when I told my parents about this, they couldn't understand how it was possible or why I would keep doing it. Even if they never said it, I knew that they found me peculiar. They were far too normal to have a daughter like me. A daughter who wanted to be an artist and move up to London – which, whenever they visited me, they viewed with the detached curiosity of a pair of aliens at a zoo.

They are kind people, of course. They always did what they could to support and protect me, but I knew from an early age that we were very different. And so, as I sit in my cabin, with all my dead friends nearby, I think of Mum and Dad and how they would react if they could see me.

Oh, Clara-bear, my father would whisper in that kind but disapproving tone of his. *What have you got yourself into now?*

Mum would stand and shake her head. It was the same when they discovered I was pregnant. I felt that I had let them down again. I don't want to feel that way anymore. I want to be proud of myself and everything I've achieved. I don't want to be a victim or a failure. I don't want the one defining event in my life to be a love affair with a famous singer who didn't deserve me in the first place.

Eventually, I move to the bed and decide what has to happen next, just as I did when I received Ade's invitation. It makes me feel a little better about the world, though this confidence is erased when the lights suddenly turn off and darkness fills the room. The numberless clock beside the bed tells me that the power has gone out.

Horror sets in again and I'm back in my house, looking up at the wallpaper that my parents quietly removed one day when I was at school. I wait for the inevitable knock on the door, but it takes Ade longer to come down than I expected. I hear his footsteps first.

They are slow and heavy, and I imagine he pauses to look at Jake along the corridor, just as I did.

"It's over," he calls in a sad, slurred voice. "Clara, can you hear me?"

I don't reply. I can't. I run to push against the door, as if that will be enough to keep it shut with the electricity turned off. For a moment, I wonder if he is responsible for this. Is he about to burst in here now that the locks aren't working?

"Clara?" He's come closer. I can hear his shoes as they scuff against the floor outside my room. "Did you hear me? I've killed Tom." He talks so matter-of-factly that it stuns me a little. "The danger is over. He's dead."

I consider staying quiet, but then he might try the door. "Why would I trust you, Ade?"

I hear a slight thud, as if he's pressed his head against the hollow metal that separates us. I imagine viewing the impossible cross-section with me on one side and him on the other with his hands flat against it.

"I don't know how to answer that." His words come out in a rasp.

"Did you turn off the power?" My voice is small and weak compared to his, and I try to sound more confident. "Is that why the lights went out?"

"No, darling. No, of course not. It must be because the crew are locked away below deck. You can't just leave a vessel like this to look after itself, especially in bad weather. Captain Andy has been doing what he can, but you saw what he had to deal with. The man is as scared as the rest of us. I've told him that one of our friends had a breakdown and killed the others. He says it won't be too long until we're rescued."

I open my mouth to reply, but all that emerges is a shallow breath.

"We're all right now. Everything will be okay."

I feel as if his words are invading the room. They creep under the doorframe to touch me like fingers, and I realise how dumb I was not to have found a weapon as soon as I came down here.

"How can I..." I begin, but my voice fails me, and I have to try again. "How can I trust you, Ade, after what I just saw?"

He bangs one hand against the door, which is unlikely to assuage my fears. "I didn't want to hurt him, Clara. You must see that. I didn't want to kill Tom, but I had to protect you."

"That's not how it looked to me." I've found some confidence. I no longer sound like myself. "I think you enjoyed it. That's why I ran down here. I couldn't stand to see the pleasure on your face as you murdered him."

"I didn't murder... You must see..." He is shouting now, but he realises his mistake and tries to calm down. "Listen. I'm not going to open the door and come in there. Surely that proves you have nothing to fear. If I wanted to hurt you, it would be the easiest thing in the world to slide this door open, but I'm not going to do that."

I try to make sense of his reasoning, but before I can, he speaks again.

"I'll go and tell the crew that there's nothing to worry about anymore. I won't let them out until the police get here. I don't want anyone to interfere with the evidence. I doubt that Tom thought to wear gloves, so his fingerprints will be everywhere." The way he says this doesn't ring true. There's no guarantee that any evidence remains to pin the murders on Tom. "I'm going to find something to eat. I'll be on the upper deck if you want to join me."

I put my ear to the door to hear whether he really is leaving, and it certainly sounds that way. I can just about hear his boots on the metal stairs. I slide down to the floor and close my eyes. I would like to go to sleep, but it feels like I've spent the night downing one samovar of coffee after another. The muscles in my arms and legs are jumping. My thoughts bounce around like pinballs. I am both flat-out exhausted and full to the brim with energy. It's a horrible combination, but there's nothing I can do about it.

I sit where I am and listen long enough to be sure he's gone. I don't know if it's ten minutes or an hour. After everything that I've experienced, time is a fairly insignificant concept, but I eventually decide that I can't hide here any longer. It may be the stupidest thing I ever do, but I grab the only weapon I can find, slide the door across and step out into the corridor.

I can't say why, but I feel as if my senses are brighter than usual. It's dark here, without even the dim light from the night sky reaching me, but I can see perfectly well. The noise of the engine and the cresting waves are perfectly clear in my ears too, and they almost sound like they are working in unison.

There's another sense – one that doesn't have a name – and I'm more aware of it than ever. I suppose you might call it paranoia, but it's more useful than that term implies. It's an awareness of danger that admittedly may not even be there. I turn the corner, expecting to see Ade with a knife or a bow, but there's no one and nothing.

I pause again and listen. The waves crash more softly than before, and there is no rain or sound of human life. I continue on up the stairs, and though a constant sting of fear won't leave me, it seems that Ade told the truth. I don't look into the lounge to see what he did with Tom's body. I press on to another set of stairs and go up to the table where we had dinner on our first night on board. There are two chairs laid out, and he's sitting facing me as I approach.

I won't sit down yet. I stand some metres away, watching to see what he will do. The table has a selection of tempting foods arranged on it, and the briefest glimpse of them makes my stomach ache. I am suddenly so hungry that it pulls me a few steps closer.

Ade looks at me affectionately across the table. "I'm glad you're here." He sounds so sweet and understanding. "I'm glad we're finally alone together."

THIRTY-SEVEN

He beckons me to him, and I'm still powerless to resist. I sit down in the free chair and unwrap my cutlery from the linen napkin he's brought up from the galley. If this will be my last meal, at least I will enjoy it. I put down the biro I had taken from my bedside table as, for one thing, that was never going to save me, but I also now have a knife if I need to use it.

We eat in silence. There's quiche, slices of cold meat and a selection of cheeses. I stack little chunks of them on bits of bread, which I load onto my plate as if I'm afraid he'll take it all away again.

"You do understand, don't you?" he eventually asks, and he's wrong, but that doesn't mean I intend to answer him. "You understand that this was all for you?"

Perhaps it's just the dawn gradually lightening the skies around the ship, but the whites of his eyes seem clearer than they have all night.

"Maybe..." I take a deep breath and try again. "I don't know what you want me to—"

I'm relieved when he cuts me off. "You must realise that I brought everyone out here so that I could see you. I thought you would be more likely to come if the others were here. I was worried you never forgave me for what happened."

For a moment, I think he's going to say it. The solemn expression on his face suggests he'll admit what he did, but then he smiles his innocent smile and keeps talking. "It's not just guilt that drove me. I missed you. I've thought about the life we could have had together so often. You know, it probably stunted me in some way. It's like I could never move on from that time when we all lived together. No matter how much success I found. No matter how famous I became – all I wanted was to travel back and put things right."

If we'd had this conversation the day before, I would have made the right noises in response, but I just let him talk now.

"I thought of calling or writing or visiting you so many times, but I didn't know how to broach the feelings I've held on to all these years. I'm sorry..." He stops himself for five seconds and then continues as if nothing happened. "I'm sorry that I have to tell you in these terrible circumstances, but I refuse to waste any more time."

I can see how hard it is for him to say all this, but that doesn't make it easier to hear.

"I never got to tell you that I loved you, Clara. You're so different from every other girl I've known. I'll never forget the moment we met. You were happy to watch the rest of us, and you did so with the most incredible smile on your face. You looked so contented in yourself, and I wondered how I could feel the same."

"I suppose that..." I say without knowing what should come next. "I suppose that everything looks easy from the outside."

I keep eating as though there is nothing out of the ordinary about us sitting here together. The tiredness I've been ignoring all night suddenly hits me, but the food makes me feel a little stronger.

Ade seems more interested in me than what's on the table. "I dated other girls, of course, but that only proved how far above them you were. Over time, I think I even became a little shy of you."

"Of me?" I blurt out, as the very idea of such a thing is beyond my comprehension.

"I mean it. You are more beautiful than you will ever realise." As much as I appreciate this sentiment, it sounds as though he's reciting a cheesy song. "When it was just the two of us, I found true contentment, but I didn't share my feelings because..." He puts one hand to his head as if he's still suffering Tom's blow. "... because I was afraid I would mess everything up. It was easier to accept that you weren't the kind of girl a rock star should date, and so I convinced myself we couldn't be together."

I laugh at this, as it's still so far from what I imagined. After the night we spent together, I was sure he'd made use of me because I happened to be the only girl home that night. I really don't think I have it in me to believe this rosier version of events.

He can't stop smiling as he tells his tale. "I wanted to believe you really did like me, but I hated the idea of starting something and destroying the dream of what we had. That would have screwed me up even more than I am now." He guesses what I'm thinking and quickly corrects himself. "I'm not asking for your sympathy. I just mean that if we'd made a go of things and it hadn't worked out, I would have lost my faith entirely. I can't imagine being a torch singer who doesn't believe in the possibility of two people falling in love."

I consider giving a nasty response, but I do understand what he's trying to say.

"I'm not expressing myself very well, am I?" He gives a brief, sad laugh and I wonder whether he even remembers that our friends are dead on the decks beneath us. There's a perfectly round bruise on his right cheek where the skin has turned glossy, and I focus on it to remind me of what he did to our friend.

"What I'm trying to explain is that I was a coward, and I was selfish, but I did love you. I do love you, Clara." He sounds even younger than when we first met. He sounds like a little boy confessing to a crush on his teacher. "We can still be together." There's a sudden pitch change, and these words become a plea.

For a short time, I let my teenage self enjoy the idea that he's telling the truth. For a few brief, delicious moments, I picture our wedding and the house we would have back in Britain. I think of the life we would share, travelling the world on this yacht.

But then I remember all the pain he's caused, and I fix my eyes on him down the table. "That's not going to happen, Ade." I maintain an even tone but, really, I want to scream. "You brought me here for forgiveness and then failed to apologise for the very worst thing you did."

"You don't think I killed our friends, do you? I mean, apart from Tom." He laughs again, as he apparently forgot he was a murderer for a moment.

"I'm not talking about this week." The rage that has been building inside me won't be held down any longer. "I mean back then."

He turns his head to the side. "I said I was sorry for not being around when you found out about our daughter. And you know now how ashamed I am of not telling everyone how much I adored you. What more can I say than that?"

He rolls his sleeves up ever so carefully, and I have to look away now. I study the scene as if I'm taking in the view, but my eyes see nothing of the churning waters around the near stationary yacht.

"What do you remember of that night when we were alone in the flat and you kissed me?" I choose my words carefully. I don't want to lead him to the answer. I need him to say it for himself.

I see his Adam's apple move as he shakes his head. "It was the best night of my life." His eyes are so wide, so full of emotion, that it looks like he will cry.

"Well the best night of your life was the very worst of mine."

He pulls back, as if I've just taken the knife and tried to slash him with it. "What do you mean? I remember the way you looked at me." His breath becomes more ragged as he tries to solve this equation. "I can still feel your lips on mine. And I will never forget how close my heart came to bursting as I stared into your eyes."

I try to control my emotion, as I have for so long. I try not to show how every word he says is like a needle sticking into me, but there are two traitorous tears peeking out of the corners of my eyes and, in a few seconds' time, they will tumble down onto the tabletop.

I have to tell him before they can give me away. "I said no, Ade." I pull in a gulp of air between my lips before continuing. "You kissed me, and it felt like heaven, but then you started pulling my clothes off, and I said no."

He smiles again, and it's too much to bear. The look that I once found so charming makes me want to jump from the yacht, just as I did on our first day here.

"No, you're misremembering." His tone is so soft that it's easy to believe he's not trying to contradict me but support my unique perspective. "That's not how it happened. I promise. I've thought about our time together so often. There's no way I would have done anything to hurt you."

"And I've thought of little else for the eleven years since." I keep my voice low, but the fury still pours out of me. "I spent half of that time trying to put my life back together."

He bites his lip and, in order to be the decent, sensitive person that everyone thinks he is, takes his time to consider my response. "Honestly, Clara. I promise I have no memory of that. All I remember is how perfect we were together. I slept there in your bedroom, our bodies connected, and I felt so loved and understood. I was sure you saw it the same way."

I close my eyes for a minute, as it's one thing to hear all this, and another to have to look at him as he says it.

"You touched me, and I said no. You laughed and kept pushing, and I tried to pretend it was no big deal, but I wasn't ready. I said it again and again, but you didn't care." I force myself to keep talking because I know I'll lose my courage otherwise. "I said no."

This refrain is followed by a sharp, desperate sound from the base of my throat.

As I struggle to find my words, he takes control. "Listen to me,

Clara." He's more serious now. His brows knitted, he peers down his nose at me and says with all the authenticity he can muster, "I have never abused a woman like that. I unequivocally deny that I would ever have touched you if I didn't think that was what you wanted."

This reply sounds rehearsed – perhaps even coached – and it enters my mind for the first time that he may have had this very same conversation with someone else.

My eyes flick open, and I bounce his words back to him. "Listen to me, Ade. I kept saying no, but you didn't care. And there came a point when I couldn't say it anymore. You pushed me onto the bed and removed my clothes, and I just froze. All I could do was pretend it wasn't happening."

He finally realises that I mean what I'm saying, and his pupils shrink as he looks up at the lightening clouds. "You wanted me. I know you did."

I whimper in reply. Despite my best efforts to be strong, I whimper before I find my words again. "You're right. I wanted to be your girlfriend. I wanted to make love to you one day, but that doesn't mean that what happened that night was okay."

He doesn't reply immediately. He looks back at me, and I still want him to say that he remembers what happened and feels remorse.

"I am sorry for the feelings that you have carried with you all these years." He chooses his words to avoid taking any responsibility, and each of them is a lie.

"That's not an apology, Ade. You're saying that you're sorry for the way *I feel*, not for what you did or the pain that you caused. I shut myself away afterwards and had to live with a pregnancy that I didn't want and then the agony of losing a baby that I'd come to love. I've spent most of the decade since in absolute fear. I spent years in therapy to get over it – took every kind of medication the doctors would give me – but nothing truly worked. You ruined my life, and all you can do is apologise for the way you say I've misinterpreted my own feelings."

There's no more hesitation. He knows his script and will continue to recite it. "I hear what you're saying, Clara. I promise I do. But the fact is that we remember two different experiences, so who's to say which of us is right?"

I can stand it no more and scrape my chair back to stand up. My cheeks are wet. My pulse races.

"You ruined my life," I say or perhaps shriek as I back away from him towards the staircase. "And that's why I despise you."

THIRTY-EIGHT

I run to the bridge deck and circle it so that I'm standing in front of the tall, tinted glass doors. I can see no sign of the captain inside, but that doesn't mean he's not there, and there's nothing I can do about it now anyway.

I realise that the tip of my finger is bleeding and, when I look down at my hand, I'm still holding the knife. I don't remember picking it up or running my finger over its appropriately savage point, but I'm glad I have it.

It isn't long before Ade follows me. When he arrives along the walkway, he no longer looks besotted or concerned. He's just confused.

"Why would you say that?" he demands as he comes to a stop a few metres away.

"My goodness, Ade. You really aren't very clever, are you?" I'm beyond pretending now. I want him to know how much I detest him. "I didn't come here to reignite an old flame. I came to confront you. I wanted you to know how much I've suffered."

Despite his good looks and silver tongue, despite the millions he has earned from his really quite good music, Adesina Okojie is not the brightest boy around – even out here in the middle of the ocean.

"Then you lied." He looks so hurt and, for a moment, I feel guilty that I have no sympathy left for him. "You should have told me from the beginning how you felt instead of leading me on."

"Yeah, Ade. I led you on." I fail to suppress a laugh, and it spurs me to tell him a truth that will upset him even more. "I was also the one who sent Ryan his ticket." I wait a moment for this to sink in. "I regret it now, considering how he ended up, but I knew about your record label taking him to court, and he'd written a really not very well disguised blog post about the night you went out in Soho together."

I am no longer the meek little girl he believed he was in love with, and it frightens him.

"Why would you do something like that?" Whatever charm he had has gone. He's as dim as a dead bulb.

"When I received your invitation, I screamed and cried and cursed you. I couldn't believe that you thought a first-class ticket on a plane could make up for raping me."

"No, don't use that word," he shouts back at me. "It wasn't like that."

"I decided it would be better to get even than get mad. I wanted to see your face when the man you'd wronged arrived here. I wanted to see whether there was an ounce of shame in you. I used all my savings to buy Ryan a ticket on the same flight that I was on, and then I sent him a reworked copy of my letter. I found his address online, and Dawn had told me she wouldn't be coming, so I knew there would be space for him. It almost fell apart when your man at the airport realised there was a problem, but just as I'd hoped, you were too vain and too curious to stop your party-crasher coming aboard."

He looks down at the floor now. He's morose and despondent, but he still doesn't understand what I'm trying to explain.

"For all the love you claim to have for me, when Ryan stepped off the helicopter, it was him you kept looking at, and I knew what you were really made of." I find myself smiling as I say this. "You cared more about his front at appearing here than the chance to see the girl you loved again."

When he looks back up, he puts his hand out towards me, and it still makes me flinch.

"That doesn't matter now, Clara. I don't care about any of it. I just want us to be together."

"Wow!" I say, and the laughter rises up once more. "Do you really not get it, Ade?" I hold the knife a little tighter. "Do you not see?"

"I see that you are the only woman in my whole life who has ever meant anything to me." This misanthropic statement is not one I would want to read on a Valentine's card.

"You are so thick." I never imagined this would be the criticism I levelled against him, but it is very much deserved. "Have you forgotten that Dawn is my friend? She told me that you slept with Sasha again just days after you were with me. I know all her secrets, and she knows mine."

"What happened between me and Sasha meant nothing. And when she came to me last night, I told her that I didn't want her."

"It's not about Sasha. Dawn knows what you did to me; that's why she wouldn't live with you any longer. She was the only person I could trust. The only one of you who cared enough to check that I was okay after I left London."

He at least holds his response in for a few moments and considers what I've said. "I'm sorry for however I've hurt you, Clara. But you are the only girl who has loved me for who I really am and not who I became."

"Or am I the only one who said no?"

"It's not like that!" He shouts these words with all the heartache and melancholy he invests in his songs. "I love you."

"I killed Sasha," I say straight back.

I might just as well have stabbed him for the impact it makes. There are ten long seconds when the only sound is the lapping sea and the wind whistling past our ears. "What did you say?"

"I knocked on her cabin door to get her to come outside, and then I pushed her off the boat. I killed Ryan too, and Bridget and Jake. Mick really did have an overdose. That wasn't my fault, but it put the idea in my head." It feels so good to say all this. If he'd let go of his neck at the very last moment, this is the exact same feeling of relief that Tom would have experienced. "You must understand that I didn't come here set on revenge. I was only going to kill myself, but when that didn't work, I came up with a better plan."

His lips are open a fraction as he stares at me.

"A few hours in your company was enough to make me jump off the boat. I thought a suicide would be bad publicity for a star like you. It was a petty kind of revenge, but I didn't see what else I could do. If Bridget hadn't saved me, you would have continued on your trip to the Maldives and got on with your lives as if nothing had happened."

His jaw falls lower, but no response comes.

"It was a neat twist of fate that Ryan thought someone tried to push me. Though, in the end, it just complicated things. If Jake hadn't realised so quickly that there was a killer on board, I could have got through my plan a little quicker."

"Your plan?" He's shaking, and a single droplet of saliva shoots from his mouth as he speaks. I imagine there's already enough of his DNA all over me, but this won't hurt.

"Try to keep up, Ade. It might seem extreme but, last night, when you danced with me in the lounge, and kissed the top of my head when no one was looking, I decided to destroy you. You'd abused me once and clearly thought nothing of it, so I knew what I had to do."

He's the one whimpering now. His cheeks glisten and there are tears in his eyes. He takes a step forward, but he's so shaken by what I'm telling him that he comes no further. "Then why hurt our friends? Why not just kill me?"

It's a question I've asked myself fifty times over the last day. I loved Bridget. She was like a sister to me, but I put a bunch of antidepressants in the vodka she'd brought on board. I had no idea whether it would work, but she helpfully drank it down. Jake and

Ryan were perfectly nice to me, Sasha was always fun, and I murdered every last one of them.

"They weren't my friends though, were they? As soon as I left uni, they forgot all about me."

"We never stopped thinking about you. We just didn't know whether you wanted to hear from us."

"Yeah, well, killing you alone wouldn't have been enough. I wanted to make your life a misery, just like you did to me. And the only way I could do that was to take something away from you that you actually treasured."

"What does that even mean?" His voice is weak now. He's barely got the composure to reply. "There was nothing I cared about more than you."

"You say that, and it's really very complimentary, but think back a few hours." I sound like the confident, capable person I always hoped I'd become. "You said it yourself. Your reputation is more important to you than any other thing you possess."

I'm not sure he hears much of this. His lip trembles as he stares down at his hands. "I killed Tom," he suddenly remembers. "He was innocent, and I killed him."

He's a mess, which is funny as I thought I would be the one struggling to hold it together if I ever got this far. Something about his expression makes me want to tell him to pull himself together, but then the page turns, and his anger emerges.

"How could you do this?" I'm glad this is a rhetorical question, as I don't want to have to go through it all again. "How could you think that anything I did was worth taking someone's life over?"

"I didn't kill anyone," I say in my most innocent voice, as I take the knife and slash my chest and my left arm in a few different directions. I hold the blade away from myself to make it look as though someone else is responsible. "That was you, Ade. You did all this, and you'll be the one who's punished for it."

"What are you talking about?" The poor guy sobs as he watches his life catch fire.

I swap hands and do the other arm before wiping my fingerprints off the knife and tossing it along the floor past him. "You must get it by now. You can't be that slow. I mean, I know rock stars are supposed to be kind of dumb, but I've explained the whole thing in pretty basic terms."

I proudly turn my arms out to display the blood running down them.

"You mean that..." He's finally got it. "No one will believe you!"

"They don't have to, Ade. There's already plenty of evidence of the crimes you've committed. Just think of the marks on Tom's neck. It certainly wasn't my little hands that did that."

I back away towards the barrier. There's a long drop down to the metal floor below, and my movement pulls Ade forward.

"You psychopathic little—"

I wonder what's going through his head at this moment. Is it the thought of the fortune he'll lose or how his fans will respond? I almost want to reassure him that, with a good image consultant, famous people can get away with anything these days. Of course, mass murder may be a step beyond redemption.

"How could you?" He shakes his head, and huge tears fall to the deck, like raindrops in a monsoon.

The story is over. There's only one thing left to do.

"Because you deserve it. You brought this on yourself." I whisper to burrow even deeper under his skin. "You killed your friends because you were jealous of the lives we lived out of the spotlight. Fame has twisted your mind, and you orchestrated this whole thing, from sending out invitations to stabbing and drowning and poisoning your way through the lot of us."

I watch the muscles in his arms tense as his hands turn into fists.

"You're a monster, Ade, and the police will be here soon to arrest you."

He's right up against me, and I see the moment when he realises that nothing he does now will make a difference. It's both liberating and frightening for him. He knows he's doomed, and he might as well make the most of it, so he extends one arm in my direction, and I smile as he makes contact with my chest.

The next thing I feel is the barrier as it slams against my back. The force is enough to send me over and, as I fall to my death, I see his beautiful face looking down at me. I hear the captain come running out of the door at the back of the bridge, and a feeling of true happiness washes over me because everything worked out perfectly in the end.

EPILOGUE
BRIDGET

Now that everyone is dead, I pick my way through the bodies.

I can't say what woke me. Was it an explosion or just a slamming door? To be honest, it's difficult to know anything with any certainty. The pain in my head is all-conquering. It feels as if I've spent the last day hooked up to a whisky drip and the hangover has just kicked in. I stumble from my room and along the corridor, clutching railing after railing to stop myself falling with the movement of the ship.

On the stairs above, I spot that unique shade of red in a great long splash up the wall. There's just enough blood to tell me everything I need to know; more people have died.

I remember now. Flashes of panic and anger come back to me and, a few moments later, I find the first body on the main deck. Following handprints and dirty red smudges, I make my way towards the back of the boat where a woman lies motionless. There are cuts all over her arms, but she's clearly fallen from one of the balconies above. Maybe the sound of her body smashing against the floor above my cabin is what brought me here.

A half-formed question of whether someone pushed her is quickly resolved as I look at the awkward position in which she landed. She's on her back, her legs twisted, and her arms stretched wide. Surely she'd be face down if she'd jumped. It could have been an accident but, given the circumstances, I truly doubt it.

Her face is pointed away from me, but I recognise who it is from her neat, unexciting clothes.

Poor Clara, I say to myself. *What could she possibly have done to deserve to die like that?*

I suddenly realise that I need a weapon, which isn't that easy to find on the deck of a fancy yacht. It's almost minimalist and, short of standing beside an immensely heavy chain and hoping the killer will submit to being knocked out with it, there isn't much at hand.

The fog in my head has, if not cleared, then at least parted for a moment. I remember that there are bedrooms along the walkway on this side of the ship, so I move to try the various doors.

The first I come to is a storage cupboard with nothing for me except an unwieldy mop. But I keep on. I persist. I won't give up. The wooden path curves around, and I find what I need. The door slides open a little too easily, and I stumble into a musty room and onto the bed. I push myself off the surprisingly hard lump under the covers, but I won't peek to see who's lying there. I really don't want to know.

The cabin is similar to my own, so I get to my feet to rifle through a chest of drawers on the off-chance one of my friends has brought a handy hunting knife or perhaps a small gun. Boxer shorts and T-shirts aren't going to help much, and I'm about to give up and try another room when I spot the bedside lamps. They're shaped like candlesticks, as they are in every bedroom. I grab the closest one and, with the shade removed and the cable detached, the metal body will just about do the job.

Back outside, I feel like every stupid hero in every stupid action movie I've ever mocked. I'm aware how ridiculous it is to even consider fighting a killer with half a lamp, but my friends are dead, and I have no desire to be next.

I hold the makeshift weapon in both hands and slowly mount the stairs to the bridge deck. My footsteps sound louder than at any moment in my life, and the wood beneath me creaks like it wants to let the killer know exactly where I am.

Just as I stop at the top to look around – just as I notice a knife on the floor and two definite pools of blood – a perfect shiver races through me.

I hear a sudden intake of breath, and a voice behind me says, "I didn't do it. I promise it wasn't me."

I turn to see Ade sitting on a bench beside the door to the bridge. The captain has a firm hand on his shoulder, as if they're playing cops and robbers.

"Bridget, you have to trust me," my friend begs. "You know I'd never hurt anyone."

But I don't know anything anymore. To be honest, I'm struggling to make sense of the scene before me. The one clear thought in my mind – the one idea that I can hold on to with any certainty – is that I might finally have found a story worth writing.

A LETTER FROM THE AUTHOR

Many thanks for reading *The Yacht Party*. I hope you enjoyed this departure from my usual mysteries. It was certainly a lot of fun to write. If you don't know my other books, you can check out my three far cosier series and get to know my detectives Marius Quin, Lord Edgington and Izzy Palmer. If you'd like to hear about my new releases, you can sign up to my readers' club where you'll join other readers in accessing free novellas and receive my monthly rambling newsletters.

benedictbrown.net/benedict-brown-readers-club

If you enjoyed this book and could spare a few moments to leave a review, that would be hugely appreciated. Even a short comment can make all the difference in encouraging a reader to discover my books for the first time.

Becoming a writer was my dream for two decades, as I scribbled away without an audience. Finally being able to do this as my job for the last few years has been out of this world. One of my favourite things about my work is hearing from you lovely people who all approach my books in different ways, so feel free to get in touch via my website.

Thanks again for being part of my story – I hope there are many more adventures still to come.

Benedict

benedictbrown.net

ABOUT THIS BOOK

Well, there you go, folks. That's definitely the most intense ending to a book I've ever written. And despite being a *mystery* thriller, it has a very different feel to my usual murder mysteries. That being said, I hope it's still recognisably me, and there's certainly a lot of stuff in this book that comes from the people I know and my background as a writer.

Obviously, the starting point for any book like this one has to be *And Then There Were None* by Agatha Christie. That novel didn't just set the *killer-methodically-despatching-foes* template which has been aped by so many murder mystery novelists, I would argue it established the model for slasher films that reached the peak of their popularity forty years later. If you compare that book with much of Christie's work, it seems like a massive departure, but the structure, setting and techniques she uses are so familiar that I've never seen it referred to as an outlier. Though a truly depressing book, I'd say *And Then There Were None* is one of the most perfectly plotted novels I've ever read, and I've always wanted to write something similar.

The first few chapters of this novel could be mistaken for one of my Izzy Palmer books, and I do think that there's still a lot of humour in this frankly terrifying scenario, despite the high body count. I really do wonder if I have the capacity to write a book without at least wry humour here and there, and I certainly didn't avoid it this time around.

A major influence on the plot was my first term at university, which I've already written about in the very silly *A Corpse in the*

Freezer. That period, when I was still not much more than a child and moved away from home to be dropped into a group of people who I instantly believed would be my best friends for evermore, left a massive impression. Perhaps mainly because I was a moody teenager, I fell out with my housemates, had a terrible time and swapped to a nicer flat shortly after.

Nonetheless, I know a lot of people who romanticise their time at university as the best days of their lives, and I liked the idea of someone holding on to that belief even as they achieve fame and fortune. I should probably mention that I didn't go to Goldsmiths College, though my brother and several friends did, but I needed an artsy university in London, and Goldsmiths did the trick. I'm sorry if the real arts degrees there are not populated with world-famous rock stars and serial killers. One of the fun things about writing a contemporary thriller is that I can play a little more freely with reality than I choose to in my historical novels. So hurray for poetic licence!

The character of Jake is based on my real best friend when I was a kid. I asked his permission before writing this book and, as he'd already written a play about elements of his former life on the wrong side of the law, I didn't think he would mind too much. Jake and I grew up together in South London, but he broke his back playing rugby when he was seventeen and had to miss a year of school, which I think had a massive impact on him. We were in a band together, with him as the frontman and me hitting the drums in the shadows behind, and he was always an incredible actor and a big character. He has a cheeky charm which is still hard to resist.

However, he got into trouble with the police a few times when he was at university and ended up spending six months in prison for a bar fight. When he came out, I suggested that he could have an easier life out in Barcelona, where I was teaching English. He moved there but, after a few months teaching, he ended up working on boiler room scams – selling fake shares to unsuspecting victims. Seeing him at that time, when he would reappear after weekend-long benders and be so low and so contrite that he was almost in tears, was heartbreaking, and I'm glad to say that he eventually turned his back on that life.

He's dealt with addiction and had a really hard time over the last twenty years, and I'm proud that he's come through it and is a good father to his two girls. We grew up like brothers and, just like with my real brothers, it's important to forgive the mistakes people make and learn to cherish what's great about them.

The romance plot was inspired by another of my close friends, who has been in love with his ex for the last fourteen years. It's a really painful thing to hold on to, and I hope he finds closure one day – and doesn't end up getting shot with an arrow! If you look for it, there is a bit of hope buried in the finale of this book, but I didn't want to spell it out, so consider that a hidden mystery for you to unpick.

The character of Ade was influenced by stars like The Weeknd and Kele Okereke, not least in the intensely emotional music they make. It's always seemed mad to me that, considering we have archetypal rock 'n' roll stars in Jimi Hendrix and Prince, there are not more hugely successful black front men and women. I'm not saying there aren't any (I also like TV on the Radio, Alabama Shakes, Thin Lizzy, Twin Shadow, Black Pumas, etc., and I'm not ignoring all the other genres where the balance is different) but there's a gap in the rock 'n' roll landscape for a world-conquering star.

There is also a real-life Bridget, who was one of my closest friends in Barcelona and always reads my books each time before anyone else. She is a qualified psychologist and nothing like the character in this book, but I previously came close to naming a nasty character after her, so I changed that and found a nice one instead. Phew.

As is often the case when I need to access a tricky piece of information, it turned out I knew a lot of very useful people to help with writing this novel. Clare, a friend of a friend I'd met a couple of times in Barcelona, works on superyachts as a steward and helped answer my questions. Another of my friends is married to a London stockbroker, so Sasha's account of Tom's life is taken pretty much word for word from cases that Gemma described. So thank you, both!

There are various other elements in the book which were taken from real things that have happened. One of them is where Ryan was sued by Ade's record label for selling bootleg CDs. This was inspired by a news story in Germany where a widow sold her dead husband's Eric Clapton CD online for €9.95. She was taken to court and made to pay Clapton's €4000 legal fees, even though her husband had bought the CD in a German high street shop and she had no idea the recording was unlicensed. Seems a bit harsh, if you ask me.

The look of the *Tanis* (named after my friend Tanis, who requested this in exchange for letting us stay in her apartment in Barcelona last year – a very fair deal!) was based on a few different ships, but the external layout was inspired by the 73-metre superyacht *Planet Nine*, which is currently on sale for the bargain price of €80 million (though, if that's too steep, you can charter it for €650,000 a week).

I chose that ship not just because it's hella-fancy, but because it has a helipad. From the opening chapter, I knew I needed upper decks which someone could fall to her death from. Most superyachts have tiered decks, so she'd only be falling a couple of metres, but the helipad means the decks cut off more sharply. The *Planet Nine* also has the beach club at the back (with sauna and steam room), a sunken hangar for the helicopter, a "vast" 3000 ft^2 master suite and merely a "large" cinema. The listing I found doesn't fail to mention all that teak, the guest elevator, or the space for two 32ft tenders. However, there really is no accounting for taste when it comes to some of the terrible art on display. I think I'd prefer pics of my kids.

I chose Mauritius in the Indian Ocean as the jumping off

point, as I went there on holiday with my wife ten years ago. It was to be our last big foreign trip before we had kids, and though we might have planned it as a beach holiday, that idea didn't last long, and we did just about everything we could on the island and beyond. I have to thank our lovely receptionist at the hotel where we stayed, who I've remained in touch with since, as the real Sendilen was helpful when I had questions about Mauritius before writing this book... and back when we were staying there, now that I think about it.

The island that the yacht stops beside is a short boat trip north of Mauritius and is called Flat Island. I'd first read about it in the ecologist Gerald Durrell's account of his trip to Mauritius, *Golden Bats and Pink Pigeons*, which I really recommend. The island wasn't as ecologically diverse as the neighbouring Round Island, where Durrell went in search of near-extinct lizards, but it is a beautiful spot for a day of snorkelling.

While there we saw magnificent birds, including the white-tailed tropicbird and red-tailed tropicbird that are described in this book, not to mention white-eyes and pink pigeons (that Durrell helped bring back from the brink of extinction) on the protected nature reserve Île aux Aigrettes. What I don't think we saw were frigatebirds, but they are sometimes spotted around Mauritius, and they are incredible creatures who have been known to land on boats. The red breast that Bridget mentions shows that the one in this book is a male, and it's actually a kind of pouch which the bird can inflate to attract white-breasted females.

I don't know if this will be the first of many thrillers or my one stab at them, but I have really enjoyed writing it. I also loved returning to the present day, as since I finished writing my Izzy Palmer books, everything I've written has been set in the 1920s. It's nice to not have to think about the language I'm using or read too much about the history of everything I mention, if only to make the writing process a little quicker. Of course, trying a new genre is actually far trickier and involved more redrafting when compared to my usual approach. I have a few more ideas for non-maritime-based thrillers, but it all depends on how well this one sells, and what time I have between my other books as to whether they get written. I really hope you enjoyed this book and will check out my other mysteries if you don't already know them.

Thanks for reading.

www.ingramcontent.com/pod-product-compliance
Lightning Source LLC
LaVergne TN
LVHW031537060526
838200LV00056B/4544